She would not allow her determination to crumble now. She had spent the past few days concentrating solely on getting here and not on where she was going, keeping her focus on following the Elders' directions through thick forests and narrow paths. She had faced every challenge in her life with exactly that fierce determination.

But what was the point? All along she had been driving herself toward a future that no longer existed. Her shoulders slumped, and suddenly her foot felt too heavy to lift. She was seventeen years old, and she felt as ancient as the rocks surrounding her.

And there was nowhere to go except forward, deeper into those rocks, where her death lay waiting.

LEAH CYPESS

DEATH SWORN

GREENWILLOW BOOKS
AN IMPRINT OF HARPERCOLLINSPUBLISHERS

Death Sworn

Copyright © 2014 by Leah Cypess

First published in 2014 in hardcover; first paperback edition, 2015.

www.epicreads.com

The text of this book is set in Centaur MT. Book design by Sylvie Le Floc'h.

Library of Congress Cataloging-in-Publication Data

Cypess, Leah.
Death sworn / by Leah Cypess.
pages cm
"Greenwillow Books."
Summary: "When a young sorceress is exiled to teach magic to a clan of assassins, she will find that secrets can be even deadlier than swords"—Provided by publisher.
ISBN 978-0-06-222121-6 (hardback)— ISBN 978-0-06-222122-3 (pbk.)
[1. Magic—Fiction. 2. Secrets—Fiction. 3. Assassins—Fiction.
4. Love—Fiction. 5. Fantasy.] I. Title.
PZ7.C9972De 2014 [Fic]—dc23 2013037379

15 16 17 18 19 CG/RRDH 10 9 8 7 6 5 4 3 2 1
First Edition

Greenwillow Books

To Aaron

This is the first book I started and finished while we were married.
Also, I've decided to scrap the book with the
red-haired scientist character.
So this one's for you.

CHAPTER I

The first step should have been the hardest. The cave entrance angled so sharply that one step was all it took: plunging her from light to darkness, from the fresh scent of snow to the smell of musty earth, from the touch of the breeze to the weight of dank stone. Ileni stopped for a moment, and not only to allow her eyes to adjust. Melted snow trickled down her hair and dripped on the back of her neck, and her skin was chapped by the wind, but inside the entrance to the Assassins' Caves, the air was dry and still. She could hear the slow drip of snow melting off rocks, but with her next few steps, she would leave snow and wind—

and sunlight, and falling leaves, and everything she had ever known—behind her forever.

She took the second step, ignoring the screaming desire to run back outside and keep running. She would not allow her determination to crumble now. She had spent the past few days concentrating solely on getting here and not on where she was going, keeping her focus on following the Elders' directions through the thick forests and narrow paths. She had faced every challenge in her life with exactly that fierce determination.

But what was the point? All along, she had been driving herself toward a future that no longer existed. Her shoulders slumped, and suddenly her foot felt too heavy to lift. She was seventeen years old, and she felt as ancient as the rocks surrounding her.

And there was nowhere to go except forward, deeper into those rocks, where her death lay waiting.

On the third step, the darkness deepened. Ileni clenched her fists so hard that her fingernails dug into her palms. She had known exactly what she was getting into when she accepted the Elders' mission; she had faced it, unflinching, the moment she said yes. She would spend her life within the Black Mountains, surrounded by assassins, with no defense when they decided to kill her. If she could agree to that, she wasn't going to falter now just because she could feel the stones closing in around her. She forced herself forward.

A shape hurtled silently out of the shadows and slammed her against the rough stone wall.

Ileni screamed once, short and shrill, then gasped into silence. A muscled arm pressed against her chest, and something sharp and cold whispered across her throat. A knife blade.

But she was still alive. The knife was only touching her skin, not slicing into it. Ileni's heart pounded against her chest, and she instinctively reached for her magic before remembering that she shouldn't. Instead she brought her hands up and pushed with all her strength at the arm holding her prisoner. She might as well have tried to move the wall behind her. Her assailant didn't so much as acknowledge the attempt.

Ileni forced her hands back to her sides and said, in her coolest voice, "The knife seems unnecessary, then, doesn't it?"

As she said it, she called up a magelight.

The effort made her shoulders clench and her eyes sting. A few months ago, she barely would have felt a spell that small. She ignored both pains and focused on the face of her attacker, illuminated by the ball of white light hovering above.

It was a sharp, almost triangular face, with high cheekbones slicing from his chin to his coal black eyes. He looked slightly younger than she was, but something hard lurked in those eyes, something that marked him as an assassin.

"I'll decide what's necessary," he said. His voice was terse, with a gravelly edge. "How did you find the entrance to our caves?"

It took great effort to act cavalier with that knife's edge on her skin, but Ileni rolled her eyes. "How do you think? The Elders told me."

He stepped back so abruptly that Ileni lost her balance. By the time she steadied herself, the knife had disappeared beneath his gray tunic.

Ileni drew in a deep breath, relieved to feel cool air instead of steel against her skin. Not that he couldn't kill her with his bare hands, of course . . . and nobody knew exactly how Absalm and Cadrel had died. "I'm a Renegai sorceress," she snapped. "Who did you think I was?"

"I didn't—" His dark eyes narrowed. "The Renegai have

never sent a woman to serve as our tutor before."

"Is there something in our agreement that forbids it?"

Her words hung in the air like a challenge.

Melted snow crept from her neck down her back, curving lazily along her spine, and she itched to reach back and rub it away. She restrained herself from saying something just to break the silence. Finally the assassin turned and said, "Come with me."

Ileni drew in a deep breath and hoped he hadn't heard it. She followed him down the dark corridor, the magelight hovering at her shoulder, wondering if it made sense to feel as relieved as she did. Not getting killed within two minutes of arrival was . . . well, it was something. It was a start.

It was probably better than anyone back home expected of her.

The Elders had explained, kindly but bluntly, that they were sending her because she was expendable. If she managed to find out who had killed her predecessors, that would be helpful, but if not—and they didn't hold out much hope—at least she would buy them time. She supposed she should feel grateful to them for not lying, for granting her that much respect, but she couldn't quite manage it. Her bitterness was a barrier against any conciliatory thoughts.

More than anything, she was tired of being bitter. Bitter, and sad, and angry. She missed her former self—a self she barely remembered, even though it had vanished only six months ago—and a life that had been happy and filled with purpose.

The assassin walked with a steady, implacable stride. Ileni refused to go faster to keep up with him, so within seconds he had disappeared into the blackness ahead of her. The magelight traveled with her, casting enough light for her to see jagged rock walls on both sides of her. Stalactites jutted from the low ceiling, like blades, just high enough that they didn't touch her head—but low enough that she worried they were going to. They had probably been designed this way on purpose, to frighten anyone who dared enter the Assassins' Caves. She did not duck her head.

Around the next bend of the tunnel, the darkness disappeared. She stood at the threshold of a large cavern filled with a maze of unearthly pillars and lit by dozens of glowing stones set into the arching walls. Fingers of multicolored stone hung from the ceiling and rose from the ground, reaching toward each other. It was like a majestic hall, except that the eerie shapes of the stones and their unexpected shimmering colors were nothing a human mind could have invented.

The assassin crouched atop one of the shorter, thicker pillars, his body a curve of taut muscles beneath nondescript gray clothes. He looked more like a weapon than a person. "Pretty, isn't it?" he said. "Didn't the Elders tell you about this?"

"Of course," Ileni said stiffly, letting the magelight vanish. (What they had said, actually, was, *Parts of the caves are very beautiful, but don't let that distract you from the evil within them.*) "I didn't realize I would see it so soon."

"We built the entrance here on purpose," he said. "It impresses the . . . impressionable."

"Such cutting wit," Ileni said. "You had better take me to my rooms so I can recover."

He blinked. Perhaps the other tutors, despite their status and supposed immunity, had been reluctant to openly insult trained killers. But Ileni had been riding a fatalistic recklessness for the past six months. A large part of her didn't care if he killed her.

The rest of her was greatly relieved when he merely inclined his head and said, "Of course. I'll walk more slowly this time, but let me know if you have trouble keeping up."

She lengthened her stride as he hopped from his perch, and when he reached the other side of the cavern, she was only one step behind him. She flicked her fingers against the back of his neck, pulling out a tiny strand of hair. He whirled with lightning swiftness, one hand clamped around her throat before she even realized he was moving.

His fingers curled around her neck without exerting any pressure at all, but she could see, in his merciless eyes, how easy it would be for him to tighten his grip. It took every ounce of courage to keep her voice not just even, but irritated, distracting him while she slipped the piece of hair into the sleeve of her tunic. With luck, he would think she had only flicked him to get his attention. "Attacks at knifepoint are one thing. Impudence is another. I won't tolerate that from my students."

He released her, his hand falling back to his side. "It is not wise to surprise an assassin."

"Sometimes I'm not wise."

He evaluated her coldly, as if deciding whether to kill her after all. Then he turned his back on her and resumed walking.

Ileni touched her throat gingerly and followed. "Are you taking me to . . . to the master?"

He bowed his head slightly without turning to face her. "No. I am taking you to your room."

Ileni shivered in relief. The Elders had warned her about the master of the assassins, who knew everything that happened in these caves and wielded absolute control over his disciples. He was so old nobody knew when he had been born, and was called by many names—the Wielder of a Hundred Living Blades, the Puppetmaster, the Architect— but when people said "the master," everyone knew who they meant, even among the Renegai. He was the most dangerous man alive.

Ileni didn't want to face him. She knew she would have to, eventually . . . but not right now, when she had just entered his caves. Not yet.

Three passageways opened at the end of the majestic cavern, and the assassin swerved smoothly to lead her down the one to the right. "Afterward, I'll show you the training room, where you will be teaching those of us who are skilled at magic."

"Will you be one of them?"

"I will." He left the *of course* unspoken. "I showed the most skill at magic under your predecessor."

It could be true. Ileni couldn't sense much power in him,

but sometimes even people with little power possessed great skill. As she should know.

"That doesn't mean much," was all she said. "He wasn't alive long enough to do any meaningful testing."

The assassin's smooth stride faltered, for less than a second. Because she was behind him, Ileni allowed herself a smile.

He glanced over his shoulder. The way the light hit his hair made it look as golden as Tellis's—which made her heart first leap, then hurt. "I also showed the greatest skill under *his* predecessor, who lasted much longer. And was a better teacher besides. The quality of our tutors seems to be continually declining."

"Along with their lifespans, perhaps," Ileni said. "These caves have become a dangerous place for sorcerers."

"These caves have never been a safe place for anyone, Teacher."

Was that a warning or a threat? "My name is Ileni," she said finally.

"Mine is Sorin."

The walls on either side of her were smooth and even, inlaid with glowing stones that cast a soft white light through the tunnel. Except for the dryness of the air and the oppressive sense of heavy stone suspended over her head—both of which might easily be products of her imagination—she could have been in a completely man-made structure. Like the stone prisons within the Empire where, she had been told, anyone who opposed the emperor was sent to never see sunlight again.

She was too tired to keep track of the numerous turns they took, through arched doorways and smooth rectangular openings that led to yet more curving corridors. By the time Sorin stopped in front of an actual wooden door, she felt they must be buried deep in the earth, with tons of solid rock pressing down above her.

"This will be your room," Sorin said, pushing the door open. No lock, Ileni noted—but she felt the wards thrumming through the wooden door, layers of interlocking spells, reinforced over and over by the succession of sorcerers who had lived here. One of the tasks of the Renegai tutors was to ward the Assassins' Caves against magical attack, but these wards, smaller and tighter, were directed against anyone and anything. Once she was inside, nobody else would be able to open the door.

She swallowed hard, unbearably grateful for a place of safety—however small, however confined.

Of course, Cadrel had lived in this room a few weeks ago, and Absalm before him. The wards hadn't kept either of them alive.

To her surprise, the room was decorated, with a brightly colored rug thrown over the stone floor and a tapestry hanging on the wall by the bed. Nothing elaborate, by any means—to most people, the room would probably have appeared sparse—but it was opulent compared to her room in the sorcerers' training compound, which had been a rectangular cell with a bed, a clothes chest, a small window, and nothing else. And the introduction of beds had been fairly recent, hotly contested and eventually allowed only because mattresses on the floor were more quickly infested by insects. Austerity, they had been told, was necessary for the development of their magic.

She felt her lip start to curl, and turned to Sorin for distraction before the bitterness could come flowing in. She caught him watching her speculatively, and once again had the sense that he was deciding her fate. She met his gaze, feeling like prey. She had seen how fast he moved. If he decided to kill her, she probably wouldn't realize it until she was already dying.

Maybe that would be a mercy.

But he only leaned back against the doorpost and said, "I'll show you the training area now. You start teaching tomorrow."

"In a little while. I'd like to unpack first."

Sorin looked at her pack, which was barely the size of a cooking pot, and then at her. Ileni smiled blandly.

"All right," he said. "I'll return after I report your arrival."

Ileni waited until he had shut the door behind him, then pulled a roll of clothing out of the pack and emptied the rest of its contents onto the floor.

Twelve flat black stones thudded onto the rug. Ileni tossed the empty pack onto the bed, dropped into a cross-legged position, and carefully arranged the rocks in an asymmetric pattern around her. She worked fast, half her attention on the door, but took an extra moment to make sure the pattern was exactly right. No point in accidentally blowing up her room on the first day. Later, maybe, if it seemed called for.

If she was still able to.

She pushed that thought away, closed her eyes, and envisioned the words she wanted to say. To her they always appeared in color, glowing slightly from within, looped together in the sinuous musical script in which she had learned them. She retrieved the hair she had plucked from Sorin's neck and held it with the tips of her fingers.

Stringing the syllables of the spell out between her teeth, she touched the hair quickly to each rock, then stretched it taut between her hands. The words of the spell made no noise, though she spoke them; instead of sound, pure power emerged from her mouth. It shattered the air, and she spat the words out faster and faster to keep them from getting away from her. By the time she reached the climax of the spell, she was shouting, though the room was still silent.

With the last syllable, she let go of the hair. Instead of floating downward, it disappeared, as soundlessly as the rest of the spell.

Ileni lowered her hands, throat raw. A bead of sweat tickled the outside corner of one eye. This was getting harder and harder. That spell, a year ago, would have been a warm-up exercise for her. Back then, she could have done it without the stones. Tellis, thankfully, had refrained from mentioning that when he gave them to her.

She hadn't allowed herself to dwell on Tellis for days, and the sudden memory hurt like a blow to her stomach. Before she could stop them, the images flooded her mind: Tellis's lean, rugged face, the blond hair falling over his dark blue eyes. The way those eyes had once made her feel, as if she could barely breathe.

His eyes when she emerged from her second Testing. The expression on his face that told her he already knew what the Elders had said. That he accepted what had to happen now.

That look had driven her to accept the Elders' mission, to come here to these caves filled with killers, where two of her people had died within the past half year. She had sworn to find out *why* they died, before she met the same fate, but it was an empty promise. What were the chances that she—a seventeen-year-old with rapidly fading powers—could survive whatever had killed two older, seasoned sorcerers?

But she hadn't cared how dangerous it was, or how lonely. All she had cared about was putting physical distance between herself and all the people who thought she was worthless. No one *here* would look at her with pity.

Ileni's lips quirked upward—not much, but it was the first time since the meeting with the Elders that she had seen any humor in her situation at all. The people here wouldn't pity her because they would be too busy trying to kill her. At least it would be different.

Now that she was leagues away from that humiliating

parting, she could finally be glad that Tellis hadn't allowed her to refuse the warding stones, his last gift. If Sorin tried to harm her in any way, he would find her better defended than she appeared.

The stones tumbled against each other as she gathered them into the pack. *One down, several hundred to go.*

She pushed the pack under her bed and waited for the assassin to come for her.

CHAPTER 2

High in a tiny black room carved from stone, the old man watched the slippery rocks outside the Assassins' Caves, empty now that the sorceress had picked her way across them. A light snow swirled through the cold gray air, already covering the marks of her passage.

It was the first time the Renegai had sent a woman, and it was also the first time they had sent someone so young. The girl was not particularly striking, at least not from this distance: she was thin and short, and her thrown-back hood had revealed matted brown curls. She hadn't seemed bothered by the snow whispering across her face, and had approached the entrance carefully but without hesitation.

Her predecessor had been visibly shaking as he walked across the rocks. And *his* predecessor, grandiose from the start, had levitated several feet above the rocks and sailed coolly to the entrance.

The door opened behind him. The sound didn't surprise the old man; he knew exactly how long it would take Sorin to escort the sorceress to her room, and he had been sure the girl would ask for some time alone. The only thing he hadn't been certain of was whether the boy would change his clothes before coming here. He had mused it over for a minute or two and guessed that he would.

He had guessed wrong—something that rarely happened to him anymore. He could smell the damp sweat clinging to the boy's tunic as Sorin crossed the small room and bowed low. "Master."

"Sorin," the master of the assassins said, and his disciple rose from his bow with sinuous grace.

"The new Renegai tutor is here," Sorin said. "I was watching the entrance when she arrived, so I escorted her to her room."

His voice revealed no anger over the fact that he had not

been told to expect a sorcerer, which pleased his master. Sorin must realize that this was a test: that he had been assigned to watch the entrance this week, and not told what to expect, on purpose.

"What do you think of her?"

"Nothing," Sorin said instantly. "I interacted with her for no more than a few minutes. Any thoughts about her now would be premature, and merely prejudice me later."

"Very good," the master said. "That is the correct response. Now, tell me what you really think."

Sorin turned, young dark eyes staring straight into old blue ones. Not many students in the caves could hold their master's gaze for more than a few seconds. "That is what I really think, Master," he said.

The master believed him, and that made the second time he had been wrong in the space of an hour. A lesser man might have been irritated, but he was intrigued. There was very little that could still take him by surprise. "You will rise high, Sorin," he said. "And there will come a day when you will not be able to gather all the information you require, and will have no choice but to guess, based on nothing more substantial than what you saw today."

"Of course," Sorin said. "But I have no reason to believe that this is that day."

The master smiled, pleased and amused. "Well, gather information as swiftly as you can. I am making her your responsibility."

"Yes, Master."

The old man regarded him, wondering how much the boy suspected. He still remembered the day Sorin had been brought into these caves, half-crazed and all-wild, willing to die for the sake of nothing but his fury. Now that anger had been channeled and focused, making Sorin an exemplary assassin— one of the best, but still a tool, even if a finely honed one. Sharp, deadly, but very straightforward.

So his master thought, most of the time. But then there were those moments when his guesses turned out wrong.

He still hadn't figured out why, so he kept throwing tests Sorin's way. If nothing else, this assignment should provide him with new and interesting information about the boy. Even if Sorin died, that information would be useful.

Information always was.

"Go, then," he said. "Make sure you take her to the training area while the advanced students are practicing, so she can see what we are capable of." He chuckled, more to himself than to the boy. "Or rather, some of what we are capable of. The rest can wait a few days."

"Yes, Master."

Sensing a note of doubt in Sorin's voice, the old man stopped smiling and met his eyes. Sorin jerked, then bowed his head as if under a sudden weight.

"Go," the master said coldly. "She is your charge. Take this assignment very seriously. I don't want what happened to the others to happen to her."

What did one say when strolling through an underground corridor with a trained killer? As she followed Sorin through a passageway lit by glowstones, Ileni came up with and discarded several possible openings, ranging from *The weather down here is surprisingly pleasant* to *So, how many people have you killed?* Sorin, striding grimly a step ahead of her, showed no inclination to start a conversation on his own.

The corridor sloped downward in a steady curve, which made Ileni feel vaguely nauseated. By the time they encountered an actual staircase, they had walked in what she was sure was a complete circle, which meant they were a full level below her room. And now they were going even lower.

The stone walls closed in on her. Her vision blurred, and she couldn't breathe.

Stop it. She would be underground for the rest of her life. She had better get used to it.

The staircase was a steep spiral of rough white rock, so narrow that at times Ileni had to slow down to squeeze herself through. At irregular intervals, the stairs were interrupted by equally narrow passageways, each with several sharp turns. The way was well lit by the glowing stones set in the walls, but the effect was still macabre. Every time Ileni turned, she had to keep herself from cringing, her body expecting someone—or something—to be waiting for her.

The stairs were also, she noted, defensible. In case of attack, the interior of the caves could be defended by a few men against an army. The famed impregnability of these caves was no myth.

At the bottom of the third staircase, they stepped into a large cavern. This one had three passages branching off from it, and only the middle was lit.

"The left-hand passage leads to the main training area," Sorin said.

Ileni squinted. She didn't see any stones set in the walls. "It's dark."

"So it is."

She was not going to give him an excuse to be amused at her expense. "You first, then."

Sorin held up one palm, which began to glow with a yellow light. He walked into the passageway, holding his hand out to light the way.

Ileni followed cautiously. The passageway grew narrower as they walked, until there wasn't enough room for two people to walk side by side. "A regular magelight would be a lot simpler."

"Sometimes, I'm not simple."

She blinked. He glanced swiftly over his shoulder at her, not a hint of levity in his expression, then looked straight ahead.

Ileni watched his back, since that was all she had to look at. His gray tunic pulled tightly against his shoulders as he moved, and one unruly tuft of golden hair stuck out near the top of his head. "Which of my predecessors taught you that trick?"

"Absalm," Sorin said. "Cadrel was not here long enough to teach me anything."

Absalm had been the assassins' tutor for ten years before his death, so no one had been suspicious when he died earlier that year and the summons came for his replacement. The Elders had sent Cadrel, a mid-level sorcerer with a friendly smile and a talent for cooking. That had been soon after the Elders decided that Ileni's fading powers should be put to another Test, so she hadn't been paying much attention.

By the time a messenger came two months later to report that Cadrel, too, was dead, the Test had confirmed her worst fears. Even the rumors about how Cadrel had died hadn't pierced her fog. Not until the Elders summoned her had she started to take some interest. By then, of course, it was too late.

But she wouldn't have avoided the summons, even if she could have. Ever since the Elders had told her that her entry into the sorcerers' compound was a mistake, that her powers were going to fade away just as they did for the hordes of Renegai commonfolk, she had survived by focusing only on whatever step was immediately in front of her. The Elders had helped by giving her a new and almost impossible task: find out what had happened to the two tutors who had come to these caves before her.

Perhaps their deaths were accidents, the Elders had said, but without sounding like they believed it in the slightest. Truly,

Ileni didn't want their deaths to have been accidents. All that would mean was that she had no purpose at all, that she had been sent here to bide her time until her own death. That she was truly disposable. Untangling an assassin plot seemed highly preferable.

If she could do it.

She might as well get started. "Cadrel lived here for nearly two months, didn't he? Surely that was sufficient time to teach you *something.*"

"Not much," Sorin said. "I was on a mission for most of the time he was here."

On a mission. She knew what that meant. "Do you know how he died?"

Sorin stopped walking and turned to face her. The yellow glow illuminating his face . . . or maybe the knowledge that he had murdered someone a few weeks ago . . . made him look hard and dangerous. "He fell down the last of those staircases and hit his head. These caverns can be dangerous to those who aren't used to them."

"I'll be careful, then," Ileni said. She flicked her wrist, and all at once the passageway was filled with a bright white light emanating from nowhere in particular. It wasn't much harder than calling up a magelight, but she felt her power flutter weakly, deep in her stomach. "That should make it easier to see my footing."

The yellow glow around Sorin's hand was nearly invisible in the sudden brightness. "I'm sure Cadrel made it just as light."

"He wasn't as powerful as I am," Ileni said flatly. It was true, in a way. "I've heard that Absalm was more so. Did *he* die in a fall?"

"No." Sorin closed his hand, and the yellow light vanished. "Absalm drowned."

Ileni glanced around at the dark walls of dry rock surrounding them. "Drowned where?"

"We don't know where he died. We only know where we found his corpse."

Before she could ask the next obvious question, he turned his back on her and continued walking.

Ileni resisted the urge to look back toward the stairwell. Even if Sorin was telling the truth about where Cadrel had died—and it seemed like a silly thing to lie about—he had to be lying about *how*. Cadrel would have been very careful, a mere two months after arriving at the caves.

They emerged at the top of another staircase descending into a large cavern, this one brightly lit by hundreds of glowing stones set into the walls. Ileni had never seen so many glowstones in one place before. She let the white light go, and forced herself not to sigh with relief as the effort of holding it eased and the passageway went black behind them.

The walls of the vast cavern were raw and jagged, and the high ceiling dripped with stalactites. The glowstones illuminated dozens of young men, stripped to the waist and gleaming with sweat, attacking each other with swift, deadly movements. No one ever made contact, so despite the jabs and kicks clearly meant to cause harm, the bouts resembled dances more than fights. It was terrible, graceful, and oddly beautiful.

It also, Ileni discovered when she got close enough, stank.

The assassins ranged in age from as young as ten to as old as . . . not very old; none of them was even close to thirty years of age, as far as she could tell. The rank smell of sweat was almost enough to take Ileni's mind off the weapons they were training with. Not one of them held a sword or dagger. Instead they danced at each other with circles of metal, pieces of rock, wooden staffs, whirling strips of rope—the variety was as mind-numbing as it was frightening. Another myth confirmed: assassins could kill with anything.

Some of them were practicing with no weapons at all.

The Elders had told her that she would be safe, that the assassins' discipline and obedience were strong enough to protect even a lone girl trapped in their caves. And of course, they all thought she was powerful enough to defend herself with a word. That should help. Even so, she found herself walking as close to the wall as she could.

Sorin moved the way they fought, with graceful purpose, every part of his body taut and controlled even though he was merely walking. He lifted an eyebrow at her, and Ileni attempted—too late—to look unperturbed. He led her around the edge of the cavern, far too close for comfort to several of the duelers—none of whom glanced in their direction, even though they must never have seen a girl here before.

On the other side of the cavern, several narrow archways had been cut into the wall. Sorin led her through one of them into a smaller cavern, as craggy as the one they had passed through, but completely empty.

"This is where you'll be giving lessons." Sorin turned in a tight circle, his eyes darting swiftly across every surface in the room, as if searching for danger. "Absalm would only train one pupil at a time here, to avoid injuries. Though you can do what you like."

Absalm had, no doubt, made up that rule to slow down his pupils' advance. At home they had all trained together, in a large stadium surrounded by majestic trees. The memory cut through Ileni's defenses, quick and sneaky, and for a moment she couldn't speak.

Sorin looked at her sideways, and she said swiftly, "I won't be teaching spells that can cause injuries."

The side of his mouth lifted slightly. "I'm told that's what Absalm thought, too, when he first came here. It didn't take him long to learn that to an assassin, anything can be a weapon. It might take you a little longer."

Ileni turned and scowled at him, feeling dangerous. "I would advise against comparing me to your previous tutors. You might be in for some unpleasant surprises."

He just looked at her. The expression on his face was intolerable. It said, *You're not dangerous at all. I see right through you.*

He knows . . . but no, he couldn't. If they knew how useless she was, she would already be dead.

So Ileni closed her eyes and reached for the memory of the last spell she had learned. She hadn't mastered it fully yet, but she didn't care. She spat out the words of the spell, flung out her hand, and unleashed all her fury on the smirking, self-important killer in front of her.

A flare of green light hit Sorin in the chest and threw him backward, flipping him head over heels. To Ileni's amazement, he landed on his feet, dagger in hand.

And then he was in the air again, flying toward her with the blade pointed straight at her.

He was only inches from her when the air around Ileni exploded, and Sorin shouted. The dagger flew out of his hand, bouncing off one of the craggy walls of the cavern, and his body flew in the opposite direction, crumpling against a particularly jagged outcropping of rock. He did not land on his feet this time.

Ileni stepped forward, afraid she had killed him. As her wards had reacted, she'd realized the dagger was slicing at her hair, not her throat. But then he leaped to his feet, one hand pressed to his side, staring with an expression that should have gratified her: astonishment and fear.

Except he wasn't staring at her.

Ileni followed his gaze. The cacophony of clinks and thuds and grunts from the main training area had gone silent. A cluster of assassins stood in the arched cavern entrance, staring, the pretense of disinterest wiped off their faces.

Her role as their tutor, apparently, was off to a great start.

CHAPTER 3

Despite her exhaustion, Ileni had no trouble forcing herself to stay awake that night. The tiny chamber felt small and heavy, as though the mountains of stone pressing around her compressed the very air. It was cold, though not as cold as she would have expected—an effect of the glowstones, probably, that dimmed and brightened over the course of the day, following the rhythms of a sun whose light never touched them. Ileni lay in her narrow cot, staring up at the utter blackness, trying not to imagine the mountains suspended above her head.

She'd had a lot of practice, over the last few weeks, in not thinking about things. About the life she had lost, and the life she now had, and the overwhelming probability that *life* was not going to be a relevant concept for her much longer. She focused instead on the task immediately ahead: finding out if Sorin had been telling the truth about Cadrel's death.

She wove a spell to enhance her hearing, paying special attention to the accents of the ancient words. This was a tricky one, and even some of the advanced Renegai students had never mastered it. She chose it because the concentration it required left no room for her own thoughts.

There were two aspects to working magic: the power she drew from within herself, and the skill required to weave the spell. Her strength was dwindling, but her talent was the same as it had ever been . . . which was achingly frustrating, but also useful. With her skill, she could craft the magic to require as little strength as possible, and keep the dregs of her once-abundant power for as long as possible.

Pathetic, that she should be reduced to this. A familiar fury flared in her. How could the Elders have made this mistake? The whole point of the childhood Test was to confirm that a novice's power was permanent, not merely the bright energy of childhood. They had based her life on that mistake, raising her in the sorcerers' compound, training her in the spells and techniques that would soon be all she had left. That would be useless once her power was gone.

But they weren't useless yet. She finished the spell with short, precise hand movements, then sat and listened with sharpened ears to the silence that echoed against the thick stone surrounding her.

When she stood, the glowstones flickered softly in response to her movements, and she startled in reaction. Her breath caught, excitement and fear making her skin tingle. It wasn't a pleasant feeling, exactly. But it was a *feeling*, piercing the dull, numb fog she had been wrapped in for months, and she clung to it as she pulled her door open and stepped out into the hall.

The glowstones flickered on as she passed them, though not as brightly as during the day. She reached out and used a nudge of power to stop them. She wanted no sign of her passage.

With her enhanced hearing, she could use the echoes of her footsteps to sense where the walls and openings were despite the complete darkness. That, combined with her memory of the walk with Sorin earlier, got her to the spiral stairs with only a few bumps and bruises. Once there, she had no choice but to let the hearing spell fade so she could call up a light.

She tensed all over as brightness flared around her, feeling horribly exposed. She strained her ears for the sound of footsteps, even knowing that she would never hear a trained assassin coming.

The stairs stretched steeply below her, their edges worn into round smoothness. Her light was small, and below her, all was dark and silent. Suddenly dizzy, she braced one hand on the wall. So this was where Cadrel had died.

If Sorin had told the truth.

She descended slowly and carefully, keeping her hand on the smooth, cool wall for support. When she got to the bottom, where the stone widened into a large cavern, she leaned against the wall. She was so tired. Maybe she should have given herself a night to sleep, and to adjust, before attempting this.

But even as she rubbed the back of her other hand against her gritty eyelids, she knew it was a foolish thought. She might not have time to adjust to anything before she became the next Renegai to die in these caves. Absalm had been here ten years, Cadrel only two months; who knew how long she had?

Ileni reached beneath her tunic and pulled out a square of silk, which she shook out into a gossamer-thin cloth that shimmered in the magelight. She draped the cloth over the stone floor, twined her fingers into its corner, and took a deep breath. Her fear of being discovered was so strong that even shouting silently felt wrong. She shoved the fear away and screamed the words of the spell into the void.

Like the protection-stones, the magic for this spell had been prepared by others, allowing her to call upon it with a minimum of her own strength. Even so, the effort drove Ileni to her knees and almost knocked her sideways. She pressed her knuckles to the stone and held herself up, forcing her eyes open and hoping some part of the cloth was touching a spot where Cadrel's blood had been.

The cloth turned black-red, and the stench of rotting flesh assailed her. She gasped with relief. The cloth disintegrated, falling apart in a sprinkle of blood-black ashes, and in its place was a dead man, flat on his stomach with his head twisted to the side.

She had seen Cadrel several times before he left, and this was him. The deep-set eyes were bulging, the thin mouth open. He lay on his stomach, dressed in brown breeches and a tunic that was, in places, still white. But most of it was covered with a dark, jagged stain. A long knife hilt jutted from his back.

He fell. Ileni snorted under her breath and crawled to the side of the body. The knife hilt was simple and unadorned, carved with a spiral design. She reached for it, and her hand went right through it. She kept her hand there, her pale skin cutting through the straight line of steel. She could think of half a dozen spells that would tell her something about who had held it last, but not one that she had the strength for.

Shame rose in her throat. She pushed it away. She could try to call up the shadow reflections of Cadrel's last moments—but that would take everything she had, and leave her drained for the next few days. She couldn't risk it, not when she had dozens of killers to teach the next morning, not when her life was in danger every second.

She knew an easier spell, one that would help her find the real knife. Once she had that, she could use another spell to discover who had thrown it last. It was frustrating to have to work through such small, incremental spells, but she had no choice.

She opened her mouth to begin chanting, and something slammed into her from behind.

She cried out, trying to change the words into a defensive spell as she crashed face-first into the dead man's image. It shattered around her, and she braced herself for the knife thrust into her own back. Pain shot up her wrists as she rolled over and looked up into two glowering brown eyes and a mouthful of sharp teeth.

She bit off a scream and lay very, very still. The dog let out a low, rumbling growl. It was large and black, with pointed ears laid flat against the sides of its head.

Not a knife thrust, then, but teeth tearing into her throat . . . Ileni half-sobbed. Animals were difficult to control with magic. Even if she hadn't just drained most of her power, she wouldn't have dared try. She brought one arm up to shield her throat. Still, the dog didn't move.

Ileni sucked in a long, shaky breath and forced down her panic, trying to think. It was guarding her, waiting for . . . what?

For its master. Ileni flexed one hand—slowly, so as not to startle the dog—and said softly, "Azkarabilin—"

"Don't!" Sorin said sharply. "Don't hurt him. He's not going to attack you."

Ileni didn't move, not even to glance toward the assassin's voice. She knew how hunts worked. The dog brought down the prey, and the hunter finished the job. "If you don't want him hurt," she said, "call him off."

Sorin was silent for so long that Ileni feared he would

call her bluff. Then he said, "Down, Fang."

The dog sat back on its haunches, mouth still open. Ileni curled her fingers into a fist and turned her head in Sorin's direction. She could make out his shape in the shadows. "Is he yours?"

Sorin stepped into the glow of the magelight, his body a harsh outline against the dim light. His angular face was completely without expression. "That's not the most important question right now."

"It is to me." Ileni did her best to sound unafraid— as unafraid as she could while flat on her back with terror coursing through her. He had caught her sneaking through the caves, here where death must be the punishment for any infraction. The only reason she was still alive, probably, was because he had questions. Once she answered them . . .

So perhaps she should avoid answering them.

She glanced again at the dog. "When do you have to kill him?"

Sorin stopped in mid-step. "Kill him?"

"Isn't that how it works? You're given the dog when it's a puppy. You raise it and care for it." Ileni glanced at the dog, who lolled his tongue at her. "Then, when your training is done, you have to kill it."

Sorin leaned back slightly, his body poised, perfectly balanced. "Is that the story they tell of us?"

"One of the stories," Ileni said evenly. Cautiously, she levered herself up onto her elbows. "They also say that your first kill, once you're through training, has to be your parents. That you believe your master is a god. And that from the time you enter these caves, you are given a drug that induces unimaginable ecstasy, but that will kill you slowly if you ever stop taking it."

He cocked his head at her. His skin was near white in the magelight, his eyes even blacker by contrast. "And which of those stories do you believe?"

"I don't know," Ileni said. "Yet."

He regarded her silently, then gestured at the dog. "He's not mine. We have a kennel so we can be taught to deal with guard dogs. I was practicing when I heard you."

"In the middle of the night?"

"We're trained to go without sleep."

Ileni risked pushing herself up to a sitting position. The dog growled softly but didn't move.

"Why were you following me?" she said.

His eyebrows arched slightly. Had he actually expected her to believe his ridiculous story? "Because you left your room. Did you think I wouldn't be able to tell?"

"So you were watching my room?"

Sorin moved closer, and her breath hitched, but he merely knelt beside the dog. He ran one hand over the animal's head, scratching behind the ears, and the dog half-closed his eyes without removing his gaze from Ileni. Sorin's gaze was every bit as steady, but colder. "This is not distracting me from the more pressing question. What are you doing here?"

Unfortunately, Ileni still hadn't thought of a reasonable lie. Possibly because there wasn't one. She hesitated, then said, "I'm trying to find out who killed Cadrel."

Sorin frowned. "Cadrel's death was an accident."

"I'm sure it was. Merely a coincidence that he was surrounded by hundreds of trained killers at the time."

Sorin dropped his hand from the dog's head and shifted toward her—a slight motion, but suddenly Ileni couldn't breathe. The unspent power in that movement, the focused strength in his body, made her feel soft and helpless. He could kill her. She reminded herself that her ward would protect her against a direct attack . . . but it would do nothing if he unleashed the dog on her. She could die like Cadrel had, deep in these caves, and they would call it another accident.

With her blood pounding through her, all she could think of was to tell him the truth. Or part of it. "I would rather not be the next Renegai murdered down here. I came to find out what Cadrel's body looked like right after he died."

Sorin pivoted with sinuous grace, coming to a crouch right beside her. He was so close she could feel the heat coming off his skin, and she drew away as subtly as she could. The dog was still watching her closely, sharp teeth very much in evidence.

"And what," Sorin said, "did it look like?"

"He had a knife in his back."

Sorin went so utterly still she could have sworn he stopped breathing. "Describe it."

"A straight steel knife. The hilt had a spiral design."

"That's a standard assassin's knife. It doesn't tell us anything."

"It could have, if you hadn't interrupted me. But it *did* tell me Cadrel didn't die in a fall."

Silence. Apparently she had gotten so in the habit of defiance that even abject terror didn't stop her. She told herself that was a good thing, even as her muscles clenched so hard they hurt. If she was as powerful as he believed she was, maybe she really wouldn't be afraid of him.

Sorin's eyes narrowed. Softly, he said, "Are you calling me a liar?"

His tone sent a new bolt of fear through her, and with it a sudden, fatalistic recklessness. She might be about to die, but she didn't have to do it cowering. "You *are* a killer," she reminded him. "You might not know it, but to most people, that's worse than being a liar. Don't expect me to trust you."

He didn't react. "If I hadn't interrupted you, could you have discovered who last held the knife?"

If she said *yes*, and he was the one who had killed Cadrel, her life would end within the next few seconds. But she didn't think his surprise had been faked. On the other hand, he was probably far better at faking reactions than she was at reading them.

"Yes," she said. And then, when his mouth tightened: "But I can't do it again. That spell only works once."

To her relief, he seemed to accept that. He sat back on his heels. "What will you do when you find the murderer?"

She shrugged, relieved that he had said *when*. Her illusion of power was successful, then. That was probably all that was keeping her alive right now. "I expect that will depend on who he is."

He looked at her more carefully. "You won't kill him?"

"My people don't kill."

"How inconvenient," he murmured. "Even if you're probably his next target?"

"I . . ." She hadn't actually thought that far ahead. Neither, apparently, had the Elders. Maybe because *they* didn't expect her to succeed.

"I'll tell you what." Sorin got to his feet, smooth as a snake unwinding. "I'll make it easier for you. I'll help you find him, and when we do, *I'll* kill him."

"You . . ."

"I'll start," Sorin said, "by helping you back to your chambers." He half-turned his head, his entire body shifting subtly with the movement. What would have been a simple motion on anyone else looked, on him, like a preparation to strike. "This time, Teacher, I suggest you remain there."

CHAPTER 4

The next morning, Ileni stood in front of a roomful of killers and tried to look like she knew what she was doing.

Dark gray mats were arranged in four neat rows on the stone floor, too thin to offer much comfort. The twenty students sitting cross-legged on them did not, in fact, look comfortable. They looked . . . ready. They sat silent and straight, all wearing identical gray tunics and woven gray pants, watching her expectantly. She would teach three classes every morning, sixty students in all, picked from the older assassins who possessed magical skill.

Ileni felt ridiculous.

It didn't matter, she told herself. She wasn't truly here to teach; turning these dangerous young men into sorcerers was far from her goal. She simply had to get through the class while using as little of the power remaining to her as possible. That meant a lot of theory—unfortunately, the Renegai didn't care much about theory, so she would have to make some up—and a lot of practice exercises.

She wished she knew what they had already learned.

Sorin sat at the rightmost edge of the back row, as poised and alert as the other students. Last night, he had led her back to her room in silence, and this morning, as he led her to the dining cavern for breakfast and then to the training area, he had said nothing that wasn't strictly necessary. Ileni carefully avoided his dark eyes as she began.

"My name is not important. You may address me as Teacher." That was how the Elders had advised her to begin, though it made her feel even stupider. "I am here as required by the truce between our people, to school you in the art of magic so you may better accomplish your missions. Much as I abhor your ways, I will faithfully fulfill my people's part of the bargain."

No one moved or blinked. They had, of course, heard this before. The introduction had been composed by the

Elders long ago, apparently with no thought of what it might feel like to recite it to a roomful of trained killers.

She took a deep breath and continued. "Four hundred years ago, when most sorcerers swore their allegiance to the Rathian Empire, my people separated from them. We were labeled renegades and hunted down. We fled here, to these mountains, to maintain our ways, build our strength, and wait for the right time to return. In exchange for my presence here, your master will leave my people in peace to pursue our task."

The wall of blank stares was not encouraging. So much for the official speech. "I don't know how much my predecessors taught you," Ileni said, "so we'll start with a simple demonstration of skill. Please observe carefully."

With a dramatic flourish, she held out her hand, and a light appeared above her palm. It was the same spell she had used in the passageways yesterday, a minor magic that didn't even require speech. She muttered a short spell to add a little dazzle to it, making the light shoot off sparks as if its power was difficult to contain.

"Can any of you duplicate that?"

The silence stretched—did it feel heavy, or was that simply the weight of solid rock above them? She closed her fist and banished the light with a frown that hid her relief.

"Well. We had better start with the basics, then. Do you know the eight preparation exercises?"

"Of course we do," one of the boys said. He was taller than the others, with the almond-shaped eyes and blue-black hair of imperial Rathian blood. How had one of the high nobility of the Empire ended up training to be an assassin? "If we are taught something, we know it. Not just because our lives may depend on it someday, but because we would disappoint the master if we didn't. We do not disappoint the master. Don't insult us with stupid questions."

Ileni had no patience for smug, narrow-minded, overconfident enthusiasts. She had been one herself until half a year ago, which did nothing to increase her tolerance. "Your name?"

"Irun." He leaned back on his hands, posturing for the other students, who were watching him. All except one; Sorin's eyes were still on her. "And Absalm didn't waste time on flashy light tricks. He was teaching us things that would actually be useful to us. Like fire spells."

"You're not ready for fire spells," Ileni said.

"Aren't we?"

His snide tone was all the warning she needed. She flipped up a defense spell, spitefully adding a mirror-aspect that would double whatever he threw at her before bouncing it back at him.

But he didn't aim his attack at her. Instead he half-turned and, with a flip of his hand and a sharp, vicious phrase, sent a bolt of green fire directly at one of his classmates.

Ileni dropped her shield and, with a word, threw her own bolt of pure white fire. It shattered Irun's attack seconds before it would have hit its intended victim. The two spells formed a blazing ball of energy, and she had to cast another spell to keep the impact contained. The ball collapsed in on itself and disappeared, leaving the cave looking even darker than before, and Ileni barely able to stand.

She hissed between her teeth. She had better things to spend her strength on than protecting killers-in-training. She whirled on Irun.

"What *exactly* was that?"

"A demonstration," he said, "of what we *have* learned. Though none of your predecessors taught us that defense. Perhaps that could be our next lesson?"

His tone was . . . no longer snide. And though his eyes were still on hers, his head was slightly lowered, enough to give the impression that he was looking up at her. Ileni quickly scanned the others' faces and saw no shock or outrage on any of them. Was there respect, or was she imagining that?

She focused on Irun's intended victim—who would certainly have been badly hurt had she not stopped the attack spell. He looked young, with round cheeks and red-brown hair. He sat as still as if the attack hadn't happened, his hands rock steady. But when he met her gaze, his eyes were those of a hunted animal.

Ironically, he practically blazed with magical power— power that her training allowed her to sense, but that *his* training, obviously, hadn't equipped him to use. She had noticed him as soon as she entered the room.

Ileni drew in a deep breath, gathering energy with it. With luck, she could remain upright long enough to finish the lesson.

"The first thing I teach," she snapped, "will be control. I've never seen such a waste of power." Here, she realized suddenly, was the excuse she had been looking for. "The most important part of your training has been sorely neglected. Before you can perform any act of magic, you need to strengthen your minds. That requires daily practice. We'll begin with the nine-pointed meditations."

Irun's chin came up, and she met his defiant eyes squarely. She didn't have to feign her lack of fear. She was too exhausted to feel much of anything. After a moment he looked down again.

"Absalm didn't teach that way," he muttered.

"He would have, if he'd had time to finish his teaching. He certainly did not expect you to use that spell without adequate preparation. You will not attack one of your fellow students again without my permission. Is that understood?"

He nodded curtly.

"Good." She swept her gaze around the rest of the room and saw that everyone's eyes were respectfully lowered. Maybe that expenditure of power had been worth it after all. Or would be, once she could breathe without effort again.

Later that night, as she slept fitfully on her narrow bed, someone touched her elbow. She rolled over and murmured sleepily, "Tellis?"

And thudded off the bed onto the floor.

The fall drove the breath out of her body, leaving an empty space that was immediately flooded with grief. She gasped, not caring that she was flat on her stomach, completely vulnerable—

—to whomever had woken her in the first place.

She scrambled to get to her feet and turn around at the same time. Sorin took several slow strides back, his hands held up before him.

After a moment, Ileni decided to be furious rather than frightened. If he had come to kill her, he wouldn't have bothered to wake her first. "What are you doing here?"

By the faint light of the glowstones, Sorin's face looked sharp and feral. "Who is Tellis?"

"No one you have any right to ask about. Any more than you have a right to be here, in my room, in the middle of the night! How did you open the door?"

He smiled at her, a quick flash of white teeth. "It was already open."

She stalked past him. There—a thin wedge of cloth, jammed into the corner between the doorpost and the floor. It would have kept the door from closing completely, and, therefore, the wards from working.

Furious—mostly at herself, for not being more careful— she kicked the cloth out into the corridor before turning back.

Sorin was watching her in a way that made her suddenly remember she was wearing only a long sleep-tunic. He was in the same gray tunic and gray pants he wore during the day. She fought not to blush, failed, and lifted her chin.

He spread his arms out from his sides, in a manner she suspected was supposed to look innocent. It didn't. Like every move he made, it radiated honed menace. "It is not your room. You have been given the use of it, that is all. Everything in these caves belongs to the master."

"Thank you for the lesson in assassin ideology—"

"And he wants to see you," Sorin said. "I was sent to summon you."

In the ensuing silence, Ileni discovered that it was possible to be simultaneously furious *and* frightened. "All right," she said finally. "Will you wait outside while I dress?"

"No."

"Excuse me?"

"The master wants to see you immediately."

"I think you're being a bit too literal—"

"He said specifically that you weren't to get dressed first." Sorin's face was like stone, all hints of emotion wiped from it. Did that mean he was embarrassed?

"Does he think I have spells woven into my clothes?" But even as she said it, Ileni knew that wasn't it. He wanted her vulnerable; wanted her to understand that she was under his control. That, as Sorin had pointed out, everything in these caves was his. Including her.

She understood it perfectly. But she would be buried before she paraded the fact in her nightclothes.

Sorin was silent, waiting. She said, "All right, then, don't leave," and walked past him to the clothes chest near the far wall.

His eyes widened slightly as she pulled out a skirt. She could practically see him running his options through his mind. He didn't have many—at least, she didn't think he did. She hoped he wasn't coming up with any she hadn't considered.

Apparently not. As she reached down to lift the hem of her sleeping tunic over her head, he spun around and stared hard at the wall.

Ileni dropped the hem, instead pulling the long brown skirt over it and lacing on her scuffed leather shoes. She did it so quickly that the right felt too loose and the left too tight, but she didn't take the time to fix them. Impatience and disapproval radiated from Sorin's tight shoulders. "I'm done," she said.

"Then come," Sorin said tersely, and strode out the door without bothering to turn around.

He walked fast, making Ileni scurry to keep up. She considered demanding that he slow down, but having won the argument about her clothes, she wasn't about to start another, especially one she would probably lose. The top of her left shoe cut into her ankle with each step, which did nothing to improve her mood.

Sorin led her through the dark corridors, in the opposite direction from the dining cavern and training area. The faint light of the glowstones was barely enough to let her see his back and the ground in front of her. She concentrated on memorizing the way.

After numerous twists and turns—some of which, she darkly suspected, were unnecessary—Sorin paused in an irregularly shaped cavern. Masses of thin stalactites hung from the ceiling like tiny knives, the dusky light of the glowstones reflecting off them as if they were macabre chandeliers. In the center, a large stalactite hanging from the ceiling and an equally large stalagmite growing from the ground had met and fused together, forming a long column of almost pure-white rock, thick at its base, narrowing at its center, and then thickening again when it met the ceiling. Hundreds of little marks were carved into the sides of the natural pillar.

"What is that?" she asked, glad of an excuse to pause and lean against a wall. Sorin's quick pace, and the itching pain in her left ankle, had drained her surge of adrenaline.

Sorin stopped a few feet away from the column and braced his legs wide, as if balancing to attack. But it was just his natural stance; he glanced from the column to her with pride. "That's the Roll of Honor. It lists those who successfully killed their targets."

The painstakingly carved names took up the entire surface of the white rock, from its base through its narrow middle, and then circled around the column where it began thickening toward the ceiling. About a quarter of the names were not merely chiseled but inlaid with gold, glimmering by the dim light of the glowstones.

Each name represented a death, a man or woman whose life had ended suddenly and brutally. Ileni wrapped her arms around her body as a shiver ran through her. It had been a mistake to stop, to give herself time to think.

"The master suggested I show you this," Sorin added. "Since it's on the way."

Ileni forced her arms to her sides. This was meant to scare her. Well, then, she refused to act scared.

Sorin was watching her, his forehead wrinkled, probably trying to judge her reaction so he could report it to his master. It was hard to believe he couldn't see her terror. She said the first thing that came to mind. "Are you on it?"

"Yes."

Said with quiet pride, but with a defensive curve to his

shoulders. A part of her wanted to ask who he had killed, but she thought better of it. "Why are some of the names in gold?"

"They not only killed their targets, but stayed alive afterward." Sorin tilted his chin, looking up at the column. "On their first missions, at least."

So his name was one of the gold ones. "Is that considered especially impressive?"

"We are permitted to stay alive, if we can do so without compromising our mission. But the mission comes first."

"I'm sure," Ileni said.

"We are not afraid to die. And we know how to overcome our own petty desires and fears." He met her eyes. "Something you might consider learning."

"Really."

"I don't mean to be insulting," Sorin said, managing to make it sound completely sincere and completely untrue at the same time. "I can help make your time here more successful, if you'll listen to my advice."

"How kind." At least this was distracting her, and delaying the inevitable.

Sorin's shoulders rose and fell with his sigh. "I want you to succeed."

"You do?"

He looked faintly irritated. "If I didn't, why would I be helping you find Cadrel's killer? Magic helps us accomplish our missions. We all want you to be our tutor for as long as possible."

"All?" Ileni said. "That wasn't my impression."

As soon as she said it, she wished she could take it back. She hadn't meant to show how much Irun's attack had shaken her. But Sorin's voice softened. "Irun is . . . a problem. He's an imperial noble."

Ileni blinked. Back home, *imperial noble* was the filthiest insult possible. The thought that Irun had actually been one of them . . . well. It made sense. "If he's a noble, how did he—"

"He was kidnapped at a young age. No one knew why at the time. It was years before the master revealed his reasons."

Ileni chewed her lower lip. "Kidnapped? Does he know?"

"Of course."

"Is that how all of you—"

"Not usually. About half of us are abandoned street children. The other half are sent by secret pockets of supporters throughout the Empire. They send us their sons, when they can."

"Supporters of what?" Ileni said. "The right kind of knife thrust?"

Sorin's lips tightened, but he went on without responding. "We're also not . . . discouraged . . . from fathering children, while we're on our missions. If we have time."

And did you have time? Ileni's cheeks flamed. She had heard that assassins had a reputation in the Empire, that women found them irresistible . . . and she didn't particularly want to hear the details. But she was too curious to stop. "And then you go collect them afterward? How do their mothers feel about that?"

"It doesn't matter," Sorin said. "The children belong here."

A shudder ran through her. "Do you remember *your* mother?"

Sorin's face returned to complete blankness. "I don't. My earliest memory is of living with a group of other children, digging food from garbage heaps, stealing it when I could. For all I know, she abandoned me at birth."

Like other Renegai children with both talent and power, Ileni had been taken to the training compound at an early age, so she didn't feel the connection to her mother that ordinary children did. But she had always known she *had* a mother, who loved her and was proud of her. She had refused to see her mother after her final Test, afraid all that love and pride would be gone.

"When I was five years old," Sorin said, "I was caught stealing. The punishment was to cut my hand off." His voice was as flat as his expression. "That's the punishment for theft all through the Empire, no matter the age of the thief. I had taken two silvers from a nobleman's belt-pouch. He wouldn't even have missed them."

"Sorin—" She shifted her feet, but stayed where she was. She knew, of course, how brutal life in the Rathian Empire was. She had heard dozens of stories, each more horrible than the last. But she had never before met anyone who had lived there, who had been forced to endure it.

"I got away from the nobleman. And I killed one of the soldiers who came after me with his own knife." His shoulders hunched slightly. "But there were too many, and I was a child. They broke my arm, and I was sentenced to death." He spoke in a calm, even monotone. "Fortunately for me there had been an assassin in the square, on a mission. He saw what I did, and he was impressed. After he completed his kill, he got me out of the prison and brought me here."

The stone wall was cold through Ileni's thin shirt. Her

back pressed against it so hard she could feel the tiny ridges in the stone. "Which one is he?"

For the first time, Sorin's voice betrayed an emotion: surprise. "That was over ten years ago, Ileni. He's dead."

She could think of nothing to say to that. *I'm sorry* seemed ridiculous, when he didn't sound sorry himself. And of course, the man *would* be dead. How long did any assassin live?

Sorin leaned back to gaze up at the column of names— his mentor's name must be on it, somewhere; she wondered if he had the space memorized—then glanced sideways at Ileni. His expression seemed unreadable, but then she placed it; it just wasn't one she had expected. Or wanted. Pity. He shook his head and said, "Are you ready to continue?"

Ileni pushed herself off the wall. "I've been ready all along."

He gave her a longer version of the same look, then led her through several corridors until, in the middle of a downward-slanting passageway, he turned sideways and vanished. It took Ileni a few seconds to find the narrow slit in the rock he had disappeared into, half-hidden by a curve in the wall. Sorin was already yards ahead of her by the time she squeezed through and emerged into the long narrow passageway on the other side.

Something in her rebelled. The Elders' voices whispered in her mind: *The master sits at the center of a web, spinning intrigues and deceits across the Empire. Death is simply one of his tactics.*

What if she didn't follow Sorin at all, what if she turned and went the other way, and never faced what lay ahead?

Then she would die anyhow, alone in the dark, when her magic ran out and she starved to death. And she would die without helping her people, without finding any answers, without even buying time. A death as useless as her life.

She strode after Sorin, following him through a series of twists and turns that made it feel like they were walking in circles, until they reached a steep stone staircase that wound upward into darkness.

Sorin glanced at her sideways and said, "You should go first."

"Why?"

"So I can catch you if you fall."

"I don't—" she began, and then suspicion made her go silent. His face was perfectly stolid and unsmiling. "Are you making fun of me?"

"Do you truly imagine I would ever do that?" he said, still not cracking a smile. "It wouldn't be properly respectful."

"Good thing I'm not in my nightclothes, then," Ileni snorted, and started up the stairs. She was almost sure she saw his lips twitch as she went past.

It was a long, weary trek to the top of the stairs. By the time the end was in sight, Ileni was no longer sure that Sorin had been joking about catching her. She was dizzy, and wished she had thought to insist upon something to drink as well as clothes. Her calves ached, and her left shoe had rubbed her ankle raw.

She looked at the heavy wooden door that ended the stairway, then turned to Sorin. He was standing a few steps below her looking irritatingly unaffected by the long climb. Ileni pushed strands of hair off her sweat-slicked forehead. Her voice shook. She hoped he would think it was because of exertion. "What am I supposed to do—knock?"

"Is that how they do it where you come from?"

Ileni turned, placed both hands flat on the door, and pushed.

The door was heavy, but swung inward far more easily than she had expected. Ileni managed not to stumble, but she rushed into the room with a bit less dignity than she had planned. She let go of the door and heard it slam shut behind her. Sorin hadn't followed her in.

That seemed like a bad sign. She dug her fingers into her skirt. The room was irregularly shaped, about six paces across, and there was no one in it. Two lamps, set in the black stone walls, lit the space murkily. There was a patterned rug in the center of the floor, a high-backed cushioned chair in the corner, and a window in the far wall.

Ileni headed for the window. It was deep and recessed, but placing her elbows on the sill, she could lean out far enough to see the dark velvet of the sky, carelessly embroidered with tiny pinpoints of stars. Ahead of her was nothing but blackness. She knew the darkness hid trees and mountains, but it was as if she was staring straight into a sky that folded back on itself to stretch over her head. A shiver ran through her. She hadn't realized how badly she missed the sight of sky and open space, the feel of the wind, after only two days underground. What would she feel like in a week—a month—a year? The rest of her life?

Someone cleared his throat behind her, and she remembered that the rest of her life might not be that unbearably long. She pulled back in and turned.

She hadn't heard the door open, and she hadn't heard footsteps. But a man now sat in the high-backed chair, his face and form almost hidden by the dark.

CHAPTER 5

A prickle ran up Ileni's spine as she pressed her back against the windowsill, looking at the tall dark figure in the chair. It wasn't magic that had gotten him here so silently; she would have sensed a spell. The wooden door was still closed, and Sorin was nowhere in sight.

The man was so still he might have been dead. Ileni opened her mouth and couldn't think of anything to say. Her mind whirled in panic as she stood frozen to the spot. What she came up with, finally, was, "Nice view."

It wouldn't have been so bad if she had managed to sound sardonic, or even cool. Instead her voice emerged shaky and frightened. The master leaned forward, bringing his face out of the darkness and into the shadows. She still couldn't make out his features, but his eyes, fierce and bright, shone in the lamplight like those of a hunting animal. The silence settled as heavily as before.

Ileni drew in her breath. The pressure of his gaze made her feel as if she was forcing out words. "Where's Sorin?"

The master's voice was soft and dry, and unexpectedly gentle. "He doesn't need to be here."

Why not? Her own heartbeat filled the dark chamber. She felt tiny and powerless, like a mouse in the shadow of a hawk. "Why do *I* have to be here?"

"I never got to meet Cadrel before he died." The voice was almost a purr. "I don't want to make that mistake again."

"Of not meeting me before I die?" Her voice shook. She couldn't help it, but she was starting not to care.

Instead of replying, the master rose.

That was all he did, yet she felt as if a dozen daggers were pointed at her chest. She had thought Sorin and the other assassins exuded menace, but they were pale imitations of this man. *He can kill with a flick of his fingers*, the Elders had said, and she believed it.

She wanted to back away—no, she wanted to *run*—but

his eyes pinned her where she stood. Small and dark though they were, they took over his entire face, and their focus on her drove the breath out of her body. She wanted to look away, but she couldn't. His eyes burned like flames, lit up from within by . . . wisdom? power? madness? Something else, something that was all those things and more.

He smiled sympathetically, as if he understood. Very slowly, he moved his head to the side and shifted his gaze away.

Ileni gasped, and air came pouring back into her lungs. Her legs felt as if they couldn't support her body, but there was no other chair in the room. Besides, she was afraid to move.

"Sorin says you seem different from the other tutors," the master of assassins said. "And he's a perceptive boy. Have you found him helpful in easing your adjustment to your new life?"

"I . . ." She tried to think. "Not . . . not really."

"That's unfortunate." He swung his head back toward her, but this time the effect of his gaze was muted—deliberately, she thought, and was grateful despite herself. She had no desire to be trapped again in that black stare. "Sorin is in many ways the best of my pupils. He has influence with the others. You are at a disadvantage to begin with, being so young. . . ." *And female*, he didn't add. "How do you plan to deal with the fact that your students will not respect you?"

A flash of defiance made it through her fear. "I plan to not care."

"I wouldn't be so sure you have that option."

Ileni managed a shrug. Her voice emerged slightly firmer. "Even if one of them is going to kill me, that doesn't mean I have to care what he thinks."

For the first time, she thought she got a reaction out of the man. Nothing obvious, no movement or actual change of expression, but his face went still for a second.

"You don't want to be here," he said, his voice gentle, "but you are. The sooner you accept that, the easier it will be for you.

Ileni set her jaw. "I volunteered to come."

"Did you?"

"I was chosen, and I did not refuse."

He studied her, and she felt pierced, as if he was seeing through her words and through her skin. "But you would have, if there was anyplace but here you could get away to."

How could he possibly know that? She hadn't told anyone. It wasn't until the journey was nearly over that she had realized it herself.

"I want to be of service to my people," she said. Her voice sounded shrill and childish in her ears.

"Even though you hate them?"

Her hands came halfway up, as if she was defending herself against a physical blow. *That*, she hadn't even admitted to herself.

The master chuckled, low and dry. "I am not calling you a liar. You can want more than one thing at once. You can desire the respect of people you resent. You feel that way about Sorin already."

Stop, she thought. When someone knocked on the wooden door, she almost gasped in relief.

The master didn't take his eyes off her as he raised his voice. "Come in."

Sorin pushed the door open and stepped into the dim room. A short, thin boy followed him.

Finally, the master turned away from her. He sat back down, placing both forearms on the arms of his chair. "Jastim, is it?"

The boy nodded stiffly, his face bleak as stone. Terror radiated from him so palpably that Ileni nearly backed away.

"You honor our cause."

It wasn't a question, but the pause that followed seemed

to demand an answer. The boy jerked his head in another nod.

The master's voice turned rhythmic—almost lyrical. "You honor it more subtly than others do. But you honor it nonetheless. Your courage will be remembered."

The boy met his master's eyes, and some of the terror went out of his face. He lifted his chin, and this time, his nod was smooth and firm.

"Please show the sorceress," the master of assassins said, "how completely my commands are obeyed in these caves."

Sorin stepped back, and Jastim moved across the room, straight toward Ileni. He was short, but ropy muscles twisted through his arms. His mouth was a thin, determined line, and his eyes were shining. With fear . . . no, pride. Or at least, mostly pride.

Panic gave Ileni strength to pull up a defensive spell. It wavered unevenly, a lack of finesse that would have been unthinkable for her a year ago, but it held.

He walked right past her, his face exultant, and vaulted onto the windowsill in a fluid movement. He poised there, crouched, his body taking up all the space in the square opening. He didn't have enough room to look back in at them, had he wanted to.

"Jump," the master said.

Jastim launched himself into the night.

Ileni screamed. She was at the window instantly, half-expecting to see a slim, dark shape soaring up toward the stars.

Far below, something hit the ground with a distant, sickening thump.

Bile rose in Ileni's throat, and she forced herself to swallow it. Her fingers dug into the stone windowsill so hard they hurt, but she didn't turn around, and she didn't—she *didn't*—look down. She stared straight out at the black mountains and blacker sky, at the view that no longer looked like freedom.

The Elders' voices were dim and distant in her mind: *He will kill for reasons that make sense to no one but him.*

But he always has a reason.

"Thank you," the master said behind her. Who was he saying it to? "You may go."

She whirled, tears tracking down her cheeks. The master's eyes were still gentle—terribly, horribly gentle. He smiled at her, utterly calm, as if Jastim was a chess piece he had flicked off the board, not a human boy with scared blue eyes whose blood and bones were now splattered on the rocks below.

Ileni walked across the small room, feeling the master's

gaze on her back, between her shoulder blades. Sorin waited until she was only a step away, then turned and led the way out.

The master's voice stopped her when she was already in the doorway. "Sorceress?"

She stopped with one hand on the doorpost, not quite able to look back at him.

"If you assume everyone here is about to attack you, you'll go through a lot of defense spells." He chuckled, low and dry. "And you'll need to preserve your power, won't you? For as long as you can."

He knew. How could he possibly know?

She gave up on the pretense of dignity and fled, almost falling down the stairs in her haste to get away.

She and Sorin were halfway down the steps before she could speak. "You knew what you were bringing that boy up there to do."

Sorin said nothing. He was a step ahead of her, so she couldn't see his face.

She stumbled, and reached out to steady herself on the wall. "How could you do it?"

"Would you have me arrange for him to live forever?" Sorin asked softly. "We all die, eventually. Jastim's death had a purpose. Death, to us, is not something to fear. It is simply a tool. Any one of us would die if so commanded by our master. Any of us would be *glad* to." His tone twisted slightly. "I wouldn't expect you to understand."

"So you would waste your life—"

"Not wasted." Sorin's voice was firm. "The master does not waste lives. If he spent Jastim's death to impress you, there's a reason that was important."

She couldn't imagine the master caring whether she was *impressed* with him. Even if she was the most powerful Renegai sorceress born in centuries. Or had been thought to be so, once.

But the master knew she wasn't. He had gained that information, somehow, just by looking at her, just by talking to her for a few seconds. She wrapped her arms around herself, then forced them back to her sides before Sorin saw.

When would the master tell him—tell everyone? He could jerk away her pretense of power, and leave her at his students' mercy, any time he wanted.

They reached the bottom of the stairs, and she quickened her pace. But Sorin sped up, too, so she was still staring at the back of his head. "So you're just his tools? No thoughts or will of your own? You don't care?"

"Not quite." Sorin still hadn't glanced back at her. "I assure you, every person in these caves is doing his best to ensure he is too valuable to be given that command."

He did slow down then, and Ileni found herself striding beside him. He didn't look at her—his profile was carved in stone—but it was as good as an invitation to keep talking. "Your master said you could ease my transition. Is that your task—to make sure I obey, and kill me if I don't?"

Sorin turned sideways, cutting in front of her. She half-pulled up a defense spell before she realized that they had reached the narrow entrance back into the main caverns, and she had almost walked past it. She sighed and let the spell go. The master of assassins was right. If she didn't become less jumpy, her power would be completely drained in a week.

Tonight's events were certainly not going to help her be any less jumpy.

"My task is to protect you," Sorin said.

"And you don't think there might be more to it than that?"

Sorin made an irritated gesture. "I don't presume to guess the master's motives. I can't fathom his reasons for wanting me to help you, just as I wouldn't try and figure out his purpose in tonight's summons."

"Then you're stupid," Ileni said, more sharply than she had intended. "I know what his purpose was. To make sure I'm as afraid of him as everyone else in these caves."

"Did it work?" Sorin asked.

His dark eyes were grave and serious, and he watched her with an odd intentness, as if her answer was important.

Ileni couldn't bring herself to shoot back a flippant reply. So she told the truth, grudgingly. "Yes."

Sorin sighed, a sound so small it could have been merely an uncontrolled breath. Then he walked on, and they made their way through the long passageways and empty caverns in silence.

After the sorceress and Sorin left, the master sat silently for several heartbeats, contemplating the empty window where the boy had crouched. A few brief minutes ago Jastim had been alive, his mind bright with fear; now he was a crushed pile of bone and blood. At times, even after all these years and all these deaths, the contrast still struck the master. Once, it had seemed important.

He tilted his head and said, "What do you make of that?"

A man stepped out of the shadows on the far side of the room. He was thin to the point of gauntness, the bones of his face jutting out around his narrow features. He watched the master, his hands clasped behind his back. "I think it was effective."

"She wasn't completely cowed. I like that." The master stroked the side of his chin. "And so, I think, did Sorin."

The thin man pressed his lips together. "We'll have to put a stop to that."

"Will we?" the master said.

His voice was smooth and level, but the thin man cringed slightly. "I mean—I would suggest that we don't allow any interest to develop. It could be dangerous."

"Or it could be useful."

The thin man tugged at his earlobe, and immediately regretted it. It was a nervous habit of his, and he wished to appear calm . . . not that he thought he could fool the master. But there was no need to be obvious. "I know your pupils' reputation out in the Empire. But this girl is no easy picking. And it would not be wise to encourage your students to . . . think of her that way. It's risky enough as it is, bringing a girl into these caves."

"Is it?" The master smiled faintly, and the thin man bit

his lip. He knew that smile. It meant he had fallen prey to the master's misdirection, had missed some crucial part of his plan. Or plans. The master always had more than one. "I don't think so. My students are, as you have seen, well trained in controlling their natural instincts."

"Not that it wasn't impressive." The thin man cleared his throat. "But killing yourself takes only one second. Control takes *every* second. Your students are extraordinarily disciplined, but they are still boys beneath it all."

"True enough." The master seemed to be considering this, though the thin man knew, from long experience, that he must have already considered it. Now he couldn't tell if the master was truly reconsidering, or just testing him in some way. He waited, resisting the urge to fidget.

Finally, the master nodded. "If necessary, someone other than Sorin can be assigned as her guardian."

"Who would you trust more than Sorin?" the thin man objected. "He is a perfect assassin."

"Yes," the master said, almost to himself. "But there is a part of him that wishes not to be."

The thin man blinked. "A part of him that objects to killing?"

The master smiled faintly. "Of course not. He is far

beyond that. But there is a part of him that objects to perfection."

The thin man did not understand, but he was used to that. He had seen the master's plans turn out successfully too many times to worry—much—about what he didn't understand.

The master turned his attention back to the window. "I believe I will take the risk."

"We should not take any risk," the thin man said. "Not with this. Not with her."

"Don't grow too attached to your plans, old friend. She is a useful tool. But if a tool turns out to be flawed, one discards it, yes?"

The thin man lifted his hand toward his earlobe, then caught himself and scratched his chin instead. He bowed his head briefly, then turned and left.

The master of assassins thought for a long time, his fingers drumming steadily on the arm of his chair, his eyes on the bruised purple hues the sky took on with the fading of night.

CHAPTER 6

Much to her surprise, Ileni fell asleep instantly after she crawled into her cot. She dreamed of falling, of toppling over the edge of a stone windowsill, of the master's cold eyes watching her from the hard ground below. She woke up sweat soaked, sandy eyed, and in no mood to tutor a group of killers who would die as easily as they would kill.

Sorin, when he arrived, looked as rested as if he had spent the entire night asleep in his cot. With him was a boy, wearing the assassins' typical gray clothes, who couldn't have been more than eight years old. Without a glance in her direction, the boy went to her bedside, picked up her chamber pot, put an empty one in its place, and left the room.

Sorin made no mention of last night's events as he led her to the dining cavern for breakfast. Ileni kept glancing at him sideways, searching for a trace of the vulnerability she had seen—or imagined—at the Roll of Honor. She might as well have been looking at a marble statue.

Like the day before, he left her at a small round table on one side of the rectangular cavern, then crossed to where twenty young men sat together at a long table. There were five such tables, all occupied by the older assassins, and one of them must have an empty seat today. Did the other assassins know yet what had happened to Jastim? That his life had been ended for her benefit?

Was that something the master of assassins did for every new Renegai tutor? Sacrifice one of his killers to show how absolute his control was?

If that was even why he had done it. *I can't fathom his reasons*, Sorin had said. Remembering those dark eyes, that cold, knowing smile, Ileni believed him.

She stirred her spoon through the thick porridge she couldn't bring herself to taste. The students probably had no idea, but maybe one of the teachers would know if this was standard procedure or a special performance staged just for her.

At the sixth table sat a dozen older men, some of whom she recognized from the training arena, some of whom she didn't.

A fit of recklessness came over her. She was a teacher, wasn't she? She should sit with the teachers. Tell them what had happened, see how they reacted. She certainly wasn't going to learn anything by sitting here alone, watching her porridge grow cold.

She picked up her bowl and was about to swing her legs over the bench when the door opened and a tall man walked in, so lanky his arms seemed awkward despite his assassin's grace. He was older than any of the teachers at the table, with white-flecked gray hair. Ileni had never seen him before.

"A summons from the master," he said, and the room was instantly silent. Every person in it bowed his head briefly.

Ileni fought an urge to bow her own head with them, and even that small defiance made her heart hammer as if she was doing something wrong. Her glance darted toward Sorin, but he wasn't looking at her. His eyes were fixed on the tall man, and for once his expression was transparent: hope, so intense it was almost painful to see.

That same hope was mirrored on every boy in the room. With some, there was a bit of trepidation too. But not with Sorin.

"Ravil," the man said, and the black-haired boy next to Sorin leaped away from the table, his face shining.

"I am honored to serve," he said.

The gray-haired teacher turned and walked out, and the young assassin followed, ignoring the envious and speculative glares aimed at him. Ileni watched him, too, her whole body tense with the excitement thrumming through the air.

As soon as the door closed, the cavern exploded with noise: "I thought it would be Jadbez—" "Do you think he's being sent to the Imperial Academy? I heard—" "He's been doing extra training in Tanfirian. His target must be—"

Sorin's face had gone stony, and he was staring at his bowl without eating. Every line of his body was rigid with tightly controlled . . . not anger, exactly. Rebellion?

It seemed impossible, but once she thought the word, she recognized it. She had felt the same herself, when her destiny started slipping away, wanting to strike out and change the path narrowing in front of her. Wanting to be free of her own future. She, too, had always controlled herself.

Something sharp and daring surged through her. She

picked up her bowl, walked over to the place Ravil had vacated, and pushed his abandoned bowl away to make room for hers.

Everyone stared at her, but it was Sorin's eyes she met. "Am I allowed to sit here?"

"I don't know," Sorin said evenly.

"So I suppose I should play it safe?" She made it a challenge.

He looked back at his own plate, but not before she saw the gleam in his eyes. It was the sort of gleam that, on anyone else, would have been accompanied by a smile. "You should," he said. But it didn't sound like a warning. It sounded like an invitation.

She slid onto the bench next to him, her sleeve almost brushing his. The boy on her other side, gangly and blond, watched with thin lips pressed together. "Where is he being sent?"

Sorin spooned some porridge into his mouth. "I don't know."

"Why weren't *you* sent?"

Only the faint rippling of muscles beneath gray sleeves gave his tension away. He chewed and swallowed before answering. "I don't know that either. But if the master believes Ravil is best suited for this mission, he is right."

Ileni raised her eyebrows. "How trusting of you."

He shot a sideways glare at her. The gleam was gone. "You've met him. Do you think he's a man who makes mistakes?"

Ileni swallowed. The tingle of daring vanished as fast as it had come, leaving only the sour taste of fear in her mouth. She moved her arm, which had almost been touching Sorin's, closer to her body. She had been reckless enough for one day, and obviously this was a conversation best backed away from. "How many missions have you—"

Sorin moved like a snake uncoiling, lunging forward. She jerked to the side instinctively, and his arm brushed her hair as he grabbed the upraised arm of the blond boy on her other side.

"Don't," Sorin said. His voice was low and perfectly calm.

The other boy did something complicated with his wrist, almost pulling his arm free. Sorin did something equally complicated, and his grip held. The other boy glared at him. "She insulted the master!"

His voice was deliberately loud, and once again the room was dead silent. Everyone was looking at Ileni, a hundred pairs of hard eyes and faintly curled lips. The weight of their disgust was palpable, making her small and loathsome.

So they kill me now, Ileni thought, and was surprised by her sudden, fierce desire to live. She gathered up what magic she had, knowing it was not enough.

"She asked a question." Sorin, too, raised his voice. "She has been answered. It's over and done."

"She spoke of *the master* with no respect at all," the boy hissed. "You're going to allow it?"

"I am," Sorin said. "Because the master commanded me to allow it."

The blond boy stared, breathing heavily. But he leaned back a fraction.

"What were his exact instructions?" Irun asked lazily, from the far end of the table. "That she be kept alive? Or that she also not be chastised for even the most filthy speech?"

The blond boy looked up eagerly, and Ileni made the mistake of meeting his gaze. The hatred in it took her breath away. The Renegai respected their Elders, too, and Ileni would never have spoken of one of them so dismissively. But if she had, she would not have been afraid for her life.

"If any of you try to *chastise* her, the master will hear of it," Sorin said. He sounded almost bored, but he was still gripping the blond boy's wrist, despite the other assassin's obvious attempts to pull away. Sorin's arm was still inches from Ileni's cheek, and she could feel his muscles trembling slightly with the strain. "He commanded that she not be harmed."

"Well. That's not precisely true, is it?" Irun stood and sauntered closer. He was on the opposite side of the table from them, but Sorin transferred his focus immediately to him, as did everyone else at the table—everyone else, Ileni realized, in the cavern. Irun was the center of attention. "He didn't command any of *us* not to harm her. He just commanded *you* to protect her."

"Which is," Sorin said, "what I'm doing." He twisted his hand. The blond boy let out a muffled whimper.

"Ah, yes. Because you've always been so obedient." A ripple of laughter went through the cavern. "Your dedication does you credit."

"Thank you." The words were a snarl.

Irun grinned. "Will you fight me for her?"

Sorin dropped the blond boy's arm and sprang into a crouch on the bench. His spine formed a taut curve, pulling his gray shirt tight. But his face was completely calm. "I'd fight an imperial dog like *you* for a copper coin."

Irun stalked closer, moving like a hunting cat, and the

assassins on his side of the table sidled away. "How fortunate for you, then, that I don't consider the foul-mouthed whore worth even that much."

Sorin leaned forward, poised and deadly. Ileni could feel his eagerness. The gleam was back in his eyes.

Irun crossed his arms over his chest and sneered. "What, were you commanded to guard her against insults, too?"

Ileni laughed. It started out too loud and forced, but her hysteria gave it an edge, made it real. Every face in the room turned to stare at her.

"It's adorable," she told Irun, "that you think anything that comes out of your mouth could bother me enough to count as an insult."

His face went blank with shock, as if a dog had started lecturing him.

"If you're done eating," Ileni added, "you should spend your time working on your hand motions for the fifth exercise. They were quite sloppy."

In the utter silence, she got to her feet and started toward the door. She hadn't gone two steps before Sorin was beside her.

She managed to walk steadily until she reached the hall outside, and then the rubbery feeling in her legs was too much. She knew, dimly, that she should keep up the pretense in front of Sorin, but she couldn't. She leaned back against the wall and closed her eyes.

No tears. She at least wasn't going to do *that* in front of him. She squeezed her eyes shut so tightly it made her head hurt.

After a few moments, while Sorin did nothing—what had she thought he would do?—she opened them again. He was leaning across the opposite wall, which seemed as far from her as he could possibly get.

"That wasn't wise," he said.

"Which part?"

"Any of it."

"Including calling Irun an imperial dog and telling him you would fight him over a coin?"

A smile seized Sorin's mouth and was gone, so fast she wasn't sure she had seen it. "I tend not to be at my wisest around Irun."

Ileni wrapped her arms around herself. "I don't think he likes me."

Sorin laughed, startling her. The laugh was astonishing. It softened the sharp lines of his face, just a little bit— but it was enough. Suddenly he didn't look dangerous at all. He looked . . . handsome. In another time, another place, he might have looked a bit like Tellis.

But it was an illusion, Ileni reminded herself.

Sorin shifted his weight away from the wall. "He won't hurt you. I won't let him."

"Thank you," she whispered, and then realized she shouldn't thank him. He was following orders.

"Try to make my task easier, by keeping your . . . opinions . . . to yourself. Especially about the master." He lowered his voice as he mentioned his leader, reverence slipping into his cool tone. "You can't say things like that. When you've been here longer, when you see how his plans unfold and realize what he's capable of, you'll understand why we follow him."

"Sorry," Ileni said, before she had time to wonder whether she should. Even she could hear the lack of sincerity in her voice.

Sorin's long jaw clenched. "You asked, last night, if I am just his tool. The answer is that I am. We all are, and we're proud to be. Whatever he demands, whatever he does, it's worth being part of." He did look at her then, and a self-mocking expression crossed his face. "Never mind. You don't need to understand. You don't need to know anything, really."

She slid across the wall, farther away from him.

Sorin looked at her carefully, his face . . . not softening, exactly, but becoming a bit less harsh. "You don't have to be afraid of *me*."

It would be extremely stupid to believe that, no matter how badly she wanted to. Ileni met his eyes.

Sorin blinked. Then he held his hand out abruptly. "Here. A peace offering."

At first she couldn't see what was in his palm. Something small and round and dark. She looked up at Sorin's expectant face, trying to guess how that could be a weapon.

"Dessert," he said. She thought she read a challenge in his eyes.

"Poison?" she said, as archly as she could. She wondered if her ward would react if it was. Probably not. He must know a dozen subtle ways to kill her without triggering the ward.

Sorin snorted. "Your class wasn't *that* bad."

What game was he playing at? She reached instinctively for magic, to tell her what he held, and the master's voice whispered in her mind: *You'll need to preserve your power, won't you? For as long as you can.*

Her stomach twisted into a knot. She reached out, plucked the ball from his hand, and popped it into her mouth.

89

It tasted bitter and sweet, solid and melting all at once, and lingered in her mouth as if she would taste it forever. She gaped at Sorin. *"Chocolate?"*

"You like it?" Sorin said.

This wasn't a gift. It was a bribe—or a promise of future bribes. What did he want from her?

She was sure she would find out soon enough.

Ileni decided not to think about that, because the velvety taste was still lingering in her mouth, coating it with rich sweetness. She ran her tongue around the inside of her teeth. She had only had chocolate a few times in her life—it was made in the southern continent and was incredibly expensive. The few traders who ventured this far into the mountains rarely bothered to carry it.

"Where did you get it?"

He looked at her. She sighed. "Let me guess. This is one of the things I don't need to know."

"You're learning," he said approvingly.

Ileni crossed her arms. She didn't need—or want—the approval of a killer. "And is this allowed? Should you be giving me . . . gifts?"

"Definitely not."

"Then why are you doing it, if it's against the rules?"

"That *is* why." The gleam was back in his eyes, this time accompanied by the hint of a grin.

I don't believe you. She turned away.

His voice stopped her. "You really thought it might be poison, didn't you?"

Without turning around, she said, "Yes."

"Then why did you eat it?"

She looked at him over her shoulder. "*You,*" she said, "haven't learned anything at all."

He made no response. In the echoing silence, she started down the corridor toward the training cavern. She didn't look back, and he walked in perfect silence, but she knew he was following her.

Sorin escorted her to the front of the class, then went to sit on his mat. Ileni looked at him, then at the nineteen other faces staring at her. Irun was one of them, leaning back slightly and smirking at her. Some of the other boys exchanged glances. They had all heard the argument in the dining cavern, and it seemed to her their stares held an edge that hadn't been there yesterday, a scarcely veiled hostility.

She was not finished proving herself.

But after her ill-advised defense spell in the master's

chamber, her power was weaker than ever. She had intended to stall for a few days, until some of it came back, but that was clearly out of the question. She was fairly sure that if she spent the class reviewing meditation—the Elders' suggestion, back in another world—Irun would start flinging spells around just to force her to react. And when she couldn't, they would know the truth.

She didn't know what the consequences would be . . . especially since their master already knew. Why hadn't he told them? What was his plan, and how did her powerlessness serve it? Because she was sure it did. Everything that happened in these caves served his purposes, somehow. She remembered his dark eyes, his pitiless smile, and dread crept into her.

He had brought her here to die. She knew it, deep in her bones. Maybe this was some sort of test he had devised for his students. A game. Maybe there would be a reward for the first assassin to figure out her secret and kill her for her deception.

"Today," she said, "fire spells."

Irun came to attention, his dark hair flipping back. Ileni looked away from him and said, "Bazel. You first."

Bazel was the round-cheeked boy Irun had attacked yesterday. He gave her a startled look, as if surprised she had noticed he was there. As he rose smoothly to his feet and made his way toward the front of the training room, she had the sense that he walked closer to the walls than any of the other boys would have; and when he came to stand beside her, he stood with his hands clasped behind his back, staring down at the floor instead of meeting her eyes. He had none of Irun's easy arrogance, none of Sorin's sense of controlled power.

He did have, without question, the most powerful magic in these caves.

Even just standing next to him, Ileni could feel it radiating from him: magical potential, power he was barely tapping into for these beginners' spells. He might never have the skill to use it fully, of course—strength and talent did not always go together—but had she been up against him in a Renegai magic contest, she would have been wary. He had almost as much power as she'd once had. Probably as much as Tellis did, and Tellis was—now—the most powerful Renegai alive.

She was going to have to be very careful to keep Bazel from realizing his full potential, which was why she had called him up first. She didn't want him to watch the others before making his own attempt.

"All right," she said. "All of you listen carefully, because this is complicated."

"We always listen carefully."

Irun, of course. If she had to contend with him all morning, somebody was going to end up dead. Probably her. "Noted," she said. "Now, you start by forming a mental image of a flame, and then—"

"Absalm said we would learn the spell best by watching him do it."

Ileni narrowed her eyes. Irun was sitting as upright as everyone else, his face blank, yet somehow he managed to give the impression that he was slouching back and smirking at her. "In case you haven't noticed, I'm not Absalm."

"I've noticed." He said it flatly, without expression, but one of the other students snickered. A brief, quickly swallowed sound, but one that rang in the stillness like a bell.

Ileni allowed herself to imagine how Irun would react if she demonstrated by setting his clothes on fire. Suddenly she was too aware of the power next to her, leaking from Bazel's skin and sizzling against hers. It made her itch with the desire to somehow draw it in and use it, unleash it, be herself again.

She had heard of taking another's power for your own, methods the imperial sorcerers had perfected—but that was evil magic, and her people had rejected it when they broke from the Rathian Empire centuries ago. Even if she had been tempted, Ileni had no idea how that kind of spell worked.

"If you're such an expert, why don't you try it first?" she snapped. No, that was a bad idea. She wished her head felt clearer. "Actually, why don't you all try it at the same time? Bazel, back to your mat. All of you, do as I say."

Bazel slunk back. He had not, as far as she could tell, changed expression once. She sneaked a glance at Sorin, not wanting to look at Irun. Sorin hadn't changed expression either. Of course.

Too late to back out. She cleared her throat. "Start with the following phrase . . ."

After ten minutes of instruction, they were ready. She watched as they spoke and gestured in unison, feeling the power build around her, battering at her, taunting her. Sorin's face was fierce with concentration. It was a difficult spell.

It wasn't until the last line of the spell that she realized she had failed to properly explain how to shift the accent mid-phrase. By then, it was too late to stop them. The room echoed with the last triumphant word, and the power let loose. Floating balls of water burst into being over the assassins' heads, then exploded. Water rained down in the small cavern, sluiced through hair and thin gray tunics, then ran in dozens of rivulets over the stone floor and out the opening that led into the main training area.

Total silence. Then someone snickered, and a second later, all twenty drenched young killers doubled over in hysterical laughter.

"That could have killed you!" Ileni shouted. If they had shifted the accent lower instead of higher, the water would have been boiling. She glared at each of them in turn—and noticed, suddenly, that it was nineteen drenched students. Bazel, though he was laughing as hard as everyone—albeit a bit tentatively, and keeping a wary eye on the others—was completely dry.

Ileni advanced upon Bazel. That cut off the laughter. Even a sudden, startled curse from the direction of the training area—where the assassins sometimes trained barefoot—didn't restart the snickers, though a few students grinned.

"What happened to you?" Ileni demanded.

Bazel looked blank, as if confused by the question, but he couldn't keep a hint of smugness from his voice. "Cadrel taught us rain-shields before he died, Teacher."

Silence. Ileni, glancing around the room, saw that no

one was grinning anymore. They must all have mastered the rain-shields—among the Renegai, three-year-olds used rain-shields—but Bazel had been the only one to think of using one.

The grins and easy laughter had turned to dark expressions and glares, all directed at Bazel. Sorin in particular looked thunderous, and Ileni could guess why: *he* was supposed to be the one who surprised his teachers with clever tricks, who surpassed the others without half-trying.

Ileni looked at Bazel thoughtfully. "Perhaps we should arrange some private lessons for you."

That caused another snicker—a far nastier, less friendly one. Bazel stared at her as if she had struck him, then lowered his eyes.

Ileni sighed, and turned to face the rest of the class. Nineteen hard faces: cold, resentful, and dripping wet.

It was Irun, of course, who spoke. "Why only Bazel?"

She blinked at him. "What?"

"Absalm gave extra lessons to everyone who had great power. Perhaps you should do the same."

She folded her arms. "I suppose you were one of them?"

"Me. Arkai. Elum. Efram." He pointed to each student as he said their name, then added, with a sneer, "and Bazel."

She followed his pointing finger, blinking. Sorin, watching

her closely, spoke up. "You disagree with his assessments, Teacher?"

"No," Ileni said, too stunned to lie. She didn't disagree at all. Irun had correctly identified the five students in her class with the most raw power.

But correctly identifying them was not the tutors' purpose. The Elders had been clear on that: the treaty required them to train the assassins, but they were to do it as ineffectively as possible without raising suspicion. Non-sorcerers couldn't sense magical potential, so all the teachers were to single out the least-powerful students for the most training. Creating superior killers was the very last thing they wanted to do.

What were you up to, Absalm?

"I'll think about it," she said finally. They all watched her, their faces still unfriendly, and she took a deep breath. "In the meantime, let's try this spell again."

CHAPTER 7

"You're making a mistake," Sorin said as he walked her into the dining cavern for the midday meal.

Ileni ignored him, heading for her table. She was wrapped in her own thoughts, and Sorin walked in complete silence, so she didn't notice at first that he was following her. Only when he walked around to the other side of the table did she realize this wasn't going to be another solitary meal.

The food for the meal was laid out in the center of the table—enough for only one person. Ileni reached for the stew and dumped half of it into her bowl, then tore off a chunk of the bread and dipped it in, not looking at Sorin.

Sorin settled himself on the bench across from her with his typical predatory grace. He made no move toward the food, even though he had obviously spent much of the morning in vigorous training. Sweat still glistened on his forehead and upper arms. "You're not helping Bazel by singling him out. You're making things more difficult for him."

Ileni swallowed a spicy mouthful of stew—someone in these caves knew how to cook, which was one small mercy—and said, "I'm going to train him to use his magic. Why would that make things more difficult for him? Isn't that why I'm here?"

"You're here to help us use magic on our missions," Sorin said. "You shouldn't waste your time on Bazel. He probably won't survive long enough to be sent on his first mission."

Ileni tore off another chunk of bread. "Why? What will happen to him?"

"A fatal accident during a weapons training session, I would imagine."

Ileni wasn't sure if he was joking. Sorin leaned back on the bench, regarding her with his head tilted to the side. "Shocked that we're capable of murder, Sorceress?"

She thought carefully before answering. "Of one of your own? Yes."

"Ah, you begin to understand us." It might have sounded like a compliment, but he said it too flatly. "But I said an accident. Bazel's fighting skills are . . . not up to our standards. And so people are a little less careful when sparring with him. The better to push him to improve, you understand. And the farther behind he falls, the higher the risk." He twitched his shoulders in a shrug. "It's simply the way things work."

She couldn't think of anything to say and couldn't hide the disgust on her face. He straightened. "What do you Renegai do, to people born with inadequate magical ability?"

Ileni choked on her bread, but kept her eyes on her food. He couldn't have guessed how sharp that would cut. "We don't kill them! Among the Renegai, ordinary people are allowed to live."

"Ordinary." He mimicked her pronunciation of the word, and this time she did flinch at the nonchalant contempt in his voice. An exact echo of hers. "How nice for them, if they're willing to live with that. None of *us* would accept it."

Ileni pretended to be deeply involved in removing the mushrooms from her stew, not trusting herself to speak. She could feel his eyes boring into the top of her head, but could think of no way to deflect him.

Finally he said, "Death doesn't mean to us what it does to you. We prefer it to a life of shame."

She remembered the tight fear on the thin boy's face, the grimness in those blue eyes as he walked to the window. But he had jumped. Jumped, and fallen, and then that thud . . . she forced her mind away from the memory.

"Bazel will improve," Sorin said, "or he will die. There's no in-between."

"And you'll try to make sure it's the latter option, won't you?" she said.

Even though he couldn't see her face, he must have sensed something, because his voice softened. "Remember, he's like the rest of us. Training to kill. You've made it clear you abhor us all, so why should you care about Bazel?"

Ileni tore off another chunk of bread, but couldn't bring herself to eat it. She had been ravenous when she sat down, and now she wasn't sure she could manage to swallow. "Why do *you* care?" she demanded. "Because he's not good at fighting, he's not allowed to be good at anything? Does it bother you so much, that he's better at magic than you are?"

Sorin sat ramrod straight, and Ileni knew she was right. Bazel had no right, in his classmates' eyes, to be better than they were. At anything. And by offering him lessons, she had as much as promised that his small victory today wouldn't be a fluke, that she would ensure he continued to be better. She leaned over the table, feeling suddenly savage. "Besides, you just told me he'll never be sent on a mission. So he's not a killer after all, is he?"

"He wishes he could be." Sorin leaned forward, too. His cheekbones stood out like blades below his fierce eyes. "Don't think he's anything like you. He's as devoted to the master, and to our purpose, as the rest of us."

"Purpose?" Ileni said. "You're hired killers. *Gold* is your purpose."

Sorin's jaw clenched. "Do you truly think that's all we are?"

Ileni put her bread down. "Are you honestly trying to tell me you're *not*?"

"Money is necessary," Sorin admitted, "and sometimes, yes, we kill for pay. But usually we kill because the target's death, or an alliance with the person hiring us, furthers our greater mission."

"Which is what, exactly?"

"Bringing down the Empire."

She stared at him.

Sorin pulled his shoulders back. "That has always been

our goal. It seems your Elders didn't tell you the whole story."

That stung. "Well," Ileni retorted, "you're clearly doing a fantastic job. You've only been killing people for, what, four hundred years. . . ."

"And each assassination has been a blow, disrupting the Empire, making the Rathians fear us." His voice was like his posture, the violence barely discernible beneath his calm tone. "When the Empire does collapse, it will seem to its subjects that it happened overnight. They will not see how we weakened its foundations, one chip here and another there, for centuries. No one sees the whole picture yet. No one but the master."

He said it as if it was undeniable, and the weight of his certainty crushed her questions. She looked away.

The blaze died out of Sorin's eyes, and he pressed his lips together. "I need to talk to you about something else." He stood and turned his back on her. "Follow me."

Ileni hesitated for only a moment. Then she slid off the bench and hurried after him.

Outside the cavernous dining hall, a few twists and turns through dimly lit passageways brought them to a small chamber—barely more than a widening of the passageway, but full of thickly packed clusters of long, thin stalactites that hung from the ceiling nearly to the floor. A few daggers were lodged among them. Ileni deliberately turned her back on the tendrils of stone and crossed her arms. "What is this?"

Sorin walked over to the dense block of hanging stones and dropped to his back, a lithe, graceful movement. While Ileni stared, he grabbed the bottoms of the stalactites and pulled himself beneath them, sliding along the ground. After a second she couldn't see him anymore.

Ileni stood where she was. "Um. I don't think so."

"Not willing to risk much to find out the truth, are you?" Sorin's voice was oddly distorted by the rocks between them, but it wasn't coming from below; clearly, he was standing. There must be a clear space between the hanging stones and the cavern wall behind them.

This is not a good idea. Ileni lowered herself gingerly to the ground and onto her back. She pushed herself with her heels until her head was under the stalactites. Their ends weren't as pointy as she had thought, but blunt and somewhat knobby. She was fairly sure she would still die if any of them came loose and plunged down on her.

She lifted her hands, closing them around the two

thickest-looking stones. They seemed solid and sturdy. She took a deep breath and pulled.

It wasn't quite that easy, of course. Sorin had done it in one motion, but she had to pull herself onward three times before she was on the other side. By the time she stood up, her arms and back felt covered with bruises, and dirt rained from her hair.

They were in a small space barely big enough for the two of them. It seemed pitch-black until Ileni's eyes adjusted to the faint light creeping in between the hanging stones.

"All right," she said. "Do you have a reason for these elaborate precautions, or are you just having fun?"

"Both." Sorin held his hand up, and something flashed in the dimness: a blade. Ileni leaned back sharply, bumping against a sliver of stone. Trapped. She felt for her ward, and sensed it as a faint tingle wrapped around her skin. "I found the knife. The one used to kill Cadrel."

Ileni blinked. He smiled at her, sly and proud, and she stopped paying attention to her ward. "How?"

"That's not important. Can you find out who used it on him?"

Her throat felt suddenly like a block of wood.

"Well?" he said impatiently. She felt the whoosh of his breath on her cheek.

She tried to pull up some power, knowing it would be futile. The effort—and the sickening lack of response—made her faintly nauseated. She did her best to hide it as she bent forward to examine the knife. Her mind whirled, frantically and uselessly. "I . . . I can't. Not here. There's not enough space."

Sorin rested one finger against his chin. "You think I can't tell that you're lying? We're trained to read people. Do it *now*, Sorceress."

She moved carefully this time and managed to lean against the wall without scraping any part of her body against stone. She put her hand on the knife hilt, right next to Sorin's fingers. His skin brushed hers, dry and warm, as he edged his hand away. She closed her eyes, assumed what she hoped was an expression of deep concentration, and murmured some random spell-words. They sounded thin and weak in the dry air. But when she opened her eyes, Sorin was waiting expectantly.

She took her hand away, a dull leadenness in her chest. "It's been too long, been handled by too many people. The traces of whoever used it to kill Cadrel are gone."

Sorin looked disappointed, but not—thankfully—suspicious. "Are you sure? Is there another spell—"

"No," she said. Too swiftly? She tried to sound angry and disappointed. "Nothing. Magefire!"

Sorin didn't move. He was so close she imagined she could hear his heartbeat. "You're sure?"

Ileni shifted. "I'm sure."

The space felt oppressive and small. She should have been afraid—and she was, a little bit; what if he realized she was lying?—but mostly she was ashamed. Tears pressed at the insides of her eyes. She *had the knife,* and yet she was not one step closer to learning who had used it, because she wasn't strong enough.

I'm sorry, Cadrel.

She clenched her jaw and let the silence stretch longer, so she could gain control of her voice. She had no idea what Sorin was thinking. She was sure he could feel her inadequacy radiating off her.

"Well," she said finally. Her voice was *almost* steady. "If that's all . . ."

When he didn't move, she lowered herself to the floor and began inching her way under the stones. Sorin landed on the ground behind her with a quiet thud, then shot past her.

She pulled herself halfway through, then rolled over onto her stomach and crawled the rest of the way. When she was finally out, she turned away from him as she pushed her hair from her face and combed her fingers through it to get the dust out.

Sorin's voice was sharp. "What is that?"

She stiffened. "What?"

He reached forward and brushed her hair away from her neck. The touch sent a shiver through her, and she went even stiffer.

His breath whispered against the back of her neck. "What is that?"

Suddenly she understood. She felt his finger press against her skin, right below the hairline. "What does it look like to you?"

He didn't move or speak for so long that, if not for his breath against her skin and the finger still resting on her neck, she would have turned to see if he had gone. It should have made her afraid, his hands so close to her throat—all he had to do was slip them forward and close them, and he could strangle her before she had a chance to call for help. It should have, but it didn't. She had to force herself not to turn around and meet his eyes.

"Like a picture," he said finally. "One man walking, one man falling."

"That's how it was, when the Empire exiled us. Half of us died before we reached the mountains. From starvation, from exhaustion, from arrows. Some of the emperor's archers came after us and picked us off. We managed to capture one and ask him why. He said it was for fun."

She did turn then, after the silence got long enough. Sorin was staring at her as if he had never seen her before. "That was four hundred years ago," he said.

"Yes. We don't forget." She reached back and touched the tattoo. Her fingers brushed his, and he snatched his hand back as if suddenly noticing where it was. "We make sure to never forget, because someday we will return."

He kept looking at her, and this was different from his usual controlled silence. She had actually put him at a loss for words. Finally he said, "You're all tattooed?"

"Every last one of us."

"But Absalm wasn't. . . ."

"Our parents choose where to put the tattoo. Some families like for it to be more visible than others." Tellis's tattoo was on his shoulder.

His fingers twitched, but he didn't reach for her neck

again. "Then shouldn't you be glad to tutor us? Our goal is the same as yours. We also want to release the world from the Empire's grip. We also want to make the Rathians pay for all they have done."

"Our methods are not the same." She smoothed her hair back over her shoulder, and it brushed across her neck, hiding the tattoo again. "The Renegai don't murder innocents."

"What we do is not murder." The contempt in his voice stung her. He wasn't trying to convince her; he was explaining the obvious to a slow child. "Every person we kill dies to serve a greater purpose."

"I'm sure they would be happy if they knew it," Ileni said sarcastically, but her voice sounded weak even to her. "If you would explain it to them, perhaps they would volunteer for your knives."

Sorin shook his head. "Every leader makes decisions about other people's lives. Didn't your Elders do the same, when they decided to send you here?"

She stepped back as if from a physical blow. "And who did *you* kill, on your last mission? What purpose did that murder serve?"

He turned his head away from her, and for a moment, in profile, looked as dangerous as she knew he must be. "An imperial noble. Do you have a problem with *that*?"

She shouldn't have asked. He had ended someone's life, plunged a man into terror and pain and watched the hope die from his eyes, and he was *proud* of it.

"Does it matter if I do?" she asked.

Sorin regarded her with narrowed eyes. When he finally spoke, his voice was very soft, and a shiver ran up Ileni's spine. "No. It's just . . . surprising."

"That I'm the only one in these caves who knows what life is worth?"

"I don't think you do." His eyebrows slanted in thin lines downward. "How can you know what your life is worth if you don't know what you would trade it for?"

"Get out of my way." She forced the words out, before her throat closed up and made speech impossible.

He stepped aside without a word, but she could feel him watching her as she walked back down the dark passageway.

CHAPTER 8

It took three days for Ileni's magic to come trickling back, heartbreakingly slowly. Dozens of times a day, she reached deep within herself, worrying at the emptiness where her power had been. Every time she did, it made her stomach twist, but she was unable to stop.

She had plenty of time to brood about it. She taught her three classes every morning, reviewing skills her students already knew, dodging their veiled and not-so-veiled demands to learn more. She devised dozens of ways to teach magic without spending any herself. Most of them involved insulting their competence and skills, something she found dangerously satisfying. Her unhappiness made her sharp-tongued and vicious, and even Irun began to hesitate before challenging her. At least, she thought he did.

After her third class each morning, Sorin took her to the midday meal and then to her room, where she was left to do whatever she wanted until he came to pick her up for dinner. In theory, she was supposed to be spending some of that time building up the wards around the caves, wards strengthened for centuries by generations of Renegai tutors. She wondered how long it would be before anyone noticed she wasn't doing that part of her task.

Advanced sorcerers required uninterrupted stretches of solitude for practice and preparation exercises. If she'd still had her power, those long afternoons and evenings would barely have been enough time. She had once gone through the mental exercises for hours each day, then spent more hours memorizing the rituals and incantations that enabled more complicated spells, repeating the hand motions and words endlessly until they were second nature, drawing thousands of warding patterns until she could get them right every time.

Now she had nothing to do but stare at the walls, fight off memories, and wait for whatever pathetic remnant of her power returned to her.

She tried to think of other ways to investigate Cadrel's and Absalm's murders. There must be methods that didn't require magic—questions she could ask, places she could search—but it all seemed so tenuous, so unlikely to produce answers. The knife was her best clue. And she needed her magic to pursue that.

What she did, for the most part, was sleep: for hours and hours, until it made her feel heavy and groggy instead of alert. Back home, she had slept grudgingly, always trying to get away with as little as she could. She had needed those extra hours for practice, or studying new spells, or—more and more, especially over the past year—being with Tellis. She had often thought, back then, that she was tired. But that was nothing compared to how she felt now, when the tiredness came from within her, as if her body simply had no interest in remaining awake.

On the third day after Sorin showed her the knife, she finally felt power begin to coil within her, enough for her mind to grasp and use. A part of her wanted to hold off, to let the magic build, to feel it flow . . . but that wasn't what she was here for. Besides, who knew if it would ever happen? Maybe this was all she would get.

And more than that . . . she wanted to *use* the magic.

She felt the power tugging at her, waiting to be shaped and unleashed on the world.

The problem was that now that she had the power, she no longer had the knife, and she couldn't think of how to get her hands on it again. Unless . . . she blushed, a tingle running through her. She could think of one obvious excuse for sneaking into Sorin's room, and the idea was surprisingly tempting. But she didn't trust herself to pull off a seductress act, not with Sorin. He would probably just throw her out.

She lived in danger of imminent death, yet she was afraid of a little humiliation? Ileni shook her head at her own stupidity, but abandoned that particular idea. She would have to use the magic for something else.

That night, she pulled the warding stones from under her bed, arranged them on the floor, and placed a strand of Irun's hair inside the pattern.

She had retrieved the hair from his rug after class that day. But now that she was ready, she felt a sudden, overwhelming weariness. She stared at the pattern and couldn't bring herself to sit down and start the chant.

Irun was too obvious a bully to be a real threat. The dangers in these caves wouldn't be that straightforward. She couldn't enact a protection spell against every hot-blooded young killer who wanted to prove he couldn't be controlled by a woman.

. . . Couldn't she? It had been her original intent, when she took the stones from Tellis.

With a sickening wrench, she recognized what lay behind her reluctance: fear. She was afraid her magic would fizzle out halfway through the spell.

She dropped down cross-legged with such force that she banged her ankles painfully against the floor. Judging by how empty she felt, she might live long enough to see all her magic gone. And that had never been part of the plan.

A sudden, sharp memory pierced her: the day she had first learned to use the warding stones. The Renegai didn't have many stored spells, and though they required little power, they called for great skill—that much power, wrongly handled, could easily shatter a sorcerer's control. Only she, Tellis, and two other students had been permitted to try the stones that day. Tellis had always been quicker with new spells, but she had mastered the stones first. He had been furious, and she had laughed at him, which had made it worse. He hadn't spoken to her for days. And then, when he finally had . . .

She tried to push the memories away, to focus on the

stones in front of her, the threats all around her. But it was too late. Tellis's arms around her. Tellis on the grass beside her, staring up at the stars, telling her things he'd never told another living soul. Tellis watching her at practice, as if she was the only other person in the stadium. The first time he had kissed her, leaning forward fast and suddenly. Telling her afterward that he hadn't planned to, had thought he should wait longer, but wanted to so badly that he couldn't.

He was leagues away. And even if he wasn't, it wouldn't make a difference. She would still be powerless, and she still couldn't have Tellis.

Ileni found herself sitting on the floor with her back against the bed, arms wrapped around her body, feeling as if something inside her had frozen and cracked. She had been so loved, once. She hadn't even realized how lucky she was, to be the center of someone's world, to have someone who would always be there. And now she was alone, a helpless girl in a labyrinth of caves, surrounded by people who would kill her at a word. Even back in the Renegai compound, not a single person still cared about her day-to-day life. Everyone had put her out of their minds. She was in the Assassins' Caves, no longer a part of their lives.

No longer a part of anyone's life.

It's better, she told herself. Better than staying while her magic dimmed, being an object of pity and charity. Watching Tellis find someone else to love. Even now, though she tried not to, she wondered who that girl would be, and hated her.

Not for the first time, she wished she could hate *him.* It would have made her life so much easier. He didn't deserve it, but it wouldn't hurt him, since she would never see him again.

After several long seconds, she got up and flung herself into her narrow cot as if she was trying to hurt *it.* Or herself. She closed her eyes before tears could come, and kept them that way until she was no longer conscious of forcing them shut.

The next morning, she woke early and couldn't remember why. Her sleep had, thankfully, been deep and dreamless. She lay in her cot, blinking at the black stone ceiling. Then, with a gasp, she dropped out of bed and onto her knees beside the warding stones.

She had just *left* them there—an unthinkable lack of discipline, the sort of carelessness that got sorcerers killed. A lifetime of training dropped in one hysterical bout of self-pity. If an assassin with power had come in here, and found them all set out like this, waiting to be ignited . . . an assassin who, of course, wouldn't know what he was doing . . .

He would likely have killed himself. And her. And possibly brought the mountain crashing down over their heads.

Maybe not such a bad thing.

She knelt and rearranged the stones, breaking up the warding pattern and forming a new design—slightly asymmetric, with an off-center focus that hurt her eyes. Using the stones for anything other than their intended purpose was dangerous, but if she didn't take the risk, she had no chance to find the answers she was looking for. If the spell failed, that would mean she couldn't accomplish anything in these caves anyhow, and if so, she might as well die. And she might as well do it spectacularly.

She touched one smooth rock, feeling the magic coiled within it. The warding spell she had already set against Sorin was so strong that its energy was easy to redirect—deceptively easy—requiring only the faintest flicker of power from her. But it took all her skill to keep control of the spell, to twist it exactly the way she wanted it to go.

The magic surged against her, wanting to be loose in the world. She twined her mind around it, struggling to outwit it as it slipped and slid against the bonds she was trying to set. For one terrifying second, it almost got away, and she braced herself for an explosive death even as she fought to regain control.

And then, all at once, she had it. It was hers.

She closed her eyes as the magic rushed through her, clear and cool and sweet. She had forgotten how good it felt.

Reluctantly, she opened her mouth and let the spell rush from her, a torrent of words that pulled out the magic, leaving her once again aching and jagged inside. When she opened her eyes, her vision was blurred with tears.

She swept the stones back into the bag and stood. The redirected warding spell now gave her an awareness of Sorin's location, a warning tingle designed to help her stay away from him. The purpose of the spell was to avoid him, but she could use that same knowledge to find him—and, more importantly, to find the knife that had killed Cadrel. Sorin had to be keeping it in his room. Once she got her hands on it, she would find out who had stabbed it into Cadrel's back.

It felt good to step out of her room and stride in the direction that screamed *danger* at her. She had woken earlier than usual, so it would be some time before Sorin arrived to bring her to breakfast. From her strained conversations with him, Ileni knew the assassins studied a variety of skills when they weren't in the training arena: language, spatial memorization, lock picking, skulking. (Though she suspected "skulking" had been Sorin's idea of a joke.) He had mentioned once that he had some sort of training in the morning, before breakfast, which meant he would probably be leaving his room shortly. If she could make it there before he left, she could wait outside and then get at the knife while he was gone.

The sense of danger pulled her through several dark, curving corridors, down a short flight of stairs, and into another of those narrow passageways that made her feel as if the black stones were pressing in on her from both sides. Farther and farther into the mountains. Fewer wooden doors interrupted the walls of rugged stone, replaced by rough arches and irregularly shaped openings in the rock. She didn't look through those openings, focused as she was on the spell, but what she glimpsed as she passed sent shivers through her: a cavern full of hanging ropes, crisscrossed with wooden beams; the replica of some sort of throne room; a cave divided in half by a shiny length of wood studded with sharp metal spikes.

She gritted her teeth and kept going. Finally, something wafted toward her, something she hadn't smelled in so long it took her a moment to identify it. Fresh air.

She breathed deeply, then hurried forward. The passageway ended abruptly in a wall, which she found by walking straight into it. In a blur of confused pain, she realized it wasn't a dead end, but rather a sharp turn. She followed the turn, more cautiously, her head still ringing. But she forgot the pain when the passageway truly did come to an end—not in a wall, but in an exit to the outside world.

The sky was dusky blue, streaked with pink-gray clouds, and there was no sign of the sun—but it was still lighter than it ever was within the caves, the sort of light that filled the world instead of coming from tiny stones. It was cold, too, and she welcomed that. The breeze brushed across her face, and she breathed it in, icy and sweet. She had almost forgotten what it felt like to have air move against her face. She leaned into it, her skin coming alive.

Before her stretched a large, rocky valley—surrounded by towering black rock on all sides, so not a way out after all, but it was still *outdoors*. Of course, they must have outdoor training areas, so they could learn to fight in snow and rain . . . even as she thought that, she became conscious of the unnaturally even sound of feet thudding against the ground. She drew back swiftly, just as the assassins came into sight.

A dozen of them, running single file, wearing nothing but breeches and packs. She recognized some from her first class. The oldest students, the closest to being sent out into the Empire. An older man, one of the teachers, was running behind them. His voice pierced the silence: "Faster! You call that running? *Faster!*"

The rocks on the ground were not, after all, haphazard; they were obstacles, and as she watched, the runners leaped over each one and kept running. Their uniform pace and set faces suggested they had been doing it for a long time.

When the one in the lead got close enough for Ileni to see him clearly, she realized that those weren't packs on their backs. They were slabs of stone. They must have weighed more than she could easily lift.

She retreated farther back into the cave, but not before she recognized one of the runners, his blond hair slicked back against his head.

She had been wrong. Sorin had left his room long ago.

What now? she asked herself, and had no answer. She sighed and let the remnant of the altered warding spell go, then stood pressed against the rock until the sound of pounding feet passed her and grew distant. A part of her wanted to go outside again, to feel the breeze on her skin.

She shook her head and turned back into the dark, trying to remember the way she had come.

Within seconds, she was completely lost.

After a turn that she *thought* would take her back to the staircase, she found herself instead in a large cavern full of knives, hundreds of them, hanging on racks stretched across the back of the room. Targets hung on the wall, heavy cloths cut into the shapes of people, with circles drawn over various body parts. One of the targets was child sized. She stared at them, feeling her stomach tighten. Then she turned back to the doorway, and collided with a bare, muscular chest.

She shrieked and raised her hands. Large hands gripped her upper arms, hard enough to hurt, holding her motionless. She looked up into Irun's rugged face.

"Teacher," he said, his tone a mockery of respect. "What are you doing here? And without your guardian, too. Not very wise."

She didn't bother to struggle, vividly recalling how he had leaped obstacles with a stone slab on his back. She didn't bother to reply, since she had nothing to say. She met Irun's hard almond-shaped eyes and did not move.

His thick eyebrows lifted. Then he let her go, though

he didn't move from the doorway. Ileni used every bit of willpower she possessed and did not step back. The marks of his fingers were painful on her arms.

"Good," she said, hoping her haughty tone would disguise her fear. "I'm glad you're here. You can lead me back to my room."

Irun laughed. "I don't think so. This is a good opportunity for the two of us to talk."

Ileni tried to look past him, to see if anyone else was coming. The entrance to the cavern was empty. It was just her and Irun in a room full of glistening knives.

With an effort, she hung onto her haughtiness, though she doubted it would fool him. "Talk about what?"

Irun's smirk made her attempt seem infantile. "Two weeks before you arrived, *Teacher*, I returned from a successful mission. Do you know who I killed?"

She didn't trust her voice, or her expression. She shook her head.

"The high sorcerer at the emperor's court."

She blinked, shocked despite herself. Irun shifted position and nodded. "Nobody truly believed it could be done. Certainly not that I could do it and survive. But Absalm's lessons . . . they came in very handy."

"Did you kill Absalm, too?" Her voice shook, which she hated, but Irun obviously liked. His eyes glittered.

"No. Nor Cadrel. And I won't kill you, either, if you cooperate."

"With what?"

"Next time I kill a sorcerer, I don't want to just take his life. I want to take his power."

Ileni choked. Irun waited, with exaggerated patience, for her to regain her composure. Then he added, "I want you to tell me how to do it."

"I don't know how!"

"That's . . . unfortunate." His disbelief was palpable. "Because it means you serve no purpose here."

He moved with swift, brutal efficiency. All at once she was flat on her stomach on the stone floor, her wrist screaming in pain, her face crushed into the black stone.

"Perhaps your successor will be more amenable," Irun said, stepping back.

Her mouth filled with pieces of grit. She pulled up her power, but it was so little, so weak.

This would make three Renegai killed in these caves. She wondered who the Elders would send next.

"None of the Renegai know how!" She pushed herself

up from the ground, craning her neck back to look up at him. "Taking magic from others is evil. Only the imperial sorcerers practice that sort of perversion."

"Perversion? My, what strong language."

"Hunting down those with power, breeding them as slaves, keeping them in cages, and harvesting them for their magic? That's how the Empire gathers its power. We don't—we would never—" She had to stop talking then, because she had run out of air and couldn't seem to draw in another breath.

Irun laughed, a harsh triumphant sound. "I don't believe you. When one of your sorcerers dies—of old age, *of course*—you let his power die with him? You don't transfer it to another sorcerer, or into a lodestone?"

"*No.*" She had to croak the word out, but she was past caring. "We let our people die in peace."

"You waste their deaths, you mean. And none of you are tempted, is that it? None of you ever think about what you could do with your power multiplied by two, or three, or four. . . ."

Ileni rolled over and sat up. "No."

"You're lying." Irun leaned forward. Despite herself, she cringed. Irun noticed, and smiled. "But I suppose I'll wait and see what the next tutor says."

"The next one?" Again, she couldn't quite hide the sob of fear. Not that it mattered. "Do you think my people will keep sending tutors if we all meet the same fate? The master won't be happy with you if you cause us to break the treaty."

His face twitched. With one stride, he stood over her. "You don't understand much about us, if you think I would ever risk interfering with the master's plans. Your people will do whatever we tell them, or risk annihilation."

"Did your master command you to do *this*?" Ileni said desperately. There had been a slight hint of hesitation there, when she brought up the master. Very slight, but it was her only hope.

"The master expects us to think for ourselves. Most of our missions are half a world away from him. What he needs—what we strive for—is to understand what he *would* want even when he isn't there to tell us." Irun laughed softly. "When he commands, of course we obey. But the best of us obey even before he commands. I know what he wants. He brought me to these caves to do just this." He leaned back slightly and kicked her in the ribs.

Agony exploded through her chest. She groaned and fell over on her side, curled up into a ball. Irun knelt beside her. "The pain makes it difficult to call up your power, doesn't it?" he said, and closed one hand over her mouth, clamping her jaw shut. He placed his other hand on her forehead and slowly, inexorably, tilted her head back.

She struggled to open her mouth, to scream out a spell—*any* spell, to make him stop, even if it was only long enough for a breath—but she couldn't.

She could have had all the magic in the world, and it wouldn't have helped. The room went black around the edges, and the back of her neck was about to crack. She writhed and flailed, too panicked now to aim her blows. Through the ringing in her ears, she heard Irun laugh.

Then his hands were gone, and air came rushing into her lungs again.

She gasped and gagged and scrambled to her hands and knees. She tried to stand—*run, run, RUN*, her instincts screamed—and fell over, the room turning around her. Dizziness rushed through her, and the world went black.

But air kept coming in, and she concentrated on that, crouched on the ground like a beaten animal, breathing in long, desperate sobs. It was a few moments before she could see again.

And then she saw who had rescued her.

Sorin and Irun were locked in battle, moving so swiftly

she could barely see what they were doing. There was nothing dance-like about *this* fight: it was fast and vicious and brutal. Sorin jabbed his thumbs into Irun's eyes; Irun twisted his head beneath Sorin's arms and thrust a knee at his groin; Sorin dodged low and grabbed Irun around the knees, and the two fell to the ground. They continued attacking each other as they fell. Aside from the crash when they hit the stone floor, and the thuds when their blows connected, they fought in absolute, eerie silence.

They rolled over, and then over again, their limbs in constant motion. Ileni could only catch the occasional move: Sorin's arms encircling Irun's neck, Irun's elbow slicing into Sorin's side, Sorin's heel slamming against Irun's jaw, the arc of Sorin's body as Irun flipped him over his head. She should help Sorin somehow, but the idea was so obviously ridiculous that it barely formed a thought. She forced herself onto her knees and watched, trembling.

The sudden sickening crack of bone echoed through the cavern. The two assassins sprang apart and faced each other, and now she could also hear their quick harsh breaths. Blood spread across the lower half of Sorin's face, dark red on his mouth and jaw. Irun's hand hung limply from his wrist.

Irun made a movement toward Sorin, who stepped back

and grabbed two knives from the nearest rack. Irun stopped.

"Dangerous," he observed. Despite his broken wrist, his voice betrayed not a hint of pain.

Ileni didn't see Sorin move. She saw a lock of Irun's black hair flutter to the ground, and then the knife Sorin had thrown slid neatly into a crevice between two rocks and stuck there, quivering.

"Very," Sorin agreed. For all the clipped precision in his voice, something wild ran in the tense lines of his body. Ileni had the odd impression he was on the verge of laughing. "But more so for the one who can hold only one knife. And what's life without a little danger?"

Irun drew his lips back in a snarl, and Ileni was sure he was going to attack again. Instead he inclined his head, turned, strode right past Ileni, and vanished through the doorway.

Sorin didn't waste a second before he whirled on her. "What are you doing here?"

A drop of sweat slid with excruciating slowness down the bridge of Ileni's nose toward the inner corner of her right eye. She knew it would burn when it hit but couldn't summon up the strength to raise her hand and wipe it away. She couldn't summon up the strength to lie, either.

"I was looking for your room."

"Why?"

"The knife," she whispered.

His black eyes narrowed into barely visible slits. Ileni tasted blood in her mouth; she had bitten her tongue. Now it would all come out, her lack of power, the trick her people had played. Now they would all know how helpless she was. Every single assassin in the caves would feel free to use his strength and skill against her, to reduce her to prey, as Irun had.

Or maybe she would be lucky, and Sorin would kill her now. He would do it fast, she thought. He wouldn't enjoy it the way Irun would.

"There *is* a spell you can use to find out who threw it," Sorin said tightly. "You wanted to use it without me watching."

Her head came up. She said, slowly, "Yes."

"Why?"

Suddenly it seemed she might live after all. Her hands still shook, her breath still hurt the inside of her throat, but Ileni's mind started working again.

"I don't trust you," she said, as if it should have been evident.

Sorin laughed. Its harshness reminded her of Irun's laugh, and she cringed despite herself. "I would say that was smart. But you've proven that you're not very smart at all. Don't you understand that my task is to *protect* you?"

Ileni sat back and pulled her knees into her chest. Her hands shook, and she pressed them against her calves to still them. Sorin rubbed a hand across his chin, smearing blood on his knuckles.

"I hope you understand now," he said grimly. "Get up, and follow me. No more secrets. We're going to find out who killed Cadrel."

CHAPTER
9

"No more secrets," Ileni agreed—as if she had a choice in the matter; as if Sorin cared whether or not she agreed. She forced her back straight, but didn't get off the floor. "So tell me this. Did the master order Irun to kill me?"

Even locked in battle with Irun, Sorin hadn't looked so angry. "No. If Irun was acting on the master's orders, he wouldn't have left until you were dead. Or he was."

Ileni hugged her legs tighter. "He acted against the master's instructions?"

"Of course not." Sorin glanced at the blood on the back of his hand, then spat on his sleeve and, with a few practiced, efficient movements, wiped his face clean. "At our level, instructions aren't always . . . explicit. Sometimes we don't know we're being tested until the test is over."

"Why would Irun think the master wants me dead?" She rested her head on her knees for a moment, then raised it. "He said he was brought to the caves just for this. What does that mean?"

For a moment she thought he was going to ignore the question, yank her to her feet, and march her to his room. She wondered if her ward would interpret that as a threat, and doubted it. She knew, now, what it felt like to be truly threatened by an assassin.

Sorin glanced swiftly at the entrance to the cavern—still empty. Then he turned to her. "When the master ordered Irun taken, sixteen years ago, no one knew why. It was the most dangerous mission we had ever attempted, so daring I've heard the story even though it happened several years before I arrived. The master sent four assassins. Three of them died on the mission, and the fourth died of his wounds shortly after arriving here with Irun. It wasn't until this year that part of the master's plan became clear, when Irun was sent on a mission that only someone who looks like him—like one of *them*—could possibly accomplish."

She lowered her hands slowly to the ground. "Killing the high sorcerer."

Sorin nodded, a quick jerk of his head. "But the plan goes back farther than that. The master's last kill, before he became our leader, was also a sorcerer."

Ileni braced herself on the floor behind her. "The previous high sorcerer?"

Sorin's eyes slid away from hers, then back. He reached out—unconsciously, she thought—and rested a finger on the hilt of one of the knives. "No."

A few days ago, she would have thought his face blank. Now she saw the expression on it, but couldn't tell what it meant. "Then who?"

"Not within the Empire," Sorin said. He took a deep breath. Though his face was almost clean, there was still blood between his teeth. "The sorcerer he killed was a Renegai."

Ileni started to push herself up, then thought better of it and remained on the floor. "That's not—"

"It was many years ago," Sorin said. His voice was almost sympathetic. He nudged the knife straighter, then turned away from the blades and faced her. "He pretended to be one of you, and he made it look like an accident. None of the Renegai ever found out."

"One of us," Ileni repeated numbly. Her fingers dug into the rock, gravel wedging beneath her fingernails. "And what was the purpose of that murder? How was killing an innocent Renegai going to help you bring down the Empire?"

Sorin rubbed his eyebrow. "None of us knew that at the time, either. But as it turned out, it was crucial. He showed that it can be done."

Ileni blinked at him, remembering what he had said earlier about chipping away at the Empire's foundations. She knew—everyone knew—what the true foundation of the Empire's power was: sorcery.

If the assassins were able to bring down the imperial sorcerers—a ridiculous thought, but *if they could*—the Empire would fall with them.

Could it be a coincidence that while the assassins were targeting sorcery, the two sorcerers within their own caves had been murdered? Had Absalm and Cadrel been killed for *practice*?

"You knew," she said slowly. "You knew Absalm's and Cadrel's deaths might have been part of some test, or some plan."

Sorin's arm knotted, but his voice remained even. "Everything that happens here is part of the master's plan.

What happened to Absalm and Cadrel, what happened to Jastim, what Irun did . . . it's all part of a pattern, and the master is the one weaving the pattern. But I can only see pieces of it. I don't understand the whole thing."

"Even I can see this part of it. The part where I'm going to be the next sorcerer to die." She said it without feeling much of anything at all. A film of clammy sweat covered her forehead.

"No," Sorin said, with a fierceness that surprised her. He sounded as if he really cared.

But she was only surprised for a moment. The master had, after all, assigned him to keep her safe. Had given him permission to care.

Which meant it somehow fit into the master's plans that he care. But she couldn't think about that right now. Her fear receded, very slightly, and that was all that mattered. He was on her side. Perhaps she did have a chance after all.

"Thank you," she said, and Sorin looked at her sharply.

"I can't be with you all the time, Teacher. I think it's time I taught you to fight."

She stared at him as if he had started spouting poetry. "What? No."

"Why not?"

"I'm a Renegai. We don't fight."

He laughed. "You threw me into a wall the day you arrived. What was that?"

"A defensive spell!"

"Fine. I'll teach you defensive maneuvers."

She could still feel Irun's hands on her mouth, and her complete helplessness as she struggled for air. *Defensive maneuvers* . . . But she was forgetting something. She said, as haughtily as she could, "I'm a sorceress, remember? I have certain defenses of my own."

"They didn't do you much good today, did they?"

And how was she going to explain that? "I was overconfident. I thought I had time, once he stopped talking. Next time I won't make that mistake."

"Neither will Irun," Sorin said. "He must be able to sense it when you draw upon your magic, or he wouldn't have *talked* at all before he attacked. But does it matter? Two weapons are always better than one, especially when neither has to be carried. The more skills you hold within yourself—"

"Spare me the pithy one-liners of assassin philosophy."

"It's one of the master's teachings," Sorin said stiffly.

Despite herself, Ileni thought of the fighters on the training floor, the deadly graceful dances she walked past every day. As a child she had been athletic, outstripping most of the others at races and games. She had left all that behind, of course, when it came time to focus on her truly important skills.

Sorin was watching her with smoky coal eyes. "You could never match one of us, but any ability at all would give you the advantage of surprise. And what if you were fighting another sorcerer, one more powerful than you? A physical attack wouldn't be expected among your kind. It could give you an edge."

She would never fight, or even meet, another sorcerer again. It came back to her in a second, how it felt to be surrounded by people who thought the way she did, accepted her, respected her. And then, just as fast, the memory rushed away, leaving a dull ache behind.

"All right," Ileni said abruptly.

"How gracious of you to agree." He walked over and held out his hand. "But first things first. Are you calm enough to use magic yet?"

"Yes," she said, hoping it was true. Ignoring the hand, she pushed herself to her knees, then to her feet. She swayed a little bit, but he didn't try to steady her. Instead he stepped back.

"You're not even bruised," he observed.

She wasn't? Ileni held up her unblemished arms, white but for some faint brown freckles, and saw that he was right. She still felt hurt, but that was just memory.

Healing magic had always been a focus for the Renegai, and those spells were so well practiced and so ingrained that using them was an instinct. She had used the healing spell without even realizing she was doing it. It had taken so little power she hadn't felt the difference.

"Of course not," she said, but despite her best effort, her voice didn't sound even slightly confident. "I'm a sorceress."

"Then let's get that knife." He held out his hand, and she stared at it until he dropped it. "You're going to do the spell, and I'm going to see the results. Don't even try to trick me this time."

"I won't," she whispered.

Sorin hesitated, and she thought he would say something else. Instead he turned and led her out of the cavern.

It was a long walk to Sorin's room, and on the way they passed numerous boys Ileni had never seen before, most of them younger than her students. Some were mere children. She should have pitied them—would have, an hour ago—but every time one of them glanced at her, her skin shrank inward. One was a child who looked no older than six, his face round and unformed, in contrast to the determined set of his mouth. She looked at him, at his smooth cheeks and soft chin, and thought, *Enemy.*

Despite the healing spell, she still felt as if her whole body was damaged from Irun's attack: her neck, her jaw, her side. Her sense that there was something sacred and inviolable about her own skin.

Was *attack* even the right word, when it had been so easy for him?

She found herself drawing closer to Sorin, even though he was the same: a killer, strong enough to snap her neck, trained to do so without compunction. Her ward might protect her, but she had no doubt he could find a way around that, given time. The only difference between him and the others was a command. And that command could be withdrawn at any time.

She drew near to him anyhow, until she was so close her sleeve brushed his. He moved his arm away, and she felt briefly bereft. For a ridiculous moment she wished he would take her hand in his, hold it tight, and make her feel protected.

It would be an illusion, but it would be better than nothing.

A few seconds later they were in his room, which was even smaller than hers. No tapestries or rugs softened the austerity here. The entire inside of the room was smooth black stone.

Sorin knelt, reached under his bed, and pulled out the knife. For some reason, the fact that they had the same hiding place struck Ileni as funny. She giggled, hearing the edge of hysteria in it, and Sorin turned and looked at her.

"Never mind," Ileni said, though he hadn't asked. "Are you going to tell me now how you got the knife?"

He nodded. "We keep all our blades in the knife-training room, and rotate them so they can be regularly sharpened. Any missing one would have been noticed eventually, so I knew the one that killed Cadrel had to have been returned there. I used a spell to find out which one was blooded at the time Cadrel died."

He sounded very proud of himself. It was an easy enough spell, but Ileni didn't find it difficult to say, "Very good." If he had asked her to do it, she might not have been able to.

She went to his washing bowl and spilled some of the water onto the stone floor, where it spread slowly and irregularly. Then she knelt and used her finger to trace a pattern around the shallow puddle. "Give me the knife."

Sorin knelt beside her, knife hilt out. Ileni laid it carefully in the center of the puddle and waited until the ripples had subsided.

"Absalm never showed us how to do this," Sorin said.

Ileni gathered in her power, pushed away her fear that it wouldn't be enough, and unleashed it with a word.

The puddle shrank in toward the knife, gathering around it as if toward a whirlpool. They both leaned forward at the same time, and their heads almost cracked together. Sorin pulled back just in time, but remained so close she could feel his breath on her cheek.

For another moment the water was still again, and then it rippled and shimmered, gently at first, then so violently the knife began to shake. Ileni leaned closer, frowning, and the water spurted from the floor and hit her directly in the face.

It wasn't a lot of water, but the surprise knocked her backward. Sorin reacted with a single leap that took him to the corner of the room, but by then the water was gone, splattered all over the floor and walls. A drop fell from the ceiling and landed on Ileni's shoulder. The knife remained where it was, motionless on the floor, completely dry.

"Was that supposed to happen?" Sorin inquired, from his position in the corner.

"No," Ileni said, and burst into tears.

It was difficult to say who was more horrified, her or Sorin. Ileni tried to gain control of herself, but it was all too much. Nothing, *nothing*, was going the way it was supposed to. She wasn't supposed to be this helpless, or this scared. She was supposed to have her magic to protect her. She wasn't supposed to be forced to the ground like a hunted animal, waiting to find out whether she would suffocate before her neck snapped.

She pressed her hands to her cheeks as she sobbed, her humiliation drowned in the enormity of everything else. She could be humiliated later, when she was less terrified and frustrated. The only tiny bright spot was that Sorin looked as helpless as she felt.

How to throw assassins off balance: cry in front of them. She would have to find a way to pass that along to the next tutor.

When it was clear that she wasn't going to be able to stop crying within the next few seconds, she decided to talk through her sobs. Sorin would have to deal with it. "It was supposed to show the hand that threw the knife. Instead it showed me, as best it could, what threw the knife. It wasn't a human hand."

Sorin was still watching her as warily as if she might explode. "What was it?"

The wild movement. The controlled outburst of power. She recognized it in her blood.

"It was magic," she said. She turned her head away, feeling her sobs begin to die as a cold horror wormed its way into her. This was even worse than knowing a regular assassin was after her. "A very complex spell. Nobody in these caves should have been able to perform it, but someone did. Cadrel was killed by magic."

CHAPTER
10

The next morning, Ileni began testing her students for magical skill. She couldn't really believe any of them had the ability to throw a knife with magic—while random throwing spells were easy enough, aiming and throwing a blade was as difficult with magic as without it—but she couldn't think of any other possibility. *Someone* in these caves had done it, and she had to find him before she became his next victim.

Despite the urgency, she put off testing Irun until she had no choice. On the fourth morning, after she had found every other student lacking, she finally called him up. Her skin shrank in on itself as he crossed the floor toward her, his wrist still wrapped in a tight white bandage.

In the four days since his attack on her, Irun had not changed his behavior in the slightest, and she had been doing her best to return the favor—mostly because she didn't know what else to do. Her chest constricted as he came close. She wanted to hurt him, to make him pay for what he had done. And she couldn't. She couldn't do *anything* to him.

But when his knife bounced off the far wall, hilt first, then skittered across the floor back to him, she allowed herself a faint sneer. "Clearly, this skill is too advanced. We'll go back to the basic exercises we practiced last week, and I'll try to think of a simpler technique to start with."

Irun had stepped on the knife hilt to bring it to a stop. Complete silence fell while she waited for his retort. If she had targeted any of the other students like this—even Sorin—there would have been at least a snicker. If it had been Bazel, everyone would have been smirking. But the cavern was completely silent.

"This is the first useful thing you've taught us," Irun said at last. He flipped the knife up into the air and caught it by the hilt, all without looking at it. "You do know what it is we do, don't you, Teacher?"

"I know." *Magefire.* She should have been more careful. All the students were watching them, and she couldn't think of a way to back down from this confrontation. All the respect she had gained was slipping away. "But you're not ready. Eventually—"

"*Eventually*," Irun sneered. "How typically Renegai. You know, sometimes waiting is wise, but only—"

"—if you know what you're waiting for." The students on their mats chorused it together.

Ileni turned and stared at them.

"One of his teachings," Irun explained, as if she should have known.

Ileni wanted to match his sneer with one of her own: *Quoting other people is fine, but only if you actually have the ability to think on your own.* It was on the tip of her tongue. But all at once she could feel his hand on her jaw, the helpless panic burning through her chest.

Irun was enjoying himself, she could tell. Enjoying her fear.

"Basic exercises," she said. "Now."

As soon as she said it, she was sure that he—that all of them—were simply going to ignore her. But after a long, insolent stare, Irun sauntered back to his mat, dropped gracefully onto it, and closed his eyes. The other students did the same, except Sorin. His eyes met hers, and then he, too, closed them.

They were all sitting in what she had once thought was the exact same pose. But now she could see how Bazel's shoulders were just the tiniest bit hunched, how Irun's chin was tilted a fraction higher than everyone else's, how Sorin's body was coiled as if about to explode off the mat.

Ileni knew they could hear her, but she couldn't help a small sigh as she began to walk through the training room, checking and correcting them as they went through the exercises. She might have lost their respect, but she still had their obedience.

For now.

This time, Ileni thought grimly as Sorin came toward her, his fist aimed at her jaw, *I'm going to throw him against the wall.*

She didn't, of course. Just as she hadn't the first three times that afternoon; just as she hadn't gotten anything right in the four days since they had started these ridiculous fighting lessons. The only difference was that this time, she failed more spectacularly than before, ending up flat on her back on the rock floor, sweat stained and frustrated and with a sharp pain shooting up her wrist.

One of these days, I'll forget that this is practice and my wards will react. Somehow, the thought didn't give her as much satisfaction as it should have.

Sorin sighed and lowered his arms. He looked as composed as if he had been sitting on a mat for the past hour, not a drop of sweat on his skin. "You do realize what the problem is?"

"There's only one?" Ileni said sourly, sitting up. She didn't even feel her usual surge of satisfaction when she made a crease appear in the corner of his normally grim mouth.

"The problem," he said, adjusting his tunic, "is that you don't believe you can do it. If you believed it, you could."

"Inspiring," Ileni said, getting to her feet. Muscles she hadn't even known she had ached. "Is that another of your master's teachings?"

His mouth flattened, and he sighed again. "Let's try those stretches one more time, and then we'll give it another try."

Or we could give up, Ileni thought, but didn't say. She didn't know why she should care if Sorin looked down on her, but when he stretched one leg in front of him and leaned down to sweep his hand along the floor, she followed suit. Even though she was only able to reach the middle of her calf.

Sorin swiveled his legs neatly so that he was facing forward, bending low and resting his elbows on the black rock. As always, Ileni was struck by the effortless grace of his movements. He fought the way he used magic, with something wild and unpredictable always on the verge of breaking through his perfect precision.

Except it never did break through. And he fought a lot better than he used magic.

She tried to copy him, but she lost her balance and fell flat on her face. Sorin looked at her over his forearm and managed to make it very obvious that he was not smiling.

Ileni gritted her teeth and struggled to her feet, hating her body for being so weak and unwieldy. The Renegai did not train their sorcerers in anything physical, because they had no reason to. A person who had magic had no need for any other skills. If she'd had her full powers, Ileni would never have agreed to this humiliation. How could Sorin possibly not realize that?

But then, it was probably hard for him to imagine she wouldn't care that she could be physically bested by almost anyone. He moved through the stretches with such obvious physical enjoyment that, watching him from the corner of her eye as she struggled to follow, Ileni felt a rush of envy.

It was too easy, sometimes, to view what he did as a pure skill, and forget the purpose of it.

She tried to move faster so she could finish the series of stretches and be done with it, and her back twinged dangerously. Her body was a collection of throbbing bruises, none painful enough to warrant stopping, but enough to make her feel constantly battered. She felt herself reaching for a healing spell out of habit, and pulled back sharply. They were easy spells, but still required power. So she forced herself to endure the aching muscles and dull bruises—and, even worse, the unending itch of magic that wanted to be used.

Most depressing of all, that morning she had woken up and realized that she was looking forward to this; that these fighting lessons, for all their physical pain and embarrassment, were the only true bright spot in her day. She tried to tell herself it was because she was learning something new, because she had something other than magic to focus on, but she knew it was more than that. It was Sorin.

That was clearly not good. But at least she *had* a bright spot in her day; why should she give that up? She would just have to be careful that Sorin never guessed how she felt, or he would certainly find a way to use it against her.

She finished the stretches—perfunctorily and badly, but

she finished—and sat up. "I finished testing the students today," she said. "None of them have the skill to have killed Cadrel with magic."

"Unless they're hiding it," Sorin pointed out.

"Magical skill is not an easy thing to hide. No." She had been thinking about this all morning. "It isn't one of the students, which means it must be one of the teachers."

Sorin vaulted to his feet and began a series of punches, blocks, and kicks, his slow grace masking the controlled violence of the movements. "Why would a *teacher* want to kill the Renegai tutors?"

Ileni didn't know. But there was a lot she didn't know. "Did Absalm spend a lot of time with any of the other teachers?"

"With all of them," Sorin said. He leaped into a double kick and landed in a light crouch. "He sat at their table, after all."

"You brought out the small table just for me?" She had intended it to sound light, but even she heard the bitterness in her voice.

Sorin straightened. "No. Cadrel sat alone."

"Then why didn't Absalm?"

"Absalm had the master's favor from the beginning."

"Are you saying I don't?" she asked, and surprised a laugh out of him.

"Perhaps not at the moment." He was still poised to continue his exercises, but hadn't yet moved. "In time, you'll be accepted, too."

"I don't want—never mind. It's not important." Ileni got to her feet. "It's not as if Absalm was teaching magic during mealtimes."

"He wasn't giving the teachers lessons at any other times, either," Sorin said. "No one here has much free time."

"You have time to give me these lessons," Ileni pointed out.

He gave her an inscrutable look. "Officially, you are giving me private magic lessons."

"Only you? Doesn't that bother the others?"

He looked away, his shoulders stiff.

"It *must* bother Irun."

"Irun," Sorin said, "has his own suspicions about what we are doing with this time."

Heat flooded her face. "Oh."

Something flashed deep in Sorin's eyes, something that made her wonder if he wished Irun was right. He stepped toward her, and her skin tingled all over with sudden anticipation.

Then he rushed her.

She was so startled, she reacted without thinking. She grabbed and twisted as she had been taught, and Sorin slammed down on his back.

A thrill of pure, fierce joy ran through her. She grinned savagely as Sorin rolled smoothly to his feet, and her sense of triumph didn't die until he grinned back. Then it drained away in a flash.

"You let me do that." Without the adrenaline coursing through her, it was obvious.

"Of course," Sorin said. He balanced on the balls of his feet. "But if I had let you do it last week, you still wouldn't have been able to."

Ileni stepped away from him, eyes burning. "This is stupid."

Sorin blinked. "What?"

"This is *stupid*." She glared at him, breathing hard. "And you know it. Four days of intense training, and I can manage to throw you one time, *when you let me*. I'm not going to be able to defend myself against any of you."

"Well," Sorin said, stretching his arms above his head and twisting his neck from side to side, "four days is not long. We have years to practice." He let his arms drop. "I guess that's a good thing."

No, it wasn't. She was *supposed* to die. That was why she had come here. And here she was, buried beneath the earth, practicing pathetic new skills against someone she could never really fight. Someone whose body would never betray him the way her magic had betrayed her, someone who had no idea what it was to be ordinary.

Someone who's going to die, too, she thought, and a pang twinged through her. It wasn't right that he should die. That all his skill and physical prowess, all his fierce devotion and simmering wildness, should be so temporary. One command and he would be gone, just like Jastim.

"I don't have time for this," she said, dropping out of her fighting stance. "I have to . . . to talk to the teachers." Would any of them even talk to her? So far, they all completely ignored her. "I have to figure out which one of them might have magic."

Sorin nodded. "Arkim is the only possibility I can think of."

Ileni had been prepared for an argument. "What?"

"Arkim. He's the one who summoned Ravil for his mission—he always does the final preparations for missions. He spent forty years in the emperor's court, his one and only mission, and the knowledge he gained during that time was too valuable to lose. So he became a teacher. I suppose he could have learned magic during his time in the Empire."

He could have . . . but when he had walked into the dining cavern, Ileni hadn't sensed a trace of power in him. Then again, she hadn't been paying attention. She had been too busy watching Sorin. "What sort of mission took forty years?"

"He was gaining the trust of the emperor and his family."

"And what he did with that trust was kill one of them?"

"The emperor's brother," Sorin said calmly, "the last time the emperor was considering attacking us."

"Nice."

Sorin's fingertips curled slightly inward. "That warning kept the Empire's army out of these mountains for the past half-century. Ensuring the Renegai's safety as well as ours. One death in exchange for avoiding hundreds."

"I'll bet the emperor's brother didn't see it that way."

"I don't think his opinion was requested."

"It's not *funny!*" Ileni pressed her knuckles against her mouth, then let her hand drop. "Do you truly think all the people you kill deserve to die?"

"That would be an easier belief, wouldn't it?" Sorin's face was cool and remote. "But no. We are trained to make accurate observations, not to be blinded by lies. If we allowed ourselves to believe that, we would falter when we realized some of our targets are innocent. We face the truth, Sorceress: not that they deserve to die, but that their deaths serve a greater purpose."

He stood poised on the balls of his feet, every line of his body thrumming with easy power. Ileni shook her head jerkily, her body tight. She knew he was wrong, but she was certain that if they argued, he would win.

Sorin's mouth twisted cruelly. Suddenly she was afraid of him—which made her realize that she had not, for some time, been afraid of him. *Magefire*, she was a fool. "Here's something else you should know about Arkim. Do you want to guess how old the emperor's brother was, when Arkim killed him?"

Silence.

"He was seven years old."

Ileni's throat convulsed.

"He was an imperial noble. Just not a fully developed one. And his death was necessary."

Nausea roiled up from Ileni's stomach. "Thank you," she said in a hiss.

He leaned back. "For what?"

"For reminding me," Ileni said, "what you are."

Something flickered deep in his eyes, and his mouth twisted again. "Were you in danger of forgetting?"

"Yes," Ileni said. "But it won't happen again."

She turned and walked away, out the cavern entrance and down the long dark hall, and didn't once look back to see if he was watching her go.

Ileni was getting used to being up in the middle of the night; it wasn't as if she was sleeping that well to begin with. So when the knock sounded on her door a few nights later, she was awake almost at once, both feet on the floor and her hands braced behind her on the cot.

"Ileni?" Sorin whispered through the wood, and she got to her feet and crossed the room. She put one hand against the solid wood, then pulled the door open. Sorin stood in the doorway, illuminated by the faint glow of the stones in the wall.

"What?" she breathed, and heard the fear in her voice.

"Nothing like that," Sorin said, without bothering to explain what *that* was. He was smiling, a light, easy smile that looked odd on his face. "I'm here to invite you to a celebration."

"A what?"

"Interested?"

She opened her mouth to do the smart thing and say no. Things had been strained between them since their argument a few days ago, and she knew it was better that way. The young man in front of her now, brimming with excitement and rebellion rather than with zeal and death, was an illusion. A dangerous illusion.

But the very last thing she wanted to do was go back to bed and think about what she might be missing until she fell asleep. Without a word, she went to her clothes chest, pulled on a skirt and shoes, and followed Sorin out into the dark corridor.

Clearly, whatever they were doing was against the rules, and her breath quickened. All her life she had been obedient, following the path laid out before her, asking permission before doing anything that might distract her from her goals. All her life, she had been in pursuit of something too precious to risk by breaking the rules. It was time to adjust to having nothing to lose.

Except her life. Which was not, in her darker moods, that important at all.

"What are we celebrating?" she whispered, but Sorin was

already halfway down the corridor. Swearing, she hurried after him.

The route they took was familiar, after two weeks of following Sorin to the training cavern and back. Even so, she stumbled several times while trying to match his pace by the glowstones' dim light. Too late, Ileni realized that if she'd had her power, she would probably have called up a light. She was still trying to think of an excuse for not doing that—in case Sorin asked—when they emerged into the training cavern, where all the glowstones were bright with white light.

The cavern still stank of sweat, but it mingled with the scent of wine. The combination was, if anything, even more disgusting than usual. But Ileni barely noticed. She stopped short and stared, openmouthed.

The cavern had been transformed. Not by any decoration—it was still sparse and bare—but by the young men who filled it. Gone were the deadly attacks and counterattacks, the focused aggression, the clashes of steel and rope. Instead, the weapons were shoved into piles along the sides of the room, and killers sprawled on the ground around collections of wine jugs and clay mugs, smiling and laughing. She recognized some of them from her classes and from the dining cavern, but not all of them.

Sorin led her down the stairway. Halfway down, a group of boys brushed past them, and one looked over his shoulder at her. She recognized him—he was one of her younger students, curly haired with a triangular face. His name was Esen. He grinned at her and said, "She came!" and the other boys whooped.

Ileni found herself grinning back. Someone else put a clay goblet in her hand, the liquid within sloshing. A dim warning sounded in the back of her mind—but really, if they wanted to kill her, it wouldn't require this elaborate a ruse. Besides, Sorin had been given a similar goblet and was already draining it. She tilted her head back and drank.

It tasted utterly vile, and she choked. Sorin and Esen both laughed, but their laughter had no edge, and Ileni laughed with them. The wine she hadn't spat up raced through her blood. She'd never had wine before. It would have interfered with the focus and concentration required to develop her skills, so she and her fellow students had always regarded it with scorn.

She wouldn't think about that. She *wouldn't*. She was so tired, so unutterably tired, of thinking about it. There was still some wine left in the goblet, so she braced herself and lifted it to her lips. It was over in a single grimace.

"It's not exactly the best quality," Sorin said. "I can get you something better."

"That would help." She giggled, stumbled on the stairs, and grabbed Sorin's arm to steady herself. Beneath his long-sleeved shirt, his arm was like steel. Not surprising. She didn't let go, even once she had regained her balance.

Sorin lifted an eyebrow, but didn't shrug off her hand. "Have you ever had wine before?"

"No." His expression struck her as funny, and she laughed again. Sorin lifted the other eyebrow and led her the rest of the way down the stairs.

Once they were on the cavern floor, she let go of him and looked around. When she didn't see Irun, her last edge of fear receded.

Some of the teachers were here, too, but not all of them. Not the dour-looking man who taught poisons, or the short one with the red hair whose class Sorin always refused to discuss. Arkim was absent as well. The students must have selected which teachers they wanted there. And they had selected her.

How much of that choice had been Sorin's?

A soaring melody pierced the cavern, soon joined by a fast, rhythmic beat. She turned and saw two boys in the corner, one with a flute, the other pounding at a pair of drums. She didn't recognize them; they were too young to be her students—eleven or twelve years old, maybe? The flute player had fiery red hair and an angelic face.

Did all assassins learn an instrument? Or was he being prepared for a specific mission?

"It's an Arcaian dance song," Sorin said, and she turned back to him. He was watching her with the oddest expression on his face—as if it mattered what she thought of this strange party. As if he cared whether, right now, she was happy.

That was delusion. Delusion, and wine. Sorin was a killer.

But he didn't look like one, right now, as he held his hand out to her.

She decided not to think about it—not thinking about things was feeling wonderful, and the wine and music made it easy. She took his hand.

"Arcaians truly know how to dance," Sorin said, shouting now over the sound of the music—and of the whoops of the others as they began to leap about on the floor. "Be glad you don't know the words to this song, though."

"Who says I don't?" Ileni retorted. An assassin whirled past them, launching himself off the rock floor and tumbling over twice in midair before landing lightly on his feet.

Sorin rolled his eyes and took her other hand. His hands were fine boned, but rough and callused. He pulled her close with casual strength and grinned down at her.

He was closer to her than he had ever been. His hands moved to her waist, his arms encircling her with unyielding strength. She could feel his breath as he spoke. "Can sorcerers dance?"

She lifted her chin to stare up into his face. "I think you're about to find out."

Actually, sorcerers couldn't dance—not in the athletic, graceful way the assassins could—but it didn't matter. Sorin held her close and refrained from the complex acrobatics of the other assassins. They whirled around the cave floor, Sorin looking down at her with his lips pressed together but curved upward at the corners. The music worked its way into Ileni's blood, and she moved to its beat without thinking, the fabric of her skirt brushing rhythmically against her legs. Exhilaration rushed through her, fueled by the music and the movement and the press of Sorin's hands against her lower back. Every time he pulled her close, it felt like another draught of wine, making her reckless and giddy.

"Does your master know about this?" she asked at one

point, when her cheek was inches from Sorin's.

"Of course," Sorin said. He pushed her away, twirled her around, pulled her close again. "But don't worry. He never comes. He knows we need some small freedoms."

Not true freedom, if he knows about it. But who was she to talk? She had chafed against some of her training restrictions, back in the sorcerers' compound; she had even bent the rules, from time to time, to be with Tellis. Small freedoms, every one of them, nothing that would have scandalized the Elders had they found out. For all her little rebellions, she had been content to be what she was being molded to be.

And she didn't want to argue with Sorin now. He grabbed both her hands, and she leaned back. As her hair flew out behind her, she scanned the cavern. She was still looking for Irun, but her eye fell instead on Bazel. The round-faced assassin was not part of the dancing. He stood in a corner, near the piles of weapons, small and furtive. Every once in a while, one of the other assassins would walk up to him, and Bazel would hand him something too small for Ileni to see.

Sorin followed her gaze and grimaced. "Would you prefer to dance with your favorite?"

"Why do you care?" she said archly, and then she caught his expression. It was pure scorn, without a hint of jealousy, and it felt like a slap. Ileni whirled out of his arms, taking him by surprise, and hurt flashed through her again when he released her without a fight. She stumbled, managed *not* to fall flat on the rock floor, and headed defiantly across the cavern in Bazel's direction.

Sorin hissed something behind her, but the music was too loud to make it out. She didn't care what he said, anyhow. He'd have a lot more to say when she *did* ask Bazel to dance.

She reached Bazel just as another assassin—a tall boy who wasn't in any of her classes—was saying to him, in a lofty voice, "Being rather generous, aren't you?"

"I'll be getting more soon," Bazel began, then stopped when he saw Ileni. The other assassin gave him a sideways look and glided away.

"Teacher," Bazel said stiffly.

It occurred to Ileni that if she asked him to dance, he might say no. She could feel Sorin's gaze, hot on her back, and abruptly changed her plan. "What are you giving out? Can I have a look?"

Completely without expression, he dipped a hand into the pouch at his belt and placed something small and square in her palm.

Ileni blinked, surprised at his compliance. Was she

bullying him just as his classmates did? But then she recognized the dark object in her hand, and her mouth watered.

Compunctions gone, she popped it into her mouth and closed her eyes as she swallowed. The taste of chocolate lingered on her tongue.

"Where did you get this?" she breathed.

Bazel's face closed. He stared past her stolidly, like a defeated animal waiting to be hit.

Sorin gripped her elbow from behind. Ileni looked up to see the sneer he aimed at Bazel. "Are you going to invite our teacher to dance?"

Bazel didn't reply.

"Are *you?*" Ileni asked Sorin, to get his attention away from Bazel. It worked. He looked down at her, then pulled her away from the corner. Ileni glanced over her shoulder just long enough to see another assassin approach Bazel, and Bazel's gaze lift from the floor as his hand dipped into his pouch.

Obviously, the chocolate was a secret—even if an open one. Another of those small freedoms? Or maybe this was something the master actually didn't know about. Though even as she thought it, she didn't really believe it.

She turned back to Sorin. "Can't you see he's afraid of you? Why—"

Sorin swung her around in a dizzying swirl, and her harangue ended in a tiny shriek. When he pulled her back to him, his eyes still hard, she opened her mouth and then shut it. She didn't want to fight. Besides, what would it change? Should it surprise her that he was capable of cruelty?

What she said instead was, "Where does Bazel get the chocolate?"

Sorin shrugged, his mouth twisting. "Others gather it on their missions, I assume, and he arranges trades for them. It's one way to make himself useful."

That was possible . . . but it didn't entirely make sense. *I'll be getting more soon*, Bazel had said. How could he possibly know if one of his fellow assassins was going to be coming back alive?

Through her dizziness, Ileni tried to remember if Sorin had been close enough to hear. It wasn't like him to miss things. . . .

But of course, this was just a small freedom, and it was just Bazel. Not worth Sorin's concern. If he didn't pay attention, then he didn't have to worry about *how* Bazel got the chocolates, and whether it involved more than a small

ave to think about whether it was something

pped.

convenient for him.

When Sorin offered her another goblet of wine, Ileni took it and drained it with barely a sputter. She liked his surprised grin, and the way the wine sizzled through her blood, and the fuzziness of her mind. Her worries and regrets and fears seemed dulled and distant, and she laughed again, because it was so easy and it felt so good. She leaned back, laughing, trusting Sorin's arms to support her. She wanted to feel like this forever.

"How often do you do this?" she asked Sorin when they stopped to rest. They sat side by side against the wall, him in a crouch that was simultaneously relaxed and ready, her with her skirt spread over her outstretched legs. Sorin wasn't touching her, but she could feel him, inches from her skin.

"Like it, do you?" Sorin tilted his head down at her. His arms rested loosely on his knees. "There will be more, though not very often. We celebrate every time one of us returns alive from a successful mission."

A successful mission.

All at once, everything came rushing back: where she was and who she was dancing with, her past and her present and her narrow bleak future. And what she was celebrating, what all this joy was about. The death of someone, far away in the Empire, a dagger stained with blood. The knowledge rose around her, threatening to overwhelm her, to engulf her again in a black fog of misery.

No. She focused on the present, on the music and laughter, on Sorin's face as he watched her. She reached out recklessly and closed her hand around his.

"I want to dance again," she said.

Sorin's fingers pressed, very slightly, against hers. "Already? Are you sure?"

"*Yes,*" she said, and scrambled to her feet. He stood up too, looking bemused, and followed her back out onto the training floor.

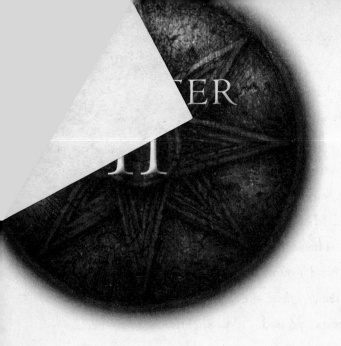

The next morning, Ileni woke with a throbbing headache she suspected was a hangover. She'd heard some of the Renegai commonfolk talking about hangovers once. Until now, she had assumed they were exaggerating.

"It's not a hangover," Sorin said unsympathetically when he arrived to pick her up. "You're just tired. You didn't drink enough to have a hangover."

But she *had* drunk enough, she suspected, to make a complete fool of herself. Her face burned as she leaned weakly against the wall. Another good reason not to leave this room ever again.

Except, of course, that she had no choice. *Small freedoms.* No matter the illusion created last night, her life here was not her own, and she had better not forget it if she wanted to stay alive.

In the dining hall, Sorin sat across from her, leaving an empty seat at his table—no, not just one. Ravil's seat was also still empty. "Was it Ravil who came back? From his . . . from his mission?"

"No. It was someone else."

"Where is that person?"

Sorin jabbed his spoon into his porridge, which he had retrieved from his own table before coming over. "With the master, reporting on what he learned. And what he will not realize he learned, until the master points it out."

His voice was terse. Ileni put her own spoon down. "You're jealous."

He stirred his porridge, then spooned some into his mouth.

She remembered how he had held her last night, controlled and wild. But most of all, joyous. She remembered her questions the first night, about how all these young men could be forced to kill. How incredibly stupid she had been. "You *want* to be sent."

"Of course I do."

Ileni picked up her spoon, slowly. "To kill someone you don't even know."

"Easier than if I did know him."

She swallowed a mouthful of porridge. It went down in a hard lump.

"That wasn't a joke. The noble I killed was a quick job—into his room and out in less than an hour. If you have to befriend someone before you kill him . . . those are the most difficult missions, the ones the master assigns only to his most trusted students."

Ileni looked down at the rest of her porridge, mostly so she could look away from him, from the longing clear on his face. She had to stop forgetting what he was.

Even though she was hungry, the sweet, thick smell from her bowl made her stomach turn over. She forced in a few more spoonfuls, then put her spoon down and endured until the meal was over, closing her eyes periodically.

It didn't improve her mood to find that her students—most of whom had been dancing all night, and had drunk *far* more than she had—were as attentive and disciplined as ever. Her attempt to get through class without expending any power seemed even more pathetically obvious than usual, and she braced herself for a challenge from Irun. But he said not a word. He just watched her grimly, his silence more menacing than an outright confrontation.

By the time she was finished with her first lesson, her mind had begun to work again. As her students rose to their feet, she said, "Sorin. A word."

The two boys next to Sorin exchanged glances, which reminded her that they had seen her display of . . . whatever that had been . . . last night. Her cheeks heated up. By the time Sorin obediently came to stand in front of her, they felt beet red.

He waited patiently, as if he didn't notice. She cleared her throat. "Did Absalm and Cadrel go to the celebrations?"

Sorin blinked, then rubbed the side of his neck. "Absalm did, yes. I don't think we had any celebrations while Cadrel was here."

"For two whole months?"

"It's not unusual. Our missions depend on events in the Empire, on who wants to hire us, and on the master's plans. Sometimes nobody gets sent for years."

"How boring for you all."

"It makes for better training." He glanced over his

shoulder at the now-empty cavern. "But since Irun's success, our missions will probably be far more frequent."

"Who invited Absalm to the celebrations?"

"I did." Sorin shifted his weight slightly. "Why does it matter whether he went? Nobody killed him for *that*."

"I don't know," Ileni said. "But there must have been *something* they did that led to their being killed. I won't know what it is until I find it."

Sorin considered her. "Ileni—"

But then the next group of students began filing into the cavern, and he stopped talking and turned away.

Ileni wondered what he had been going to say for most of the second class. By the third class, she had turned to the more productive question of what other small rules her predecessors might have broken. She had seen only one other illicit activity last night, and while she couldn't imagine someone being killed over chocolate, either, it was the only avenue she had to explore.

She waited until she and Sorin were at the entrance to the dining cavern, with Bazel only a few yards behind them. Then she turned and said, "Bazel. Sit with me, please. I want to talk to you."

Bazel blinked at her, then darted a nervous glance at

Sorin, whose expression was flinty. Ileni turned her back on both of them and made her way to her table. As she sat, Bazel headed toward her, exuding reluctance. Sorin started as if to follow, then turned on his heel and stalked to his own table.

The midday meal was some sort of clawed, buglike creature that had been served once before—a delicacy in the Empire, Sorin had informed her then, and therefore something the assassins had to learn to eat with pleasure. Ileni looked at the red legs and antennae splayed out on her plate and decided she didn't have to learn any such thing. She folded her hands together on the table and looked at Bazel, who was methodically taking apart his own food, keeping his eyes on the scaly red limbs. When she said his name, he looked up, stony resentment in his pale blue eyes.

She resisted the urge to apologize. Instead she said, "I want to offer you a trade."

He chewed and swallowed before he replied. "Thank you, Teacher. But I don't think you have anything I want."

"Then you lack imagination. Wouldn't you like to know how you can beat Irun next time he decides to attack you?"

Silence. Bazel looked down at his plate, rigid and unmoving. When he spoke, it was in a near whisper.

"Irun has a lot of magical power, too."

"He does. But power without knowledge isn't very useful. With the spells I would teach you, you could humiliate him."

Bazel's hands twitched. "In *your* class," he said finally. "I would pay for it later, in our next weapons drill. Pay heavily, I would imagine."

A fatal accident, Sorin had said. Ileni repressed a shiver. "Possibly," she said. "Of course, that wouldn't change the fact that Irun had been humiliated."

Bazel smiled. It wasn't a smile she wanted to return. It was grim, deadly, and so implacable that she suddenly wondered if this was a good idea.

Too late to reconsider. "Of course, I would have to tutor you privately. It would take a lot of my time."

"You have something better to do?" Bazel said.

Just because someone was being victimized did not, necessarily, make him likeable. Ileni lifted her chin, trying to look mysterious rather than irritated. "A great number of things."

"Like allowing Sorin to drag you along as the special entertainment for one of his parties?"

Was that why he had brought her? "What do you mean, *his* parties? You were there, too."

Bazel's face twitched. "Didn't he tell you? The parties were Sorin's idea, and he's the one who organizes them. They're not exactly sanctioned by the master."

"He does things of his own volition?" Ileni's voice emerged sharp. That *special entertainment* still stung. "How remarkable. I'm surprised he can get away with it."

Bazel smiled bitterly. "Sorin's the sort of person who likes to find out what he can get away with. In case you hadn't noticed."

She hadn't. She had thought he was a perfect assassin, that he kept any rebellious impulses under strict control. And she still wasn't sure she was wrong. A party and a dance . . . permitted transgressions, she was willing to wager. Deliberately overlooked, like her own use of sleep spells or excursions with Tellis. It didn't mean Sorin would ever dare anything truly forbidden. That occasional gleam in his eyes, the wildness she sensed simmering beneath the surface, could be safely dissipated in a few nights of celebration. The master *was* wise, at least when it came to controlling his students.

She leaned forward. "These lessons wouldn't be at your master's command, either. They would be for you."

Bazel rubbed the back of his neck, but all he said was,

"And what you want in return is chocolate?"

"Not quite. Though I wouldn't say no to a few pieces." Ileni pressed her hands hard against her knees, under the table where Bazel couldn't see. "I want to know where you get the chocolates."

He hesitated for so long she was afraid he was going to refuse. She took a risk. "Did you get them from Absalm?"

"What? No."

She couldn't tell if he was lying. She bit the inside of her lip. "But you must have used magic. I don't believe the other assassins would give you spoils from their missions."

Anger flashed across his face. She added, "Yet. I can help you change that."

He laughed shortly. "Even if I beat Irun, that won't turn me into a different person, Teacher." He blew out a short breath and nodded. "I'll show you how I get them. But I don't know when they'll be back."

Was she supposed to know who *they* were? Ileni decided the safest thing to do was nod.

Bazel inclined his head back, a barely discernible motion, then swung his legs over the bench and hurried away, leaving an uneaten jumble of claws and jointed legs on his plate.

Almost as soon as he was gone, Sorin slid into his place.

Ileni braced herself. But all he said, after a glance at her full plate, was, "Are you done eating? I think it's time you learned something new."

He didn't mention Bazel as he led her away from the table and through the corridors, walking instead in silence. Ileni, prepared for a challenge and rehearsing a dozen different retorts in her head, didn't realize where they were going until they were there. Then she stopped so short she almost fell, staring at the racks of shiny knives in the cavern where Irun had almost killed her.

"What is this?" she demanded. "A reminder of what I owe you?"

Sorin gave her a look that was half-amused, half-reproachful. "We're here for weapons training."

"Why?"

"Because, as you pointed out, the hand-to-hand lessons are somewhat pointless." He walked over to the racks, pulled a knife, and threw it over his shoulder without looking. It landed in the center of one of the targets. "With a weapon, you can be far more effective."

"Or I could cut off my own hand by mistake."

"We'll practice not doing that. It will be our first lesson."

She didn't laugh. She kept looking at the knife he had

thrown, which still quivered in the center of what would have been a person's heart. "When you and Irun . . . when you took the knives . . . he said it was dangerous."

"Because those were poisoned knives." That wild gleam leaped briefly back into his eyes. "I like to take unexpected risks, once in a while. It's dangerous to be predictable."

"Um," Ileni said.

"Most of us aren't permitted to use the poisoned knives. It requires training and preparation." He looked at the shiny blades proudly. "The poison is called vernath. There is no antidote, so we have to take care."

"Marvelous," Ileni muttered.

"Don't worry. We'll start with unpoisoned ones."

"*Start?*"

"First, let's see if you have knack for throwing—"

"No," Ileni said.

He blinked at her. "Why not?"

"Renegai don't use weapons."

"You're not exactly a Renegai anymore, are you?"

She should have seen that coming, but she flinched anyhow, so violently that Sorin saw it. He looked at her in silence, his dark eyes slits above his sharply planed cheeks, and she felt her heart thud against her ribs. He was going to figure it out . . .

he was smart, she should have been more careful. . . .

But when he spoke, his voice was soft. "You could be happy here, you know."

Her laugh sounded like a sob. "I doubt that."

"You should know . . ." He trailed off, looking uncharacteristically uncertain. "That you have choices. Even here. I understand what it's like to grow up outside and then know you'll spend the rest of your life underground. I used to be angry, too."

"Oh?" This time it sounded more like a laugh. "And who were *you* angry at?"

"Nobody. Everybody. Just like you." He walked to the target and pulled out the knife. "Undirected anger accomplishes nothing. Anger can be a powerful tool, but only if you treat it like one."

By the practiced rhythm of his words, she knew that was another of the master's sayings. "I'm fine with my anger as it is. But thank you."

"You don't have to be resentful all the time. Once you understand that your life here has a goal, and a purpose . . . you could be happy. I am." He drew another knife. The blade looked natural in his hand, like it belonged there. "Absalm was, too."

Ileni shook her head violently. "No. He wasn't. Maybe you *thought*—"

"We're trained to recognize truths, Ileni. No matter how unpleasant." Sorin was watching her so intently it made her feel almost panicked. "He wasn't an outsider. He didn't feel like an exile. We considered him one of us."

"Quite the honor. I'm sure he was overwhelmed with pride."

"He was a good teacher. A wise man. Even the master respected him."

"Don't you understand?" Ileni clenched her fists. "Absalm was an Elder of our people before he volunteered to be the next tutor. So you respected him. Maybe he didn't *care*. Maybe the respect of a group of student killers wasn't all that important to him." She spoke as hotly as if she had known the man. She hadn't known Cadrel, either. But she knew that both of them, like every tutor in the past two centuries, had viewed their sojourn in these caves as forced labor, a lifelong sacrifice made for the good of all Renegai. As she did, and would, however long she managed to survive.

No matter how tiring it became, being miserable all the time.

You could be happy.

"This is because of last night." She crossed her arms over her chest. "You think I'm one of you now. Because I celebrated a murder."

Sorin said nothing. So he wasn't denying it.

"I'm not one of you," she hissed. "I never will be. And neither was Absalm."

Except Absalm *had* betrayed the Renegai, at least once. He had told his strongest students the truth about their magic.

Ileni drew in a dry, painful breath. She had been here less than twenty days, and last night she had danced with killers and not cared why they were rejoicing. She hadn't cared because no one else in that cavern had cared. Absalm had been here for a decade. Who was she to judge him?

"It wasn't murder," Sorin said suddenly.

She blinked at him, startled by the anger in his voice. "What?"

"You keep calling it murder." He drew another knife from the rack and walked toward her, holding it out hilt first. "This is a war, Ileni. Between us and the Empire. In war people die. You have to accept that, if you're going to fight."

"But you don't," Ileni said through gritted teeth, "have to celebrate it."

Sorin looked at the rows of shining knives. Then he said, slowly, "It makes it easier, though."

Ileni didn't doubt it. She thought of the pillar carved with names, stretching up almost to the ceiling. The way they had danced last night, the exhilaration filling the cavern, the weapons piled on the sides.

She thought of the fact that she had been calling him a murderer for weeks now, and he had never before seemed to care.

"Didn't you ever wonder," Sorin said, turning back suddenly to meet her eyes, "what your people could do if they were willing to fight? Instead of sacrificing one of your own to be our tutor, you could turn your magic *against* us. Or you could battle the imperial sorcerers themselves. Magic against magic."

"The imperial sorcerers are far more powerful than we are," Ileni snapped. "They gather power from other human beings. That's dark magic that we would never touch."

"Exactly." Sorin was still holding the knife out, his hand rock steady. "What makes us stronger than you is not our training. It is our willingness to kill."

"Then you'll remain stronger than us," Ileni said flatly.

"And so will the Empire."

"If we do exactly what the Empire does, what right do we have to fight it?"

"If you don't, you *can't* fight it. And it will go on conquering and destroying and killing, while you sit in your mountain village and congratulate yourselves on how virtuous you are."

Their eyes locked. His were fathomless as dark water, unyielding as marble. Ileni knew he was wrong, knew there must be a dozen things she should say in response, and couldn't think of a single one.

"All right," she said finally, and closed her fingers around the hilt of the knife. It felt as if a part of herself was falling away. "Show me."

Two weeks later, as Ileni was drifting off to sleep, someone knocked on her door. She had been lying in bed for an hour, thinking—again—of Tellis. When she tried not to think about him, she found herself thinking about Sorin, and that was even worse. It didn't hurt the same way, but it was far more dangerous.

So the knock was a welcome reprieve. She scrambled off her bed, pulled on a skirt, and hurried across the room to open the door.

Bazel stepped into the doorway. "Rather trusting, aren't you? You might at least have asked who it was."

"What difference does it make?" Ileni retorted, trying to keep her face blank. She crossed the room before he could advance farther—that way it wouldn't seem like she was retreating—and took a seat on the edge of her bed. Disappointment formed a hard knot in her stomach; she had expected Sorin. *Careful, Ileni.* "Is there any one of you I should trust more than another?"

"A valid point." Bazel leaned against the doorpost. In the darkness, alone, he looked far more dangerous than he did in her class. "I'm here to show you where those chocolates came from. Are you going to put on shoes?"

Bazel led her through a series of passageways, then turned through a square entrance into a tunnel that was unfamiliar to Ileni. The ground was uneven and littered with pebbles, and there were no glowstones. Stalactites dripped down the walls like lines of paint.

To her relief, Bazel called up a magelight on his own. It wasn't very bright, but it was sufficient for her to see the ground in front of her. Even so, she twice sent rocks skittering along the tunnel floor. Bazel walked with his head up, arms swinging by his sides. He looked like a different person.

After ten minutes, the crumbling passageway ended in a medium-sized cavern with large boulders in a looming jumble at its far end. Bazel hopped onto one of those jagged rocks, reached up, and pulled himself over it without looking back. Ileni followed, scraping her ankle on a sharp edge.

The crack between the boulders and the ceiling turned into a low, flat tunnel. She had to lie on her stomach and pull herself forward by her elbows, twisting her hips sideways and dragging her legs after her. In front of her, Bazel wasn't exactly quiet, but he had clearly done this before, and she had a hard time keeping up with his smooth, efficient movements. The magelight vanished, leaving them in complete blackness. The tunnel got narrower and narrower, until she was pulling herself through by her fingernails, hips and shoulders scraping painfully against the rocks.

She was starting to worry about getting stuck when something thumped lightly ahead, and a few seconds later her fingers hit empty air instead of rock. She wiggled forward cautiously, reaching down and sliding her hands along the smooth rock wall below the tunnel's end. Bazel had landed with barely a sound, so the ground couldn't be too far down.

Suddenly eager to be out of the stifling tunnel, she pushed hard with her feet.

She slid out of the tunnel, too fast. Suddenly she was out and flying down headfirst. She scrabbled frantically to grab the too-smooth rock, and her sharp scream cut off as she slammed into the stone floor with an impact that thudded through her entire body. For a panicked moment she couldn't breathe, and then she gasped in a lungful of air that hissed painfully through her chest.

The magelight flared white, revealing Bazel's round face looking down at her. Ileni scrambled to her feet, a spasm of pain shooting through her back, and tossed her head. The movement sent clumps of dirt flying from her hair, which did nothing to further her pretense of cool assurance.

Bazel muffled a laugh. Ileni's fists clenched. It was one thing to be humiliated in front of Sorin, or even Irun, but in front of *Bazel* . . .

"I think that's about enough of my blindly following you," she snapped. "Why don't you tell me where we're going?"

Bazel just looked at her. Ileni was suddenly aware of how close he was, and how tall. He might be the least of the assassins, but he was still deadly and dangerous. Somehow, she had let the others' attitude infect her, and she had forgotten.

But he thought she was deadly and dangerous, too. A powerful sorceress. And unlike Irun, he'd had no experience in killing sorcerers. Ileni drew herself up. If he saw her fear, *that* would cause her death. She tried to be the girl she once had been, supremely confident in her abilities, eager to take on any challenge.

"Tell me," she said. "Or neither of us is going any farther."

Bazel set his jaw. Ileni glared at him, then lifted one hand as if to begin a spell. She could freeze him to the ground where he stood. For a moment, she believed it, and whatever he saw on her face made Bazel's eyes widen.

"All right," he said. "You should have some warning, I suppose."

"Yes." Ileni lowered her hand, but not all the way to her side.

Bazel took a step back, his eyes on her hand. "I suppose Sorin gave you the usual speech about these caves. How we're isolated and indoctrinated and trained to think of nothing but death."

"That's all common knowledge, actually."

"Right." The side of Bazel's mouth lifted in a sneer. He sidled sideways and sat on the edge of a flat black rock.

"Well, it's not that simple. Even here, the rules aren't always followed. There are entrances into these caves besides the way you came. And things can be smuggled in that aren't only about our mission."

Ileni leaned forward. "There are traders who come into the caves?"

Bazel shifted. "Official traders come to designated meeting spots, and are met with contingents from the caves. That's how we get the food we can't grow or raise nearby. And then there are . . . unofficial traders."

Ileni raked her hand through her hair, dislodging more dirt. "That seems like a rather dangerous endeavor. It must be quite profitable for them."

"It is."

Of course, the traders who ventured this far into the mountains tended to be an adventurous lot to begin with. Ileni had seen some of them when they visited the Renegai village, but never spoken to any. Sorcerers didn't get involved in the time-consuming business of haggling for chocolate and spices.

She rolled her shoulders back, cautiously. They still ached from her impact with the ground, but they didn't protest the movement. "They trade with *you*?"

Bazel put one foot up on another rock. "And through me, with the others in these caves."

"Does the master know?"

Bazel's eyes darted to the side. "If he did, he wouldn't care. It's not important enough for him to pay attention to."

Ileni lifted her eyebrows.

"If it was important," Bazel said, "he *would* know. Nothing significant escapes his notice. But he allows us small freedoms. He understands that we can't be perfect all the time."

Ileni kept her face carefully blank.

Bazel put both feet on the ground. "If that's all—"

"One more thing," Ileni said. If she was going to preserve the illusion that she was more powerful than he was, she should control when the conversation ended. "If you know another way out, why don't you run away?"

His lip curled. "There is no such thing as running away, Teacher. One can't escape the master merely by getting out of these caves. Besides, who said I want to run away?"

He turned and walked across the rocky ground, the magelight hovering at his shoulder.

Within minutes they were clambering through a labyrinth of jagged boulders that leaned haphazardly against one another, stretching as far ahead as Ileni could see by the magelight. Bazel leaped easily from rock to rock, balancing and launching himself from one precarious edge to another with practiced ease. Ileni scrambled behind on her hands and feet and knees, feeling cautiously for footholds. The rocks looked like they might tilt and fall as soon as her weight hit them.

She was concentrating so hard that it was a while before she heard it: a rushing murmur that seemed to come from all around them.

"What is that?" she demanded.

Bazel leaped to the top of a bulbous rock structure, balancing in a crouch, hands and feet gripping the stone. He replied without looking back. "You'll see."

"Or you could just tell me," Ileni muttered, but not loud enough for Bazel to hear. He pulled himself through a tiny opening between two leaning boulders, and she scrambled to catch up, terrified that he would get too far ahead and leave her alone among the rocks and the darkness.

She heard a soft thud, and pulled herself cautiously through the opening after Bazel, holding tight to the edges of the boulders and leaning over. Below her—far below— was a dense blackness and that constant rushing sound. The air smelled different, too, dank rather than musty.

A river, here beneath the earth. If she had kept going, she would have plunged right into it.

Was that what Bazel had wanted?

She pulled herself farther out, then looked down and around for Bazel. She couldn't see him—but she *could* make out the faint outlines of the rocks rising behind her, which meant it wasn't pitch-black. She twisted around to search for the source of the light, and found it when she looked up.

"Come on," Bazel said, and she saw that he was standing on a ledge several feet above the tunnel's opening. Squinting, she made out square handholds cut into the cliff above her, leading up to the ledge. Bazel's voice was muffled by the rushing river, so she couldn't tell if there was any disappointment in it.

This must be where Absalm had died. Was it how he had died, as well?

"I'll need help," she said.

Bazel sighed, loudly enough to be heard over the rushing water, and leaned down. Ileni hesitated before reaching for his hand—if he did want her to drown, this was a perfect opportunity. But it wasn't as if she had any choice. She clasped his wrist as tightly as possible, though she was under no illusions about his ability to pry her off if he tried. He lifted her up part of the way, and then he paused. Her feet dangled in thin air, and her body twisted slightly, brushing against the rock. The river rushed far below.

"Don't," she tried to say, but all that emerged was a whimper. Then he grunted and swung her up onto the ledge next to him.

The rest of the whimper turned into a gasp of relief. Bazel pulled away. "It's easy from here," he said. "The path goes down the side of the cliff until it's level with the river."

"What river is it?" Ileni asked. She could see nothing but slick blackness below.

Bazel started down the path. "A minor tributary— nothing that would be very impressive in sunlight, I'd imagine. It flows under the mountains for a bit before emptying into the Farlin River."

Which emptied into the Diannor, which flowed straight to the capital of the Empire. As a child, Ileni and her friends had cursed stones and thrown them into the Farlin, in the hope that some imperial noble would pick one up and have a run of bad luck.

Excitement fluttered within her. The river went *out*. Through the caves and out of them. Another entrance, another exit. And she knew how to swim.

Not that it mattered, since she was in these caves for a purpose. She didn't need an escape.

Yet.

She followed Bazel down a steep path, narrow and bordered by a plunge into blackness—not exactly her definition of *easy*. She pressed as close to the rocks as she could until, after a short jump from the bottom of the path, they landed on a blessedly wide area of flat stone. Here the river was at their level, a black spreading vastness, silver ripples skimming along its surface.

Ileni looked around for some sort of raft or boat, but there was nothing on the rock except her and Bazel. The cliff face rose around them, smooth and solid but for the narrow slope of the path they had come down on. "You didn't ask if I could swim."

"Oops," Bazel said.

Before she could respond, a new sound mingled with the rushing of the river: a steadier, more purposeful sound, interrupted once by a splash. Seconds later, a large canoe appeared around the bend of the river, headed straight for them.

CHAPTER
12

Torches in the bow and stern clearly illuminated the two occupants of the canoe. A blond man with ruddy skin was at the oars, his smooth strokes spreading wide white ripples from the sides of the canoe. In the bow sat a woman with short dark hair and a square face. Her gaze fixed on Ileni and didn't waver, even when the canoe bottom scraped rock and the blond man leaped out to pull it onto dry land.

"Has your master started recruiting women?" she said. Her voice was surprisingly high-pitched and feminine.

"Not quite," Bazel replied, and Ileni was startled to see that he was smiling. "Sorry to disappoint you."

The woman rolled her eyes. "Whether or not your master thinks women are capable of killing hardly affects me. Or their ability to do so, I might add." By now the canoe was firmly on the rock, but the woman remained sitting, as if she was a queen on her throne.

"This is our new magic tutor," Bazel said. "From the Renegai."

"Ah." The woman's gaze hadn't moved from Ileni's face even as she spoke to Bazel, but now sharpened. "Interesting choice on the part of the Renegai."

"Thank you," Ileni said coldly.

At that, the woman focused on Bazel. "What do you have for us today?"

"Two gold earrings, a necklace of black pearls, and a ring set with emeralds." As he spoke, Bazel knelt on the floor and laid the items out on the ground. Ileni gaped. The jewelry spread on the damp stone represented a small fortune.

"Where did you get those?" she blurted.

Bazel picked up the ring and handed it to the woman, who examined it closely. "The master doesn't mind if we keep souvenirs from our missions."

"But you haven't—" he shot her a warning look, and she finished—"any idea how much these are worth, do you?"

"The master is very rich," Bazel said. "And here in these caves, they're worth nothing."

"Officially," the woman put in, fingering the ring.

Bazel grinned at her. The woman smiled back, and he flushed ever so slightly.

"We'll give you five bags of chocolate and a cask of Vaeran red wine," the woman said, slipping the ring into her sleeve and lacing her fingers over one knee. "It's overly generous, but we're on our way to those very same Renegai, and we lost a horse in the mountains, so we need the extra space. There's a shortage of dainar in the capital right now."

"Dainar?" Ileni said sharply. Dainar was an extract of the albalia tree, necessary for a number of spells. Producing it was the occupation of many unskilled Renegai.

The woman nodded. "Valuable stuff. The imperial sorcerers pay almost anything we ask for it."

"We—the Renegai—don't trade with the Empire," Ileni said stiffly.

"No, of course not," the blond man agreed, crouching next to the jewelry. "There's no call for Empire-made goods in the Renegai village. I don't know why we're wasting our time making a stop."

The woman sighed, shooting him an admonishing

look—he smirked unrepentantly—then looked with weary patience at Ileni. "When you get over your outraged disbelief, you might think about whether you want a message sent to someone among your people. I can make sure they get it. And bring a message back, if there is one. We'll be stopping here again before we head to the capital."

Tellis. The longing that tore through Ileni hurt like the ripping open of an old wound. She bit her lip for a full second before making herself say, "No. There's no one."

The woman simply waited, as if expecting Ileni to change her mind. Did she know something? Had Tellis asked her . . .

No. That was ridiculous. Tasting blood on her lip, Ileni added defiantly, "Thank you anyhow."

"I don't think it was going to be a favor," Bazel observed.

The woman leaned over and pulled a cloth bag out of the boat. "Of course not. We're traders."

"What makes you think she has anything to trade?"

"Everyone has something to trade." The woman smiled. "Speaking of which, I have a surprise for you."

Bazel leaned in eagerly. "What is it?"

"Something new." The woman straightened, dangling the bag from one hand. "Cacao ground to powder. Mix it with water and it's better than wine. More expensive, though. You have anything else for us?"

Bazel considered. "Not yet. Sayon is on a mission now, and I know he'll bring back something to trade if he survives. I'll save some of this for him, and give you whatever he brings back in exchange."

The woman frowned. "Where was he sent?"

"Gadera. His target is one of the duke's sons, so he'll be in the castle. Plenty of opportunities to snatch some expensive baubles, and there's a good chance he'll make it out alive, too."

"Though Sayon doesn't have the greatest taste, if I recall correctly," the blond man put in, running his fingers over the black pearls. "I gave my wife one of his last acquisitions as a gift, and I slept in the stables for a week."

Bazel shrugged with elaborate casualness. "You can wait and see what he's brought, and decide then."

"We're traders," the man said, "not gamblers." But he was smiling.

The woman made a slight motion with her hand. "All right. We'll give you the powder in return for whatever Sayon brings back——"

"And," the blond man spoke up, letting the pearls drop back to the ground, "for sharing some cups with us now."

The woman turned to him, her face somehow amused despite the grim line of her mouth. The blond man propped an elbow on one knee. "Oh, come on, Karyn. To give us strength for the journey out."

She rolled her eyes. "Very well."

That struck Ileni as a bad idea. This secret meeting seemed risky enough without extending it. Clearly, however, it wasn't up to her. Bazel had already settled cross-legged on the ground, and the blond man was efficiently pulling four large cups and a stoppered clay jug from the bottom of the canoe.

The woman—Karyn—finally deigned to get out of the boat. She was wearing a long green tunic belted at the waist, thick black leggings, and boots that had seen better days. She settled next to Bazel, leaned back on her hands, and said, "How do you like living among killers?"

It took Ileni a moment to realize the question was directed at her, since the woman was looking out at the black water. Irritation prickled through her. Was this habit of not looking at the person she was speaking to supposed to make Karyn seem coy and mysterious? "About as much as you like trading with them, I would guess. Or maybe less, since I don't do it by choice."

"I come from a long line of traveling traders," Karyn

said. "Where there's great profit to be made, I don't have a choice, either."

How nicely overdramatic. "Even at the risk of your life?"

"I do what I can to minimize that risk," Karyn said. "Like instructing Bazel to always come alone."

Bazel flushed and opened his mouth. Ileni spoke before he could. "Not his fault. I forced him to bring me."

Finally, Karyn looked at her. Ileni looked back, doing her best to appear dangerous. If she had managed for the past month to hide her fear from trained killers, she certainly wasn't going to be intimidated by a trader.

Their locked gazes broke only when the blond man passed around the cups, now filled with a mixture of water and the fine brown powder. Karyn lifted hers and breathed in the scent, closing her eyes.

The chocolate drink was rich and sweet—not as good as pure chocolate, but it slid down Ileni's throat like velvet. She drained nearly the entire cup, and only when she looked up after that first draught did she realize the others were sipping theirs slowly.

How long were they going to *stay* here? Ileni didn't know how much time they had spent clambering through the caves, or when morning would come. Bazel, however, seemed in no hurry. He sat with his legs folded in front of him, taking luxurious sips of the chocolate drink and listening with a bemused smile as the traders argued over a deal they had once struck in Gadera. It was the first time Ileni had seen him completely relaxed.

"Of course," Karyn said at one point, "if the emperor declares Siman his heir, we'll have to stop going to Gadera."

"I wouldn't be so certain." Bazel stretched his legs out and took another long sip. "Siman hates the Gaderans, but he doesn't so much as choose a wine without consulting his advisers. They'll never allow him to attack."

How did he know all that? The blond man tilted his head at Ileni, inviting her to join the banter, but she kept her lips shut and raised her empty mug, pretending to sip.

"He'll need a military victory," Karyn argued. It felt like they were talking about something that wasn't real, a story about a place that had never existed. The Empire was a mirage compared to the solid rock around them, the rigid routines and hard discipline that made up her days. Everything else sounded faintly unreal.

Everything else. Ileni's fingers whitened around her mug. It wasn't just the Rathian Empire. The Renegai, too—her own village, the life she'd had, her entire world until a mere four weeks ago—felt far away and irrelevant.

"Careful, or you'll crush the cup," Karyn observed. Ileni blinked, realizing that she had missed the last part of the conversation. Karyn was watching her speculatively.

Ileni loosened her grip, and pain flowed belatedly through her knuckles. "We should go," she said. "This isn't safe."

"On the contrary," the blond man said. "This is one of the only places in the known world where discussing the emperor's choice of heir *is* safe." He grinned at Bazel. "Before we go, will you take that wager? A free bag of chocolates if Siman is still alive when we return."

"I wouldn't want to take advantage of you," Bazel said, with exaggerated deference.

The blond man let out a startled laugh, getting lazily to his feet. "Oho. Are you saying you have knowledge of his imminent death?"

Bazel widened his eyes. "I certainly didn't say that."

The man gestured for them to hand over their cups. "Was one of you sent to—"

"Enough," Karyn said. "Leave him alone. He puts himself at sufficient risk by trading with us in the first place."

The blond man stacked the cups deftly and balanced them in one hand. "I'm just talking. There's no intent behind it."

"My point exactly."

He laughed again, and the two of them unloaded a large crate and a cask from the bottom of their canoe. Bazel hauled the crate over to a small rock overhang near the cliffside and pushed it underneath, then removed a single cloth bag. Shortly after that, the canoe was in the water and the traders sprang into it. Karyn stood in its center. "We'll be back in a week's time. It's not too late to change your mind about that message."

Once again, it took Ileni a moment to realize that Karyn was speaking to her. She lifted her chin. "It's far too late."

The current caught the canoe, and the man leaped to his paddles. The woman sat without haste, balancing easily as the river swept the boat away. Her eyes remained on Ileni's face until the traders were out of sight.

On the way back up the narrow path, Ileni found herself feeling strangely desolate. Which was stupid, stupid, stupid; sending Tellis a message through a ragtag pair of traders was not a serious option. Tellis was still training to be a sorcerer, still among the elite of the Renegai. The traders had no way of getting in contact with him. And even if they could manage it, Tellis likely had no interest in receiving a message from her.

Anger flashed through her, the same unreasonable anger she had talked herself out of a hundred times. She had known what had to be done from the second the Elders told her the results, and so had he. She was the one who had said it out loud: they could no longer be together. He was going to be the one to lead the Renegai now, and she would only hold him back. His task, which had once been hers, was too important to allow their feelings to get in the way. Neither of them would have been the people they thought they were if they hadn't acknowledged that. She knew all that—and yet, unreasonably, was furious at how easily he had agreed. With obvious regret, but without a word of protest.

He wouldn't want a message from her. And even if he might, he didn't deserve one.

When they were out of the narrow tunnel, and in the cavern leading back to the built-up section of the caves, she finally caught up to Bazel. Despite the cloth bag he held in one hand, he had navigated the rocks as easily as when he was carrying nothing. He glanced at Ileni sideways as she fell into step beside him. "What did you think of them?"

"You mean of Karyn? I don't like her." Ileni snorted. "Clearly, though, you do."

It was difficult to tell by the magelight, but she thought Bazel was blushing. "She's as brave as any of us. Do you know how feared we are in the Empire? Even the emperor's armies have never dared venture into our territory. Most traders would never come anywhere near these caves."

"According to her they would, for profit."

"She doesn't do it for profit. She does it for adventure."

"And you admire that?"

"I envy it," Bazel said.

Surprised, Ileni stumbled over a loose stone. "Because your life is so lacking in adventure?"

Bazel said nothing. Thinking it over, Ileni realized that it very well might be. He had probably lived in these caves for as long as he could remember, and lessons in how to kill people were, after all, still lessons. The life of an assassin-in-training might actually be incredibly boring.

There was always the threat of imminent death hanging over his head, but that probably didn't improve his outlook much.

"Perhaps you'll be sent on a mission soon," she said.

In the long silence that followed, Ileni realized she had suggested he could improve his life by going out to kill someone.

When Bazel finally spoke, his voice was so bitter it made

her wince. "Haven't you been paying attention? No one has any intention of sending *me* on a mission. I'm going to die here." He gave her a flat look. "Like you."

Ileni decided that a change of subject was in order. "Karyn didn't seem happy to see me."

"She's obsessive about secrecy. She wants me to be the only assassin who has any hint of their existence."

"I can't say I blame her," Ileni said dryly. "I wouldn't imagine the master taking kindly to your little arrangement."

"No," Bazel said.

Ileni glanced at him sideways, trying to read the taut lines of his face. What she saw wasn't fear. It was guilt. "What would you do if he discovered you?"

"Hope he likes chocolate, I suppose."

By the time Ileni adjusted to the fact that Bazel had actually made a joke, they were back in the occupied parts of the caves and she didn't dare speak. Bazel walked her to her door, then turned and vanished down the corridor.

Ileni listened for his footsteps but heard absolute silence. She put out a hand to push her door open.

Just as her fingers touched the smooth wood, someone grabbed her from behind.

CHAPTER 13

Ileni whirled without thinking, jabbing her elbow back in one of the moves Sorin had taught her. Her assailant twisted aside to avoid the blow, and she threw her body sideways and backward, pulling out of his grasp. It almost worked; his fingers slid away, but he followed the motion of her body and grabbed again. Rough hands closed around her wrists, one foot hooked under her ankle, and Ileni slammed down on her back with her arms held together, a dark wiry form kneeling above her.

She knew who it was. She had known since the moment he reacted to her defenses. Yet her ward hadn't reacted . . . so despite her pounding heart, she had stopped being afraid once she realized it was him.

That didn't mean she should have.

She drew in a breath and said, "I'm surprised I broke your first grip. You must be tired."

Sorin's face was shadowed, so she couldn't tell if he was smiling, but there was no answering amusement in his voice. "I wasn't prepared. I was expecting you to react with magic."

But she hadn't. Instead she had instinctively reached for her limited fighting skills. The realization felt like being slammed into the ground a second time. Ileni tried to pull her arms away, but his grip was like iron, his body a solid length of coiled power above her.

"This isn't a practice session." Sorin's voice was soft, but it wasn't a comforting softness. "You *should* use your magic in a real fight."

"This is a real fight?" She tried to sound haughty and unafraid, casting about desperately for something to distract him. What possible reason could she give for not using magic? "I don't usually find them so enjoyable."

He released her abruptly and stood. Ileni pushed herself up on her elbows, her heart still pounding but her fear gone. Was he actually blushing? She couldn't tell in the dim light.

"Where were you?" Sorin demanded.

"I don't think I'm required to tell you."

He leaned forward. If he *had* been blushing, he no longer was. His face was grim and merciless. "You're wrong."

So much for having the upper hand. "I, uh—there are certain magical rites that require privacy and space. I went deeper into the caves to—"

He knelt and ran a finger over her hair, shocking her into silence. Her breath caught in her throat.

"Your hair is frizzy," Sorin said. "You were near water."

"Um." She tilted her head away from his touch, which suddenly felt cold and impersonal. "Some of the rites also require proximity to moving water."

He lowered his hand. "And you found the Black River on your own? I doubt that. Who took you there?"

Ileni scrambled to her feet and faced him. "Why?" she asked, before she could stop herself. "Are you jealous?"

"Was it Bazel?"

"*He* is ready for those spells. I'm giving him private lessons." That didn't sound remotely believable, but maybe Sorin would think they were meeting for secret trysts. She didn't know the punishment for that, but it couldn't be as bad as the punishment for meeting outsiders within the caves.

Unless the punishment for both was death.

She also hoped—stupidly, and hating herself for it— that Sorin *would* be jealous. But when he stepped closer, the only expression on his face was disbelief.

"How can you be so stupid? Don't you realize Bazel could kill you as easily as look at you?"

"Isn't that true of all of you?"

"Bazel is desperate. That makes him dangerous."

"I'm still alive, aren't I?" She turned and shoved her door open, making no objection when Sorin pushed past to precede her into the room. The glowstones flickered to life. "Isn't a willingness to risk my life something you should admire?"

"I suppose so." Sorin's voice was suddenly soft. "I just didn't expect you to be quite so . . . enthusiastic . . . about it. What was so important about this spell?"

Ileni turned to shut the door, her mind working fast. "It told me where Absalm died." It sounded weak, even to her. She swiveled to face him, putting her back to the thick wood of the door. "I thought it would tell me more, but there was nothing else. I have no idea why Absalm was at the river when he died."

"I know why he was there," Sorin said.

She lifted her chin. "Tell me."

"Tell me the truth about what *you* were doing there," Sorin countered.

Ileni bit her lip. She could guess what would happen to Bazel if his secret got out. But Bazel was an assassin, one of the enemy, and in exchange she would get a piece of the answer she had come looking for.

It should have been an easy decision.

"One condition," she said.

As far as she could tell, Sorin hadn't moved a muscle, but suddenly, instead of just standing, he looked like he was about to spring at her. "You're not in a position to be making demands."

"Aren't I? You want to find out who killed Absalm and Cadrel, too, so you can figure out how the master is testing you. Helping me serves your own interests. Whereas I gain nothing from answering *you*."

A small, reluctant smile tugged at the corners of his mouth. "You would make a great assassin."

"I thought you didn't train women."

"We don't. That wasn't an offer; it was an observation." He rolled his shoulders back. "All right. What's the condition?"

"That you leave Bazel alone. Don't punish him, and don't tell anyone."

Anger flared in Sorin's dark eyes. If Ileni hadn't already been pressed against the door, she would have stepped back. But all he said was, "Fine. He's safe. Now tell me."

She had to look away from him before she could say, "No. You first."

Sorin sketched a mocking half-bow. "Of course."

Ileni swallowed hard, feeling her shoulders relax a little. "All right. How did *Absalm* find that . . . Black River?"

Sorin's shoulders rose and fell. Shadows gathered in his eyes, and when he spoke, his voice was a near whisper. "I took him there."

"*You* did?"

"I found the Black River soon after I was brought here. I used to like to explore the wilder parts of the caves. To go places only I knew about, so no one knew where I was." He said it tightly, his eyes darting briefly away from hers. "I didn't have an easy time adjusting, from being a wild street child to this life."

Something other than shame colored his voice, something like pride, or longing. Had he ever truly adjusted to this life? "But you told Absalm?"

"He asked me about underground rivers. He said what you said—that there are spells that require proximity to running water. Is that true?"

If the spell involved manipulating the water, or breathing underwater. The sorts of spells that could only have one purpose: escape from the caves. Ileni folded her arms over her chest. "It's not your turn to ask questions yet. Was Absalm the only person you told?"

In the moment of silence that followed, she was acutely aware of the strength of his body, of the short distance between them.

"Yes," Sorin said curtly.

"Then Absalm must have been the one who told Bazel about it." Had he told Bazel about the traders, too? How had the traders known there would be someone waiting for them on that flat rock? Ileni dared one more question. "How do you know Absalm drowned there?"

"One of us found his body downstream, while coming back from a mission."

"Who? Can we ask him—" The expression on his face stopped her. Her next sentence wasn't a question. "Whoever it was is dead."

"It was Jastim," Sorin said.

The silence stretched. Ileni had a brief, vivid memory of a wiry body leaping through a small dark window. Then Sorin crossed the room and sat on her bed, without asking.

"My turn," Sorin said. "Tell me what you were doing at the river with Bazel."

Ileni tried to think about what she should leave out, what she could get away with, what it would be advantageous for Sorin not to know. But she couldn't work through all the tangles—and besides, she wasn't sure she could get away with lying to Sorin just then.

So she told him everything.

When she was done, he leaned back on his hands. Even in repose, his body seemed clenched, ready to strike.

"You," he said finally, "cannot possibly be as stupid as you seem."

"I wouldn't be so certain," Ileni said coldly.

He shook his head and got to his feet, shoving her crumpled blanket to the side. His eyes were hot as coals. "They're not traders, Ileni."

"Of course they're—"

"They're spies."

She was shocked into silence.

"Spies for the Empire. They've been trying for centuries to find out more about us, to find a way to stop us. And Bazel gave them a way in."

Ileni remembered Karyn asking, with elaborate casualness, where Sayon had been sent. And the blond man goading Bazel with questions about the succession. And Bazel—at ease, trying to impress Karyn, unafraid for one of the few times in his miserable existence—letting slip one piece of information, and then another.

"I don't think Bazel knows," she whispered.

"But he should have." The lines of Sorin's face were hard and uncompromising.

Ileni took a deep breath and stepped away from the door. "So should I."

He pressed his lips together. "You're not trained to evaluate a situation the way he is."

"Then maybe the fault lies with his teachers."

"He received the same lessons as the rest of us."

"No," Ileni said, "he didn't." She took another step toward him. "You sat in those lessons surrounded by friends. You were allowed to take pride in who you were and who you were becoming. Bazel never had any of that. Is it any wonder he let his guard slip a little, when he finally found himself among people who didn't think he was worthless?"

Sorin's fingers curled slightly as if around an imaginary knife hilt. He bit off his words as he spoke. "That's no excuse for endangering us all."

Ileni clenched her fists. "That danger started back when you all agreed to treat Bazel like a clump of mud."

"Stop saying *you* like that. It wasn't me. I never mistreated Bazel."

"You watched it happen and didn't care. And now you'll let him die—he is going to die, isn't he—"

"Of course he is!" Sorin sliced his hand through the air. "Don't be a fool, Ileni. Don't you understand the enormity of what he's done? He betrayed every single one of us! He has to die. Even you must understand that."

The contempt in his voice stung her. She looked down in the beginning of a nod, and shame washed over her. Was she really going to agree that Bazel should *die* because Sorin would scorn her if she argued?

That's it, a small part of her mind whispered. This was how her students were persuaded to kill. It wasn't just the adulation if they succeeded. It was the contempt if they refused, or even if they hesitated.

But where she had grown up, it was killing that was

contemptible. She squared her shoulders. "I do understand. That's why no one can find out."

Sorin's mouth dropped open. "Ileni—"

"That was my condition. And you agreed." Ileni drew in her breath, and her courage with it. "If you tell, I'll warn Bazel. I'll help him. I'll do everything I can to get him away. There are spells, you know, that allow a person to breathe underwater—"

"You wouldn't dare," Sorin snarled. He was crouching slightly, as if in readiness to attack. "Do that and you're dead."

Ileni shrugged. "I've been dead for almost a month. I have no particular objection to making it official."

Her damp palms belied that statement. But just a few weeks ago, she would have meant every word, and she was able to summon up that old conviction in her voice. Sorin's eyes went even darker than before.

They stared at each other. Then the fierceness drained from Sorin's body, and he sat back down on the bed. "Then I suppose I have no choice."

Ileni very much doubted that. She remained where she was, suspecting a trick. "That's very convincing."

"Ileni." His eyes were still dark, and there was a tone

in his voice she couldn't identify. Not sadness, exactly . . . sympathy? Understanding? *Tenderness* sprang to her mind, and she inwardly scoffed at herself. "I promise you, I will make it happen. Bazel will not be harmed. Nor will you."

She swallowed her thanks. "My own safety wasn't part of the bargain."

"I'll see to it anyhow."

"Really." She crossed to the other wall, suddenly unable to keep still. "How are you going to see to any of it?"

"You said the spies will return. Spend the next few afternoons with Bazel—give him those private magic lessons, perhaps. That should give you plenty of time. Convince him to tell you exactly when they're coming, and to bring you along when he goes to see them. Then tell *me*."

Ileni stared at him, at his sharp face and set mouth. The illusion of tenderness vanished. He had killed people before. He could kill Bazel as soon as he had the information. He could kill *her* right now. She was stupid to ever, ever not be afraid of him.

He met her gaze squarely. "Trust me."

"Why?" she said before she could stop herself.

He sighed. "You trust me to teach you lethal skills without harming you. You trust me not to kill you. Trust me to keep you safe. It's the same thing."

"I do trust you to keep me safe." She wasn't aware, until the sentence was out of her mouth, that she meant it. "Just not to keep Bazel safe."

His teeth flashed in a brief grin. "How perceptive. Nevertheless, I will. I'm sure if I didn't, you would throw yourself in harm's way just to spite me."

"I would try to save him," Ileni promised. "No matter the cost."

"That's what I meant." He sighed and got to his feet, running one hand through his blond hair. "Even you must realize the cost would be your life."

"Since when do you care about my life?"

"Of course I care," Sorin said. He walked toward the door and spoke without looking back at her. "I would disappoint the master if I let you die."

He pulled the door open and was gone before she had a chance to reply. That was probably a good thing.

Alone in her room, she felt suddenly drained. She checked to make sure the door was truly shut. Then she stripped off her dirt-stained clothes, pulled the blanket over her head, and escaped into a dream where she rushed down the black river and emerged under a brilliant blue sky.

◎ ◎ ◎

The next few days were more unbearable than ever. She had thought these caverns were impenetrable, that the only way out was death. But nobody was guarding that river. She had enough magic in her to breathe underwater—and besides, she could swim. She could *leave*.

But she wouldn't. She wouldn't even send a message to Tellis. She felt itchy and short-tempered, and during her classes she lashed out so often that even her younger students began regarding her sullenly.

Every afternoon, after knife-throwing lessons with Sorin, she went with Bazel to an empty cavern and taught him what she called "advanced magical theory." For the most part, she made up the theories, but she also laid the groundwork for him to perform his own spells . . . powerful spells. She wondered sometimes, watching his set, desperate face, if this was really a good idea. And she wondered all the time how long she could put off the question of why she wasn't demonstrating any of the skills herself.

She tried not to wonder whether, after the spies returned, that would still be a concern.

She made only one attempt to ask him about Absalm, a casual question about whether the two of them had been friends. Bazel pressed his lips together and turned back to the pattern they had been chalking on the floor. Just before he did, Ileni saw a twinge of—something—cross his face.

Grief? Was that possible?

She made her voice as gentle as she could. "Absalm was the one who showed you the river, wasn't he?"

Bazel was silent for so long she thought he wasn't going to answer. Then he said, "He thought it would help me. If I was the one who traded the chocolates, who had something the others wanted."

"*Absalm* was trading chocolates until then?" She forgot to sound soft; her voice went high with astonishment. But Bazel didn't seem to notice.

"Absalm made contact with the traders a few years ago. By the time I came along, they had a system, a pair of magic stones. Karyn would throw hers into a fire, and his would glow in his room, so he'd know to go meet them that night. He had been meeting them for years, and nobody knew. Possibly not even the master." Bazel glanced furtively around the empty cavern as he said it.

Ileni didn't believe that for a second. *Years?* The master had to have known. He had allowed it to go on, allowed Absalm and Bazel to believe they were getting away with it.

This, too, fit into his plans. But she had no idea how. She didn't even know how to start figuring it out.

Absalm, what were you up to? And if he'd had a way of getting messages to the Renegai, why hadn't he used it? Had Sorin been right—had Absalm stopped caring about his own people?

There was a mute plea in Bazel's blue eyes. Ileni didn't know what he wanted but was sure it was something she couldn't give him. She reminded herself that Bazel—and Sorin—had been the only two assassins who knew Absalm's secret. If he had been killed for it, it was likely one of them who had killed him.

"Do you know why he made contact with the traders?" she asked.

Bazel looked at her dubiously. "To trade things."

"But *why*? Why was it worth the risk of breaking the rules, going against your master? For some chocolates?"

"It's not just chocolate." Bazel hunched his shoulders. "It's . . . I think it was having something of his own. Something that wasn't part of the caves, of our mission. He was an outsider. He needed that."

Sure. *Absalm* needed that. Ileni thought of Bazel's laughter, of his ease as he talked with the traders. The traders who were really imperial spies. If Sorin had figured it out immediately, there was no way the spies had fooled an Elder for years. Absalm must have known the truth.

"So he liked talking to them," she said experimentally. "More than trading with them? He just wanted someone to talk to?"

Bazel shrugged. To him, of course, it made sense. Because he didn't know—or didn't want to know—what the traders really were. No matter how lonely Absalm felt in a cave full of killers, how could talking to spies for the *Empire* possibly have helped?

"What did he talk to them about?" she asked.

"All sorts of things. Imperial politics, magic . . ."

"Magic?"

Bazel glanced down at the half-drawn chalk pattern. "Well, only once. That I heard. I was too busy bartering to pay attention, usually, and it was all above my head anyhow. He was asking Karyn about the method for transferring power."

Ileni stared at him for so long that Bazel stood, still clutching his chalk. "That means something to you?"

"Transferring power is black magic," Ileni said blankly. "All people have power in them, even if most can't turn it into magic. And when a person dies, he can pass it on to a sorcerer, if the sorcerer knows how to take it. That's why the Rathian Empire is so powerful. That's why they've always been unbeatable."

"Because they kill people for their power?"

He didn't sound at all horrified. Well, he wouldn't be.

"Worse than that," Ileni said. "The power can't just be taken. It has to be *given*, voluntarily, by the person who is dying."

Bazel nodded.

"There are many things you can do to a person," Ileni said, "to make him beg for death. To give anything you want in exchange for ending the pain."

Four hundred years ago, their leader, Ciara, had been subjected to those *things*, and had managed to escape. She had written it down, every excruciating detail, before she died—in agony, but with her soul intact. The Elders recited Ciara's Lament in the square every year, at midnight on the anniversary of her death. Ileni still wept every time.

She supposed she would never hear Ciara's Lament again. Maybe she would recite it on her own, as much as she could remember, on the next anniversary. . . .

And then she realized. The anniversary had passed two weeks ago.

She hadn't even noticed.

Tears sprang to her eyes, and she fought them down. Bazel started toward her, but she turned away. She didn't want his sympathy or his mockery, whichever it was going to be. She didn't want to be here. She wanted to be home.

She took a deep breath. "The rock. You have it now?"

"Yes."

"I'll want to come with you again, next time you go meet them."

"Why?"

"Because I've changed my mind," Ileni said. "I want to send a message to my village after all."

He nodded, and only then did she realize she wasn't lying. She should have sent that message. Not to Tellis, necessarily, but to the Elders, or her mother, or one of the other novices . . . just to let them know she hadn't forgotten them.

If she had, maybe she would be getting a message back now, to let her know they hadn't forgotten her.

The knife thudded into the target, directly in the center, a killing throw. Sorin stepped back and gestured at Ileni.

"Your turn," he said.

Ileni hefted her own knife, focusing on the target. A sharp line of pain shot through her upper arm, and she cheated just a bit with a tiny healing spell. She could hit this. She knew she could.

She stepped back and threw. As soon as the knife left her hand, she knew it would fly true. When it pierced the target, she laughed out loud.

Sorin lifted his eyebrows at her. "Have you been practicing on your own?"

"Of course not."

"That's impressive, then."

She tried not to be too pleased. Over the past three weeks of knife-throwing lessons, Ileni had surprised herself by turning out to have a knack for blades. Not that she had anything approaching Sorin's level of skill, but if anyone tried to attack her while she happened to be holding a perfectly weighted knife, gave her plenty of time to adjust her grip, and stood in one place long enough for her to aim, she would be more than able to defend herself.

Sorin nodded. "Step back."

"What?"

He handed her the knife. "Take two short steps back, then throw again."

She scowled at him, but obeyed. Her heart sped up as she gauged the new distance. She could hit it from here, too. And Sorin wouldn't look impressed, but he would be.

She lunged and threw. The knife spun through the air, missed the target entirely, and hit the stone wall hilt-first. It landed on the ground with a crash that made Sorin wince.

Ileni swore, which turned his wince into a raised eyebrow. He met her glare for a moment, clearly amused, then loped over to the wall. Even just scooping up the knife, he was all smooth strength and swift movements, precise and deadly. She was starting to envy that instead of fearing it.

He handed her the knife again. "Try using your non-throwing arm to help you aim, the way we did back in our first lesson, and control the release. You threw too hard, and it spun too fast."

"I know what the problem is." And she did. She knew exactly how she had to move, what her body had to do. The problem was making her body *do* it.

He stepped to the side. "Then solve it."

As if it was that easy. But it was, for him, the same way a problem shaping a spell would have been easy for her to fix. Didn't he understand that her body wasn't honed the way his was, that she couldn't solve problems just by throwing perseverance at them? If she had her magic, she would show him. . . .

She stopped, knife in hand, poised in mid-throw.

"Ileni?" Sorin said.

She threw without paying attention, with predictably disastrous results. The knife spun wildly and hit the wall to the left of the target. It thudded to the floor, and she turned to Sorin. "Any assassin in these caves, even the teachers, could hit a target without half-trying."

"You're only starting to learn." He headed toward the targets yet again. "And you have a real talent for—"

"So why," Ileni said, "would any of them use *magic* to knife Cadrel?"

Sorin stopped in mid-step. "I assume it was to get through some sort of ward."

"No. That spell was to *throw the knife*. If they used a spell to get through a ward, that was a separate thing. Why would an assassin use a *spell* to throw a knife? Under what circumstances would *you* do that?"

Sorin spun to face her. "None that I can think of," he said slowly. "So there must be a reason I haven't thought of."

"It doesn't make sense," Ileni said, and then almost laughed at the understatement. Of course it didn't. *Nothing* made sense. She was lost in the dark, doing everything wrong, and somewhere, the master was laughing. Somehow, he had trapped her in the center of a web of intrigue she didn't understand, predicting every move she would make. . . .

"Ileni?" Sorin said. He was right in front of her. "We'll figure it out. If it does have to do with the spies, we'll know more about that soon. We just have to wait. Sometimes it's better to gather the pieces than to try to put together an incomplete puzzle."

By now she was well used to that practiced, reverent tone. Another of the master's sayings. The vise around her chest grew tighter. Trusting Sorin, even a little, was stupid. He wasn't his own person.

And yet. He was inches away from her, a blade in his hand, but she wasn't the slightest bit afraid of him. And it wasn't just because of her ward.

It was because she was stupid.

She took a deep breath. "So we wait."

"We do."

She held out her hand. "While we're waiting, let me try that throw again."

CHAPTER
14

Two nights later, Ileni rolled out of bed at a knock on her door, relief flooding her mind and wiping it clean of restless dreams. Finally, it would be over.

Anticipation was written in every line of Bazel's body. He greeted Ileni with a curt nod, and she nodded back. They walked without speaking through the dimly lit corridors, scrambled in silence over the labyrinth of rocks, and finally made their way down the narrow ledge that led to the river.

Sorin must be following them—he had been watching Ileni's room since the night before, when Bazel had told her the spies were on their way—but hard as she strained her ears, Ileni couldn't hear him.

The spies were waiting for them this time, lounging on the flat rock at the water's edge. Now that she knew what they were, Ileni found it impossible to greet them with anything resembling friendliness. She stuck close to Bazel, hoping his obvious happiness would somehow encompass them both. Fortunately, she hadn't been all that friendly last time. Maybe no one would notice the difference.

They didn't. They traded and bantered and exchanged jibes, and the spies were relaxed and Bazel was happy, up until the moment Sorin appeared at the bottom of the path.

He was so silent that even Ileni, who had been expecting it, couldn't have said when he stepped onto the flat rock. He was just there, his arms loose by his sides, his black eyes moving swiftly over the scene.

Bazel swore. Ileni tried to look startled, even though she wasn't certain what the point of that was. The blond man scrambled to his feet, drawing a wicked-looking blade from beneath his tunic. This appeared not to concern Sorin at all.

Karyn remained seated, her hands braced on the ground at her sides. Her attention was wholly on Sorin. "What's this?"

"His name is Sorin." Bazel's voice was flat. Every person in the small space—Bazel, the traders, Sorin—was taut with anticipation. Violence brimmed in the damp air, and a shudder ran through the length of Ileni's body. She was suddenly certain she had done something terrible.

Karyn's expression changed from anger to cold calculation. "I don't suppose you would consider keeping quiet about our presence here? In return for, perhaps—"

Bazel interrupted her with a harsh laugh. "Don't bother asking him to lie to the master."

"Well, then." Karyn leaned forward. "There's only one way to ensure his silence."

"Don't bother trying that, either." Bazel got to his feet. "He's one of the best. The three of us together couldn't so much as ruffle his hair."

Three—so he assumed Ileni was on Sorin's side. Or simply irrelevant.

"I know what you are," Sorin said to Karyn. "You're an imperial spy."

Karyn sprang to her feet, and everything happened at once. As she drew a knife, Sorin leaped, with deceptive grace, and kicked. The knife flew from Karyn's hand and thudded, hilt first, into the blond man's forehead.

The blond man staggered back with a cry. He recovered, then raised his own blade.

Bazel darted in, grabbed the fallen knife, and sliced it neatly across the blond man's throat.

He did it so easily, his movements as smooth—though not as fast—as Sorin's. Blood spurted and the blond man fell, his arms flailing sideways and his heavy body hitting the ground with a thud. He cried out again, a staccato gurgling sound, and then the only noise was the rushing of the river.

It was that fast, that easy, that . . . irreversible. Bazel stepped back, the knife still in his hand, his face showing no more expression than if he had merely knocked the man unconscious. Karyn whirled and ran for the canoe, and Bazel cut her off. Sorin remained where he was.

Ileni stared at the blond man, at the blood spreading slowly across the stone. She could smell it, sharp and metallic. His blue eyes were wide and sightless, his mouth slightly open. A few minutes before, he had been laughing.

Ileni's stomach twisted into a knot so tight she couldn't breathe; then all at once it untwisted, and she was spewing its contents onto the white rock. She dropped to her hands and knees, stomach heaving again and again, even when there was nothing left to expel.

When she looked up, her throat burning, Bazel had Karyn trapped against the cliffside. He held the knife ready—a red drop dripped from its edge and splattered on the rock—but didn't make a move toward her. Instead he glanced at Sorin.

"It's not enough," Sorin snarled at him. "This doesn't make up for what you did."

Bazel laughed wildly. Then he lunged at Karyn.

She dodged. Bazel's blade slid across the side of her neck, not deep enough to kill. At the same moment, a surge of magic pulsed through the cavern. Ileni jerked her head up as the spell washed over her.

A thin shimmer of white flew down from the top of the cliff: a rope, lashing against the rock. While Ileni scrambled to her feet, Bazel grabbed the end of the rope and leaped upward, bracing his feet against the rock wall, moving faster than she would have believed possible. By the time she had closed her mouth, he was already invisible in the darkness above, the end of the rope twitching violently against the cliffside.

Sorin swore. He took a step toward Karyn, who was still as a statue. Then he flung himself at the rope, which thudded against the cliff as the two assassins raced up into darkness.

"I think," Karyn said, pressing her hand to her neck, "that's my cue to leave."

Ileni turned sharply, her throat burning and tears stinging her eyes. Her voice came out in a croak. "You're going to abandon Bazel?"

"He's not exactly under my protection." Karyn wiped her bloody hand on her tunic, then strode toward the blond man's corpse. Ileni opened her mouth and closed it, feeling acutely helpless. If she'd had a knife . . . but she didn't have a knife. "Besides, he's probably already dead."

Ileni hoped Bazel hadn't heard that—or rather, hadn't heard the total unconcern with which Karyn said it.

Why *had* Sorin gone after Bazel and left Karyn free to escape?

Karyn knelt by the blond man's body, and Ileni thought she was going to say something, or close those staring blue eyes. Instead she slid both her arms under him, lifted the corpse, and without any sign of strain dragged it to the river and heaved it in.

The splash sent a spray of water against Ileni's face, making her flinch away. By the time its echoes died, Karyn had gathered their cups and flung them into the boat, then pushed it into the dark water. A jagged stain marked the rock where she had dragged her friend's body.

"Wait," Ileni gasped. "You can't—"

"I know." Karyn gave the canoe a final shove, sending it into the river, then leaped in. "You can come with me."

That was the last thing Ileni had expected. "What?"

"*You're* not dead—yet. Wouldn't you like to stay that way? You can jump overboard as soon as we're out of the caves and return to your own people."

Your own people. People who wouldn't be trying to kill her, or turn her into a killer. Her teachers. Her fellow students. Tellis. Ileni shook her head, her hair whipping into her eyes. "Why should I believe you?"

"I don't care if you do or not. You can risk coming with me, or you can stay here and die for certain." She lifted the oars.

The canoe picked up speed. The stretch of water between it and Ileni was now too wide to jump; she would have to swim. Ileni strode to the water's edge, then stopped.

"I can't," she said. "I can't leave. My people sent me here for a reason."

Karyn snorted. "What reason? To die?"

"Yes," Ileni said.

Karyn shrugged and began turning the boat. The

canoe raced forward with the current, turned around a bend in the river, and was gone.

When Sorin returned, he was alone. Ileni heard his feet thudding against the cliffside as he flew down the rope, but didn't turn around until he had leaped to the ground and was standing a few feet away from her. He looked completely unruffled except for a faint smudge of dirt on one cheekbone.

"Where's Bazel?" she asked sharply.

Sorin ignored the question. He frowned at her, a crease between his eyes. "I thought you wouldn't be here."

"Sorry to disappoint." Ileni knew her bitterness should be directed at herself—*stupid, stupid* kept going through her mind—but she couldn't help aiming some of it at Sorin. She hated him for making all of this happen, for the blood on the white rock, for the dead man in the water, for the canoe racing away down the river. "Don't worry. I'm sure your master will figure out a better way to have me killed."

Sorin went on looking at her. Ileni leaned down and scooped river water into her mouth, spitting it out along with the acrid taste of vomit. Then she turned and stalked across the slick stone, giving the puddle of blood a wide berth. She started up the path.

"Why didn't you leave with her?" Sorin asked.

Ileni whirled, putting one hand on the white rock to steady herself. She had a sudden feeling that she had miscalculated badly. "Wouldn't you have stopped me?"

"I was up on the rocks. How could I have stopped you?"

That was why he had gone after Bazel. To give her a chance to escape.

The door to her prison had been wide open, and she had turned away.

Ileni felt her lips twist as she gave him the truth, knowing he wouldn't believe it. "I was sent here for a reason. And I'm certainly not leaving until I find out who killed Absalm and Cadrel."

Something passed swiftly over his face, something that wasn't disbelief, before it went blank again. "Or until you become the next victim?"

She turned away from him. "Or that."

Sorin had left Bazel bound hand and foot on a slippery, tilted rock, using a section of the rope they had climbed up on. There was, Ileni saw instantly, a practical reason for that cruelty: Bazel was so busy struggling not to slide off that he had no opportunity to try to get loose. But she doubted that was the only reason, and she shot Sorin a glare as they approached the trussed-up assassin.

Sorin had no attention to spare for her. He reached out with one hand, grabbed Bazel's tunic, and hauled him to his feet. Bazel stopped struggling immediately, his entire body limp, his face miserable with resignation.

Sorin looked at him, just looked. Ileni shrank away. The implacable menace on Sorin's face was terrible, and it wasn't even directed at her.

Something shivered deep inside her. Right now, she could easily imagine Sorin killing Absalm for his betrayal. For endangering the mission he was so devoted to.

She knew he could kill. He had killed before. He was no different from any other assassin in these caves.

Except none of them would have given her a chance to escape.

"I didn't know what they were," Bazel whispered. "I swear I didn't. I know what you think of me, but you can't imagine that even I would knowingly allow the Empire's spies into our caves."

"And do you imagine," Sorin asked softly, "that it will make a difference whether you knew or not?"

"No," Bazel said. "I don't."

Sorin jerked Bazel closer, so their faces were only inches apart. "That was a clever trick with the rope. How long did you have that set up?"

Bazel didn't answer. Sorin shook him. "This is your chance to make it easier for yourself. Answer me."

A defiant light flared in Bazel's eyes, without changing the defeated set of his face. "You won't get to torture me," he said. "Too many traded with me and would be implicated if I talked. They'll make sure I'm dead before I have a chance to betray them."

"Then you die," Sorin said.

"I would rather die," Bazel whispered, "than have to face the master when he finds out what I've done. And I *will* die. You can't protect me against all of them."

"I'm not so sure of that," Sorin said, "but to be on the safe side, I could torture the answers out of you right now."

"Sorin," Ileni said.

Sorin held Bazel upright without any sign of strain. In the dim light, his jaw was a grim line. "I said he wouldn't die. I made no promises about how pleasant his life would be."

Bazel's head came up sharply. He looked at Ileni, then Sorin, then back at Ileni. "Why?"

"I don't like it," Ileni said, "when people die. You wouldn't understand."

"I meant why did you *tell* him?"

The anguish underlying his voice made her drop her eyes. She was very conscious of Sorin watching her. "Because it's true. They *are* imperial spies."

"You tell me everything you know," Sorin said to Bazel, "and maybe I can figure out a way to deal with this without implicating you."

"I don't know anything," Bazel whispered. "Absalm told me about them. I don't know how he found them."

"And did Absalm teach you that trick with the rope? Or was it *her?*"

Ileni hissed through her teeth. "It wasn't me."

"Absalm always thought we might need an escape route." Bazel wriggled slightly as Sorin's fist tightened on his shirt. "He prepared the rope. It's an easy enough spell to uncoil it."

So it was . . . and would have required much less power than Bazel had spent. Was that lack of skill and training? Or was he lying?

Sorin let Bazel drop to the ground. Bazel hit the rock with a thud and struggled frantically to keep himself from sliding off, all without uttering a sound. Sorin watched him, expressionless, then drew a dagger and cut through the rope in three neat slashes. "Let's go. I think that's about enough of this."

It was enough a long time ago, Ileni thought angrily at his back. Then she devoted her attention to keeping up with the two assassins as they scrambled nimbly over the rocks and through the tunnel.

As soon as they were back in the built-up part of the caves, Bazel vanished down a side corridor, and Ileni followed Sorin to the now-familiar section where her room was. Sorin didn't say a word or even turn around, but when they reached her room, he stepped in with her and closed the door.

She turned, and their eyes met. From this close, his face was all lines and angles. She couldn't believe she had ever thought he looked like Tellis.

"Ileni." Sorin's voice was very quiet. "Why did you stay?"

"I . . . don't know." It was the last thing she had expected him to ask, but his tone was so grim she didn't even think of avoiding the question. His eyes were like night shadows, with no guessing what was hiding in them. "What would be the point of going? I was sent here for a purpose, and I haven't accomplished it yet."

"You could have been free." He was so still she could barely tell he was breathing.

"Free to go back home and be despised? To never do anything that matters, ever again?"

Something flickered in the black depths of those eyes. Respect? "You could have been safe."

"You're the one who's been telling me how unimportant safety is."

"And you've been *listening*?" he said, with such undisguised astonishment that, despite everything, she laughed. The laugh had an edge of hysteria to it, and she cut it off before it could dissolve into tears.

"Not on purpose, I assure you."

He shifted his weight toward her, and her heart began to pound. Then he turned abruptly and put one hand on the door handle.

"Sorin," she said, and he looked back with his hand still closed around the dark wood. His arm was so tense it shook a little. "Was it your master who told you to give me a chance to escape?"

He blinked. "What would the master gain from your disappearance?"

"What would *you* gain?"

His expression didn't change, but all at once she recognized it. Only Tellis had ever looked at her like that. Her throat went dry.

"Did you really think I would run?" she said.

She could hear his indrawn breath. "I hoped you would."

Ileni stood frozen, not sure what to think. All this time believing she was nothing but a duty to Sorin . . . all this time, telling herself she didn't care. When she cared so much she could barely breathe.

"I shouldn't have done it." He said it like he was angry. "I try not to think about you. But then you go and do something so *stupid*, put yourself in such danger, and if you died . . ." He ran out of breath then, and stared at her across the room.

Ileni's voice came out in a whisper. "It's all right."

His breath hissed out, and she realized he *was* angry. "Of course it isn't. The way I feel, it's not—"

"Safe?" She stepped toward him, hardly aware that she was doing it. "Do you even *like* being safe? That wasn't my impression."

"I have no right to risk my life for this." He stepped back against the door, as if she was a threat. It was the most flattering thing he had done since she entered the caves. "It means nothing. It was inevitable, even. After all, you're the only girl I ever see."

That was rather less flattering.

"I thought, once I go out on a longer mission—I mean, once I get the chance to be with other women—" Sorin's jaw clenched. "I'll forget about you."

That did it. Ileni launched herself forward, with more determination than grace, and kissed him.

After a startled moment, he responded, his hands coming up hesitantly to her face, then dropping to her shoulders. After another moment—or several—Ileni leaned back and stared at him in disbelief.

Sorin flushed to the roots of his hair and dropped his hands, a bit unsteadily, the first movement she had ever seen him make that was less than completely graceful. "I told you. You're the first girl I ever—um—"

Ileni started to laugh. "You're one of the assassins, famed for their allure and irresistibility to women. And you've never kissed a girl?"

"I've only been on one mission," he said stiffly. "And it was a short one. Who would I have kissed?"

"I guess I assumed that would be part of your training. You know, how to seduce women to make it easier to kill their husbands. Or something like that."

"Maybe it's an advanced class," Sorin said.

The terseness in his voice didn't bother Ileni; but there was embarrassment there, too, so she made an effort to look less amused.

Sorin leaned toward her, his cheeks still tinged red, and said, "Either way, I've had no prior training. You'll have to start from scratch."

Upon consideration, that didn't seem like a bad idea at all.

The next morning, Ileni caught herself whistling on her
way to the training room.

She stopped immediately, pressing her lips together.
What was wrong with her? Last night she had seen a man
killed, let an imperial spy escape, given up her only chance to
go home. . . .

And she barely cared.

Sorin strode ahead of her. She resisted the urge to smile
at his set shoulders. He had been every bit as distant on
the way to breakfast, refusing to meet her eyes. Refusing to
blush, too. She was willing to bet he couldn't look at her

without remembering his eagerness the night before.

Though really, she was in no position to feel superior. They had gone further than even she had meant to. And she wasn't sure how much further they would have gone if she hadn't remembered in time that she no longer had the magic to keep herself from getting pregnant.

How could she have even thought of taking that step with Sorin when she had held out for so long with Tellis? But back then, she had been willing to do things that were difficult and frustrating. Now there seemed no reason to resist.

She knew this would end badly. It was so ridiculous and so doomed that she could almost despise herself. Except, except . . . except her whole life was ridiculous and doomed, so if a brief interlude of happiness had come her way, why not grab that? She had forgotten how *good* it felt to be happy.

But when she stood in front of her class, watching her group of young killers work through the preliminary meditation exercises, she pushed her unruly emotions to the side and made herself concentrate. Something had been bothering her about Karyn's escape: that rope, the focused surge of magic before it came sliding down. In class, Bazel's spells tasted of power and desperation, and always leaked magic around their edges. The spell that brought down the rope hadn't felt like him at all.

"Bazel," Ileni said. "To the front of the class, please."

Bazel got slowly to his feet and walked up to stand beside her. He did not meet her eyes, did not change his demeanor, did not indicate in any way that she had betrayed him and saved his life and watched him kill a man.

"I want you to demonstrate the defensive spell I taught last week," Ileni said. "Sorin, please attack him."

Sorin rose lithely. Ileni's heart sped up as he passed her, and it seemed impossible that no one else could sense the pull between them.

But Sorin didn't glance at her. He stopped a few feet from Bazel, inclined his head briefly, then moved without warning. Bazel's head snapped to the side under the force of his blow. Neither assassin made a sound, and Sorin was back in his place so fast Ileni could almost believe she had imagined it.

Bazel's head came up, and he started forward, teeth bared. Sorin pivoted and, with insulting slowness, snapped a kick at his face.

Power erupted from Bazel, a wild torrent. It hit Sorin's

foot and knocked him backward, harder than necessary. Sorin twisted in midair and landed lightly on his feet, still in a fighting position. He leaned forward to lunge, and Ileni felt Bazel gather in more power.

"The exercise is over," she said sharply. "Thank you. Please sit."

Bazel's gaze scorched her. He was going to disobey . . . and when he did, there would be nothing she could do. That wild expenditure of power clearly hadn't weakened him at all.

He turned sharply and made his way back to his mat. Sorin rocked smoothly back on the balls of his feet, then followed him. Once again, he didn't spare Ileni a glance.

Hurt surged through her, which was ridiculous. What did she expect him to do—make calf eyes at her in front of everyone? Ileni focused on Bazel, who sat on his mat looking puzzled and resentful.

She could still feel the echoes of his spell. It felt nothing at all like the magic that had pulled the rope down last night.

Bazel hadn't pulled down that rope. And if it hadn't been him . . .

Only one other person could have done it.

Karyn wasn't just a spy.

She was also a sorceress.

At the midday meal, Sorin didn't sit with her. Ileni felt the first twinge of doubt then, sitting alone over a bowl of spicy meat and cooked vegetables, acutely aware of his presence across the dining cavern. She tried not to glance at him too often, but suspected she wasn't succeeding. He lounged among his fellow assassins, more relaxed than he ever was with her, talking and smiling and even laughing. They had grown up together. She had been here barely a month. What did she really know about him at all?

The image of Tellis's blue eyes, sorrowful and sad and utterly implacable, shoved its way into her mind. Reminding her how little a kiss, or even a promise, could mean.

When the meal was over and Sorin headed to her table, Ileni stood so quickly she hit the backs of her knees on the bench. Sorin waited patiently for her to climb over the bench, then strode toward the door without looking back to see if she would follow.

He's pretending. He had to, didn't he? They couldn't allow the other students to guess what was between them.

Unless there was nothing between them. Unless last night had been a wild aberration, and he was going to pretend it had never happened.

I don't think so. When they reached a narrow branch in the passageway, Ileni turned abruptly and headed into a rough, winding corridor. After a moment, she heard Sorin follow.

She didn't have to go far before they were out of sight. In the dim light, the curves and lines of the cave walls looked like bones, the dark cracks like malevolent narrowed eyes. Ileni turned on her heel and waited until Sorin was standing right in front of her, his mouth an unyielding line. His closeness made her blood sizzle, overcoming her nerves. She slid one hand behind his neck and pulled him even closer.

It was like trying to pull a stone. He didn't back away, but he also didn't move forward. Humiliation scorched her, and she dropped her hand to her side.

"Ileni." His voice was so low she wouldn't have been able to make out the words if he hadn't been so close. "We can't do this."

"Can't we?" She wished she could disappear into the stones behind her. "Last night, it seemed like we could."

"We shouldn't have—" He drew in a sharp breath. It

sounded like he was in pain. *Well, good.* "Don't you understand how unwise—how dangerous it is? None of us are supposed to touch you. The master commanded it."

Her eyes burned, and she had to hold them wide open to keep tears from spilling over. What was *wrong* with her? He wasn't important. He wasn't the reason she was here or the reason she had stayed.

"Afraid of danger, are you?" she said, with every bit of scorn she possessed.

"No. I don't care if I die." He said it through gritted teeth. "I care if you die."

Ileni drew in a breath. "So do I. But what's life without a little danger?"

He pushed her back against the wall and leaned in. His mouth was inches from hers. "It's more than a little."

"I know," she whispered.

"We have to go to the master and tell him everything."

"What?" Ice ran up her spine. She raised her hands to push him away, but he had already stepped back. "What are you talking about?"

"I'm talking about the imperial spies. This has gone beyond smuggling chocolates. We can't keep it from him. We never should have."

"Sorin, you can't. It's too late. If you tell him, he'll know you hid the truth until now—"

He pivoted and walked away, throwing words over his shoulder. "And he'll punish me as I deserve."

"He might kill you! And even if you don't care, *I* do—" He wasn't even slowing down. Ileni ran after him, feet pounding at the ground, and grabbed his shoulder. "He'll kill Bazel too, and you *promised*—"

Sorin jerked away from her and whirled, his face colder than she had ever seen it.

"If you talk to him, he'll figure it out," Ileni said frantically. "You know he will. Even if you don't say anything, he'll know the truth. About . . . about us."

He met her eyes. His were dark and hollow, and she recognized the expression on his face. She had seen it last night, but she hadn't wanted to acknowledge it.

It was shame.

He was ashamed of her.

She felt small and loathsome, and for a moment she hated him for that. "If you tell him, he'll kill me, too. Do you care?"

Sorin's throat convulsed. "You know I do. But I . . . Ileni, I can't—"

"Can't what?" Ileni snarled. "Keep any part of your life for yourself? Any part of *yourself* for yourself? Care about anything that's not part of your master's plan?"

"Stop it!" He grabbed her wrist, holding so tight it hurt. She was too angry to be afraid. "You don't understand—"

"I understand perfectly! He took you when you were little, surrounded you with people who taught you that nothing was important, including you. And you knew it wasn't true, but you had no one to tell you differently—"

His laugh hurt more than his grip, which was growing tighter and tighter. "Until you came along, and changed everything? Is that what you believe?"

She jerked her arm out of his grip just as the ground beneath her began to shake.

She staggered backward. The walls shuddered around her, the ground tilting beneath her feet. Sorin took one quick step sideways, then stood perfectly still. Only his head and eyes moved as he took in every inch of the shaking cavern. He held two daggers, one in each hand. Ileni had no idea where they had come from.

A heavy rumbling noise filled the cavern, like angry wind, and Sorin snapped, "Throw yourself down!"

She did, not entirely of her own volition, one wrist

buckling as it hit the ground. Shock waves ran through the rock below her and shuddered painfully through her body. Something cracked far above, and a large piece of rock slammed into the floor inches from her head. Dirt rained down on her hair. Ileni bit off a scream, covered the back of her head with her arms, and squeezed her eyes shut.

"Use your magic!" Sorin shouted. "We're being attacked—"

Something struck the back of her head. She screamed. Pain lanced through her, and then there was nothing.

It seemed only a second later that she blinked her eyes open. She was lying on her back, and a pair of arms were holding her off the ground, cradling her against a familiar gray tunic.

She blinked again, and Sorin's face came into wavering focus inches from hers. His eyes were wide, his mouth tight, an expression she had never before seen on his face.

"Ileni," he whispered, and it was there in his voice, too: fear. "You're all right?"

She closed her eyes. Not trying to see made it easier to think. "What happened?"

"A rock broke off the ceiling and hit you in the head. It should have—" His voice broke. She felt his chest rise and fall. Then his lips pressed briefly on her hair. When he spoke again, his voice was cool and steady. "Why are you not dead?"

She groped for her last memories. She had felt the impact—and had screamed, instinctively, the single word of a healing spell. She must have used it just in time.

She shifted, resting her forehead against Sorin's shoulder. "I mean, what made the caves shake? Was it an earthquake?"

"It was an attack. The Empire tried to break through our wards. They failed. Can you stand?"

"I—what?"

He rose in a single smooth motion, pulling her up by her arms. She swayed and leaned back against him.

"I'm sorry," Sorin whispered. "I . . . if you . . ." He turned her around to face him, still holding her steady. The motion made the cave rock around her, back and forth, back and forth. . . . "I'll keep you safe. No matter what the cost. I promise."

Looking at him made her even more dizzy. But she did it anyhow.

Sorin brushed a strand of hair away from her face. "Are you really all right?"

"Yes. Aftereffect of the healing spell." She had no idea

why she was lying, except for a vague sense that she didn't want to seem weak to him. "It will fade in a few minutes."

"Good." He took a deep breath and let go of her. "I have to get to the training cavern, find out what the master wants me to do next. I'm sure he has a response already planned. And you should probably check the wards, make sure the attack didn't damage them. Can you?"

"I—of course." The healing spell *had* drained her. But even without her power, she should be able to sense any problems. "Go."

Ileni waited until Sorin was out of sight, then leaned against the wall. Her head hurt so much, and the cavern was spinning all around her. She shouldn't be here, alone, with her magic gone.

Her room. She should go to her room. She would be safe there, behind the wards.

Unless the Empire attacked again.

But they wouldn't, would they? Not so soon after they had failed. *Failed.* The might of the Empire, shattered against her peoples' wards.

She concentrated on putting one foot in front of the other until she was out in the main corridor. It was so *light*. If she'd had the power, she would have dimmed the glowstones assaulting her eyes.

Which way was her room? She should know this. She had most of the corridors memorized by now.

"Are you all right?" someone said, and Ileni realized that she was sitting on the floor with her eyes closed. She didn't remember deciding to sit down. She opened her eyes a cautious slit. Arkim was crouched next to her, his forehead furrowed, his gray-white eyebrows drawn together.

"We were attacked," Ileni explained thickly.

"Yes." He reached around to touch the back of her head, then glanced at the blood on his fingers. "I'm going to take you to your room."

"I'm on my way there."

"So I see." He held out his bony hand. Ileni just looked at it. Once, that hand had held a dagger and killed a child. She looked up at his face, which revealed nothing but concern.

They were actors and liars, every single person in these caves. She had to remember that.

"Why did they attack us?" she asked.

"My guess," Arkim said, "is that we got the attention of the imperial sorcerers." He smiled at her, as if the two of them were part of the same *we*. "The master chooses his targets well, as always. The Empire can feel us closing in. They're afraid."

His hand was still out. Ileni took it and let him pull her to her feet, then swayed for a few seconds before holding herself steady. "What will we do?"

"The master will know what to do. But I suspect he'll say there's no need to do anything. The wards held and will continue to hold. The Empire might send soldiers next, but that's a losing gambit—these caves can withstand a siege for years, and the mountains are full of perfect ambush points." He let go of her hand. "This is your room, yes?"

Ileni looked at the thick wooden door. "Yes."

"I can't open it," Arkim said patiently. "You'll have to do that."

Of course. Because of the wards. The wards . . . Ileni spun away from the door, and winced as the corridor tilted. "I have to check the wards! Around the caves—"

"You have to sleep first. Then you'll do your part."

She turned again and pushed the door open. Arkim waited in the doorway until she had lowered herself onto her bed.

"Make sure to close the door all the way," she said. But she couldn't keep her eyes open to make sure he had done it.

Her part, he had said. *Her part.* Because she was one of them, a piece of the master's plan, helping to bring the Empire down.

To destroy it.

Despite the pain ricocheting through her head, she was smiling when she fell asleep.

Ileni woke a long time later—how long, she didn't know, but her mind felt clear and she was starving. The back of her head was still tender, and she winced when she touched it, but her fingers came away dry.

She had no trouble finding the dining cavern and was relieved to discover that it was time for breakfast. She had never been so happy to see porridge in her life.

The cavern was full, but Sorin's seat was empty. So was Irun's. Still finding out what the master wanted them to do?

When she walked into her class, she was faintly surprised to see the rest of her students sitting in their usual neat rows, backs ramrod straight. Shouldn't the Empire's attack change everything? Instead of going through their usual routine, they should be preparing for war.

But of course, that was exactly what they were doing. What they were always doing.

For the first time, she felt guilty as she led her students through a series of pointless meditations. They were fighting for something, these young men she trained day after day. They were hurting the Empire. And instead of helping them, she was holding them back.

And meanwhile, all her people did was sit around recounting stories of cruelty and singing sad songs about martyrs.

We are preparing to take them on. She had known that since she was a child, had the Empire's destruction as her focus all her life. But suddenly that promise seemed distant and hollow. *Someday we will be free* was the ending chant of every Renegai class, but nobody ever seemed to question when *someday* would become *now*.

For these boys, burning bright and fierce, someday *was* now. They would make the Empire pay with blood and anguish, and they would do it while the Renegai practiced wards and healing spells for the millionth time.

When the lesson was over, she held up a hand to stop the students from rising. "Where are Sorin and Irun?"

No one answered. She focused on one of the weaker students, a tall boy with curly black hair. "Do you know?"

"No," he said.

A chill ran through her. "Were they . . . are they on missions?"

"We. Don't. Know," he said patiently.

But Ileni did know. She turned away quickly, before her students could see her expression.

I'm sure he has a response already planned. And the assassins had only one response. People would die, out in the Empire, to punish them for this attack.

And Sorin would be one of the assassins administering the punishment.

He was gone.

CHAPTER 16

Ileni ate barely two bites of her lunch—the porridge from breakfast felt like rocks lodged in her stomach—before she made her way to the knife-training cavern. Some small part of her hoped, idiotically, that Sorin would be there waiting. But of course he wasn't. She had slept for half a day and a night. He was long gone by now.

He might die, out in the Empire, far away.

But first he would kill someone. That should have bothered her more.

She stood before the racks of gleaming blades. Those on the left were the poisoned ones. She reached out, daring herself to touch one.

Her fingers brushed the cold edge of a hilt, and she jerked her hand back. She thought she heard movement and looked over her shoulder. No one was there.

She reached for the knife again, her heart speeding up, fear and excitement pouring into the gaping hole inside her. It felt . . . not good, exactly. But sharp enough to pierce the dull ache of Sorin's absence. She let her fingers brush the hilt again, closer to the blade.

Was *this* why the assassins were eager to kill? Because of the thrill that came when death was so close?

A hand closed around her upper arm and jerked her away, flinging her back. Fear exploded through her, suddenly not thrilling at all. She staggered and whirled.

"What are you *doing*?" Sorin demanded.

Her heart thudded hard against her chest. He stood just a few yards away from her, lean and handsome in his gray clothes. His face was grim.

"I thought . . ." The words came out in a barely audible whisper. She cleared her throat, tried again. "Where were you?"

"Checking the impact of the attack. The master told me to inspect the far reaches of the caves." Sorin let out a long, shuddering breath. "He knew, Ileni. He knew I had explored all of them. All this time, I thought it was my one secret. But he always knew."

Ileni didn't know what to say to that. She couldn't focus on it, and she couldn't stop smiling, even though she knew it wasn't appropriate. Sorin was *here*. He wasn't leagues away. He was right in front of her. "I thought . . . I thought you would be sent on a mission."

"So did I," Sorin said.

He wasn't smiling.

Ileni felt her own smile drop off her face, vanishing along with her joy. Apparently, she was the only one happy that he wasn't gone.

But she took in his clenched jaw and hunched shoulders, and a surge of real pity took her by surprise. "I'm sorry," she said. "You must hate being stuck here."

Sorin's mouth tightened. "What I want is not important. If the master says I serve best within these caves, that is where I should be." He gestured at the rack of blades. "What are you doing with those knives? You shouldn't touch them."

She lifted an eyebrow. "There are a lot of things I shouldn't do."

He turned and looked at her, but instead of leaning in, or even raising an eyebrow back, he walked past her and drew one of the unpoisoned blades. "I want to show you backward throws."

Ileni wasn't about to be sidetracked that easily. "What did the master have to say about the Empire's attack?"

"Nothing."

"You mean, nothing you can tell me."

Sorin turned and threw. The blade thudded into the heart of the one target Ileni still couldn't bring herself to practice on—the child-sized one. The cloth figure thudded back against the stone wall. "Of course that's what I mean."

Ileni wanted to ask if Sorin had told the master about Karyn, or about the two of them . . . but somehow, she didn't dare.

I'll keep you safe. But could Sorin actually be in the master's presence and hide anything from him? Ileni didn't think *she* could.

Sorin closed his eyes briefly, then turned to her. "I'm sorry, Ileni. It's just . . . the master had nothing to say to me. He didn't speak to me at all. He had Arkim give me my task."

Ileni stepped forward, hesitantly, and put a hand on his arm, feeling the tightness of his muscle. Like he wanted to hit something. "Maybe because there was nothing to discuss. The attack doesn't change anything, really."

"Maybe." Sorin wouldn't meet her eyes. "Or maybe he's disappointed in me. And he doesn't . . . doesn't trust me anymore."

No need to ask why. Maybe there was another secret the master knew.

Ileni dropped her hand. Sorin didn't move, but his throat convulsed.

What could she say? Guilt and anger tangled up in her. Ileni took a deep breath.

"I know who killed Absalm and Cadrel," she said.

Sorin's head snapped up, and his face changed, the intensity in his eyes suddenly focused. "Who?"

"Karyn."

"Karyn? But . . . how?"

"She wasn't just a spy." Ileni met his eyes, and warm relief spread through her when he didn't avoid her gaze. But she didn't quite dare touch him again. "She's a sorceress."

She meant to explain how she knew, but Sorin just nodded. He must assume she had sensed Karyn's power.

And why *hadn't* she, back at their first meeting? She should have. Even with barely any power of her own, she should have recognized the feel of magic. Ileni frowned, suddenly less sure.

But Sorin was looking at her like she was someone to reckon with, not just a source of guilt and shame. He drew another dagger from the rack and ran his finger along its edge. "Why would Karyn be killing Renegai sorcerers?"

"Because you've been going after *their* sorcerers," Ileni said. "The emperor must think the Renegai tutors are helping you do it. So of course he wants to remove us."

Sorin's fingers clenched around the knife hilt. "Then why didn't Karyn kill you when she had the chance?"

"I don't know." Or had she tried? Maybe Karyn's offer of escape would have ended with Ileni's corpse floating down the river.

Like Absalm's corpse. Had Karyn made *him* the same offer? Had Absalm been trying to go home?

Sorin threw the knife into the air and caught it by the blade. "So the Empire attacked the day after their sorceress escaped? That can't be coincidence. She must have used magic to send them a message. This was revenge."

"No," Ileni said. "An attack like that couldn't be prepared in a day. They must have had it waiting. It was their backup plan." She stopped, thinking hard. Sorin flipped the knife again, this time to hold it by the hilt. "Whatever Karyn was doing, that was their first plan. She must have communicated to them, somehow, that it hadn't worked, so they tried the attack."

"Which failed," Sorin pointed out, a bit smugly. "So Karyn will come back and try to finish whatever she was here to do."

She's not an assassin. She's allowed to give up. But remembering Karyn's steadiness as she dumped her friend's body into the river, Ileni didn't believe it. A chill ran through her. Karyn *would* be back. An imperial sorceress could easily float a canoe upriver.

And *what she was here to do* was kill Renegai.

"We have to find her," Ileni said.

Sorin lowered the knife, his arm tightly knotted. "Why would we do that? To make it easier for her?"

"No, but . . ." Ileni resisted the urge to reach for a knife of her own. "All this time, I've known someone was going to kill me, and there was nothing I could do about it. Now I know who it is. I don't have to wait for the knife in my back. If we find her, take her by surprise—"

Sorin shook his head. "It's a stupid idea. We can take precautions—"

"And wait to find out how they're going to fail?" Ileni dug her nails into the sides of her legs. "She's an imperial sorceress. You can't possibly defend me against her. And I can't do this anymore, Sorin. I can't wait to die, not knowing when, or why, or how. I have to face it. I need to know the truth about what's going on."

"And I need you to be safe."

His voice broke, just for a moment. Ileni remembered the tightness of his arms around her, the plea in his eyes when he asked her why she wasn't dead.

She softened her voice. "Please, Sorin. I can't do it without your help."

"Good," he said flatly.

She brushed his fingers with hers, watching his cheeks turn faintly red. "I'm going to try anyhow. If you help, you can keep me safe."

"Don't." He jerked his fingers away and stepped back. "You're not very good at this."

Ileni felt blood rush to her own face, and she turned around so he wouldn't see. He was right, she wasn't. She wished that she had more practice in working her wiles. Or even that she knew what, exactly, those were. She had never needed to be cajoling or coy with Tellis. This thing with Sorin was something entirely different. It made her feel like she was walking on a knife's edge, like her breath was permanently stuck in her throat.

Tellis had made her feel safe. Sorin made her feel like being inches away from death was worth it.

"So you won't help me." She didn't bother to hide her anger. Anger felt a lot better than guilt or shame.

"I *am* helping you."

"Are you? Remind me to thank you later." She started toward the door.

"Ileni—"

"Don't follow me," she said fiercely, without turning back, and told herself she wasn't disappointed when he obeyed.

The next morning, after class, Ileni gathered her courage and approached Bazel. She had been avoiding him until then, trying not to address him unless she had to. Every time she accidentally met his eyes, she sensed a banked hatred in them, a sullen viciousness more disconcerting than Irun's openly threatening glare. But that didn't matter anymore. If Sorin wasn't going to help her, she needed somebody who would.

She felt Sorin's eyes on her as she walked over to Bazel's mat. But she didn't falter, and Sorin filed out of class along with the others.

"We should," she said, "resume your lessons."

Bazel looked at her across his mat, and she realized her mistake: she should have summoned him to her, demanded obedience, rather than going to him like a supplicant. His hatred was no longer banked. He looked at her like she was a worm that had slimed its way up his leg.

Luckily, the training cavern had emptied. She forced her shoulders straight. "You blame me for what happened, don't you?"

His mouth formed a straight, ugly line before he turned his back on her. "Can you think of someone else I should blame?"

"What if you could see Karyn again?"

Bazel whirled, with a controlled grace that made her tense for an attack. But he merely shook his head. "You expect me to help you draw her back? So you can capture and torture her?"

"I don't care about her," Ileni said. "I just want to find out why Absalm brought imperial spies into these caves."

Bazel adjusted his stance, wary. "You assume he knew what they were."

"He must have guessed, eventually." *Because anyone would have.* "And she is more than a spy."

Bazel's fingers twitched.

"But you know that, don't you? You knew Karyn was a sorceress. You lied to Sorin about who created that rope, and you did it to protect her."

A flash of fear. "Did you tell him—"

"No," Ileni lied, ignoring a twinge of guilt. "It doesn't matter to me. Whatever she and Absalm were up to, it got him killed. Karyn might be able to tell me why he died. That's all I care about."

Bazel let out a breath. "You want to use my stone to try summoning her."

"Yes."

"You expect me to hand it over to you?"

"No." That would have been absolutely useless to her. Even with the aid of those stones, communication spells required huge amounts of power. She tried to sound desperate, which wasn't difficult. "You can be there. You can even work the spell—I'll show you how—and contact her yourself."

Bazel's face was carefully blank. "I'm not stupid, you know."

Her heart thumped in her chest with sudden, paralyzing terror.

"I know she doesn't care about me." Bazel scuffed the

edge of his mat with his foot. "I know I'm just a tool to her."

Ileni's relief was so vast she spoke without thinking. "Nobody in these caves is anything but a tool."

Bazel blinked twice, and then—to her astonishment—he grinned. "Right. It's nice to be a useful tool instead of a despised one."

Ileni thought about smiling back, but it seemed too risky. Instead she nodded. "I can see that."

Bazel's smile twisted, but it didn't vanish. Before she could say anything else, the students for her next class began filing in, and he made his way into the training area.

"What are you up to?" Sorin demanded as soon as they reached her room after the midday meal.

Ileni, who was already halfway across the room, turned and crossed her arms over her chest. She was the one who had chosen to head to her room instead of the knife-training cavern, and she was surprised that Sorin had followed her. To hide her gratification, she scowled at him.

Sorin leaned against the doorpost, scowling back. "Don't underestimate Bazel. Even the least of us is dangerous. Whatever you're planning, I should be with you. To protect you."

And to wonder why she wasn't working the spell on her own? Ileni sat on her bed and lifted her chin. "To stop me, you mean? No, thank you. I believe we've already had this discussion."

"Please?"

She straightened in shock. His eyes were unwavering on hers, deep black against his faintly flushed skin. Ileni suddenly wondered if he would dare close the door behind him. Her skin tingled. That would hardly be *safe*, though, so he probably wouldn't.

Sorin's voice was tight. "I don't want anything to happen to you."

She flushed too. "Nothing will."

"How can you be so sure?" He stepped into her room. If she'd had power to spare, *she* might have swung the door shut behind him. "You've been here for weeks. Haven't you realized, yet, how close death is to life? How fragile our bodies are? It takes just a *second*—" He broke off. "Do you still not care whether you live or die?"

"I—" She dug her fingers into her blanket. "What makes you think I ever didn't care?"

"You told me. Several times, if I recall correctly."

She hadn't realized he believed her.

"And even before that, it was the first thing I noticed about you. You weren't frightened of me—not as frightened as you should have been. I could have killed you so easily. And I wouldn't have cared."

He didn't sound regretful; he sounded wistful. Like he wished he *still* didn't care.

"I wasn't quite that dumb," Ileni said coldly. "I warded myself against you."

He blinked, the certainty disappearing from his face. Ileni reached under her bed and pulled out her bag. The flat black stones spilled onto the floor.

"Warding stones," she said. "Extremely powerful ones. I set the ward the day I arrived. So you couldn't have touched me, no matter how much you *didn't care.*"

Sorin's eyes narrowed. "I thought you Renagai weren't permitted to take your magical devices out of the village."

"We weren't. Aren't."

"Then how—you *stole* them?" He seemed genuinely shocked, but when she glared up at him, his tone turned mocking. "You, the paragon of Renegai virtue?"

"No," Ileni snapped. "They were given to me." She hesitated, then added, "By Tellis."

Sorin's grin didn't fade, but suddenly it had a different

slant. "I see. Not quite as righteous as you, is that it? Or did he abandon his principles out of love?"

"I don't want to talk about Tellis."

"Good. Neither do I." He looked at the warding stones. Hurt thrummed in his voice, layered far below his outwardly level tone. "So that first day, when you plucked one of my hairs . . . ."

She blinked. "You remember?"

He gave her a sideways glance. "I remember every move you made since the moment you walked into these caves."

Ileni felt suddenly breathless again. *Don't be stupid*, she told herself, and said archly, "The advantage of an assassin's training, I suppose."

His shoulders hunched slightly. There was something vulnerable in his stance, and Ileni's heart twisted unexpectedly. She hadn't realized she had the power to hurt him. "If you're warded against me, how was I able to teach you to fight? Or are the wards so sensitive they can distinguish between true and false threats?"

"They can tell whether I feel threatened or not. And anyhow . . ." She took a deep breath. "I'm not. Warded against you, I mean. Anymore."

He straightened as if in response to an attack.

The wary hope in his eyes made her chest constrict. She forced her words out, awkward and halting. "I don't have any defenses against you, Sorin. At all."

When Sorin spoke, his voice lacked its usual smooth assurance. "You shouldn't have done that."

"I know," Ileni said.

The moment stretched, clumsy and painful. Then, with an almost inhuman swiftness, he closed the distance between them.

Her power acted without her conscious intent, and the door slammed shut. She didn't care, just then, how stupid it was. And neither, evidently, did he.

It wasn't until late that night that Ileni heard the rap on her door, but she was wide awake and still fully dressed. She pulled the door open a crack and was back sitting cross-legged on the bed by the time Bazel stepped in, his reddish hair rumpled by sleep.

Ileni inclined her head. "You brought the stone?"

"He brought something else," Irun said, and stepped through the door behind Bazel.

Ileni scrambled to her feet as Bazel stepped to the side and Irun came across the room toward her. Before she could move, or even think, he jerked her around and pressed her down with her face to the bed. He yanked her arm behind her back at an angle that sent pain screaming along her shoulder.

The thin blanket pressed into her face, suffocating her. She twisted her head to the side and opened her mouth to gasp in air. Something thick and rough slid between her teeth and tongue. She choked, heaved, and tried to reach for the gag. Irun did something to her arm that made the world go black with pain.

When she could hear again, Irun was saying—his voice light and conversational—"That's the thing about sorcerers, see. If they can't speak, they can't work any serious spells."

He spun her around and threw her on the bed. The back of Ileni's head hit the stone wall. When she had blinked away the stinging tears, Irun was standing over her. She looked past him at Bazel, who stood with his back to the door. His pale blue eyes slid away from hers.

Irun followed her gaze. "See how easy it was? Just like I said. We've lived so long in fear of sorcerers, letting them prop up the Empire, holding us back from an all-out attack. And it's so, so easy to make them helpless, once you're not afraid. We can do whatever we want to her now."

"Just kill her," Bazel said.

Irun flexed his hand. "Are you sure? If I hurt her enough, I can control her even with the gag off. I can make her work the stones for you."

"I don't want to work them." Bazel did meet Ileni's eyes then, though he was talking to Irun. "I never want to see Karyn again."

Irun stepped back from the bed. "You're a pathetic excuse for an assassin," he sneered. "Don't worry, I'll keep our bargain. You'll be protected. But what happens to *her* is no longer up to you."

"Just kill her," Bazel said again. Ileni supposed she should be grateful. She reached for the gag, and Irun backhanded her across the face. She rolled to the side, her cry strangled in her throat.

"You lack imagination, Bazel," Irun said. "There are so many more interesting things we could do first." She didn't have to turn to know exactly what his smile looked like. "Besides, I can use her to send a message to Sorin."

She flinched. Irun laughed. "Sorin the untouchable. I bet *your* death would touch him. But you didn't tell him about *this* meeting, did you, *Teacher?*"

She rolled onto her back and managed, defiantly, to nod.

"I don't believe you." He leaned over and, with a negligent motion, broke one of her fingers.

Ileni screamed through the gag, an ugly rattling sound. She shook her head frantically, blinking away the sudden flood of tears, just in time to see Irun straighten and tilt his head to the side. "Still, maybe we should make it quick. Just to be safe."

Ileni didn't see where the dagger came from, but suddenly it was there in his hand. She twisted and lashed out with her foot, a move Sorin had taught her. Irun avoided the kick easily, grabbed her ankle, and pulled up. She landed in a heap on the floor, with an impact that must have knocked bones out of place.

She tried to turn herself over, and Irun planted his foot on her back. "Would you like to do it?" he asked Bazel, politely mocking.

Everything hurt so much. Ileni reached under her bed with her uninjured hand, pulled out her bag, and flung it behind her. The movement twisted her shoulder and sent new agony arching down her back. The warding stones tumbled out of the bag and across the floor.

Irun jumped away, the crushing weight of his foot gone from her back. *We've lived so long in fear of sorcerers. . . .* But he *did* still fear sorcery, and he didn't know what these stones would do. She grabbed the nearest one and sent it skidding . . . not toward Irun, but toward Bazel.

He leaped out of the way, and Ileni scrambled to her feet and ran for the door, kicking stones wildly as she went. She wasn't even halfway there when Irun grabbed her by the hair, pulled her around as if she weighed nothing, and slid his blade neatly across her throat.

She jerked her head away, ripping hair out of her scalp, the knife slashing up along her jaw and cheek. Too late. The blade had cut through skin and breath and blood, ripping right through her airway.

It hurt like nothing had ever hurt before. She grabbed her throat, and blood spurted through her fingers in hot bursts of pain, searing through her mind and her sudden blind panic. Irun let go of her, and she fell to the floor, dying.

Except Irun had also cut through the gag.

The panic of death fueled her remaining power in one final, focused effort. The spell was short, a single word. She opened her mouth and screamed it, through the blood choking her, through the agony and terror of her death. The word rushed out of her slashed throat and into silence.

A new torrent of blood followed it, spilling between

her fingers; but then there was air instead of blood, filling her dying lungs and forcing its way through her body. She didn't even stop to take a deep breath. She leaped to her feet, grabbed the knife held carelessly in Irun's hand, and plunged it into his back.

It wasn't hard. Physically, it took all her strength, but it was still one of the easiest things she had ever done. He wasn't on guard—he thought she was dead—and she wanted him to die with every fiber of her being, wanted it so badly that when he screamed, she shoved the blade in farther. He half-turned and fell, and the knife, still embedded in his flesh, was wrenched out of her hand.

She went after it. She was going to kill Bazel, too.

She should have known better. Like her, Irun was a danger even when he was dying. He grabbed her wrist and flung her—only halfway across the room, but now Bazel was closer to the knife than she was. Ileni snarled up at Bazel from the floor, her hair clinging to her face in tangled sticky strands. He didn't need a knife; even he could kill her with his bare hands.

But he didn't have to know that.

"Araskinbalum," she shouted, lifting one hand as if to throw something at him. And she realized she wasn't pretending. She was reaching inside herself for whatever magic was left to her, ready to spend it all on Bazel's death. She didn't care. She wanted him dead. She wanted him dead *now*.

Except there was nothing left.

Not weak dregs of power, not pathetic scrapings of magic. *Nothing.* An emptiness that, as soon as she realized it was there, rose from within and engulfed her completely.

Her magic was gone. And this time, it was gone for good.

She dropped her hand, too sickened to go on pretending. It didn't matter. Bazel was gone, a flash of terrified eyes and auburn hair. The door slammed shut behind him.

I'll kill you anyhow. She threw the thought after him, and her fingernails scraped against the rock floor.

She got slowly to her feet. Irun lay twisted on his side, completely still. She looked at his dead body, at the knife she had used to end his life, and felt a sweet, savage joy. Even now that he was dead, she hated him. She wished she could kill him again.

She should have been horrified at herself. She wasn't.

She went over to the corpse, moving with ease. The healing spell had also knitted her bones and skin. Blood was drying on her neck and tunic and hair, and her throat ached, but otherwise she felt fine. Better than fine; even her muscles weren't sore, as they had been constantly since she'd started training with Sorin. She knelt by Irun's corpse, rolled him onto his stomach, and eyed the dagger hilt protruding from between his shoulder blades. She might need it.

She closed her fingers around the hilt. She looked down at her hand, at her slim fingers covered in blood. She felt herself smile.

And all at once, she knew who had killed Cadrel.

CHAPTER 17

"Absalm!" Ileni shouted. "Show yourself!"

Her voice echoed in the large, empty training area. She stormed through it, her shoes hitting the stone floor in short, hard thuds.

"Absalm. I know you're alive, and I know you killed Cadrel, and I know you're here. If you don't talk to me, I'll—"

She strode into the smaller training room, and there he was.

Ileni stopped in the entrance. Absalm sat cross-legged in her spot—in the teacher's spot. He turned his head slowly and nodded at her.

She recognized him at once. Not by his face, but by his age. She had spent so much time surrounded by young men and children that she had almost forgotten what old age looked like: wrinkled and spotted skin, deeply lined brow, hunched shoulders.

"Ileni," Absalm said. He held his palm out in the traditional gesture of greeting, Elder to student.

She almost stepped forward to lay her hand in his, but stopped herself. Traditional or not, Elder or not, she was not going to greet him with respect.

He had no right to any Renegai greeting at all.

"I should have known." She tried to sound frigid, but her voice shook. "From the moment I found out Cadrel was killed by sorcery, I should have realized who murdered him."

"Then why didn't you?" Absalm asked. His voice was gentle, probing, as if he was helping her correct an error.

Ileni clenched her bloodstained fingers into fists. "Because I had the wrong idea about killing. I thought it was hard. I thought it was something you had to be trained to do."

Absalm stroked one finger across his chin, examining her thoughtfully, and Ileni's jaw clenched. She understood, now, why Sorin had always turned away her questions about how the assassins were persuaded to kill.

He was amused, that she thought killing another human being was such a difficult thing. As if it was he, and not she, who had been trained.

"Why?" she said. "Why did you fake your death? And why kill Cadrel? And why—"

"One question at a time." Absalm raised a finger. "First. I faked my death because it was time for you to succeed me."

Utter silence. She stared at him, unable to speak.

"They were supposed to send you." He shook his head regretfully. "Not Cadrel."

"Me? Why would you expect them to send—" Her words died as she realized the answer. "You *knew* what had happened to me? That I would lose my magic? How could you know?"

Absalm's eyes were very gentle. "You don't remember, of course, but I was the Elder who gave you your first Test."

Ileni had a vague recollection of her first Test, but of the Elder who had tested her, all she remembered was a shimmering blue robe and a faceless adult. She looked up slowly at Absalm's face, at his wrinkled skin and dark gray eyes.

"You were very powerful," Absalm said. "You passed without half-trying. A child prodigy. But I could tell, even then, that your powers weren't permanent."

The attack Sorin had taught her *did* work. Ileni was across the cavern in a second, her forearm pressed against Absalm's throat, her breath hissing between her teeth.

"You *knew*?" She pressed down, hard enough to hurt, not caring if she overdid it. "You let me grow up believing I was powerful, *knowing* that when I got old enough I would lose it all—"

A blast of wind lifted her off her feet and slammed her against the far wall. Instinctively, Ileni tried to raise a defense, but it failed completely. Tears sprang to her eyes.

"It was necessary," Absalm said.

"*Why?*"

He inclined his head. "This is not the time to explain. You must gain control of yourself."

Ileni's anger was a burning space inside her chest, making it hard to breathe. She wanted to hit something. To smash things, break things, turn this cave into a shambles. To destroy something other people cared about and make them feel the way she did.

But she couldn't do any of that. All she could do was

clench her fists and spit out hot, futile words. "You're lying to me! There's no way the Elders would have gone along with—for all these years—they *believed* in me! They weren't pretending."

"No. They weren't." Absalm's voice, and his face, were infuriatingly calm. "But I knew that once the truth about your powers was discovered, the Elders would jump at the opportunity to send you here. That's why I faked my death. To give them that opportunity. I don't know why Cadrel was sent instead."

"He volunteered," Ileni said numbly. "His wife died. . . ." His eyes assessed her, unblinking. "And you killed him. So they would send me next."

"Don't blame yourself—"

"I do not," Ileni said, "blame myself."

"Or me," Absalm finished, a bit hastily. His assessment had turned wary. "I didn't want to kill him. I thought he could fake his death, as I had, create an illusion of a corpse and remain hidden. But he was . . . he wouldn't listen. I tried to explain."

"Explain *what*?"

Absalm shook his head.

Ileni's fingernails bit into her palm. "What use could I

possibly be to you? I have no magic. I'm *worthless!*"

"You are far from worthless, Ileni. You have skill. More skill than anyone I've ever seen. And you have been trained to use it to its fullest." He got slowly to his feet. He was wearing not an Elder's blue robe but the nondescript gray clothes of an assassin. "That's why this deception was necessary. So you could be trained in earnest. I truly regret the pain it caused you."

The pain it caused you. Ileni clenched her fists.

"Who else knew?" she whispered.

"No one."

"Not even the master of the assassins?"

"Well. Of course the master." He sounded shocked. "Korjan and I have been . . . friends, I daresay. Since we were young. He was the one who showed me how much could be accomplished if only the Renegai and the assassins would combine our talents."

"Since you were young . . ." She drew in her breath. "You mean, since he spent time in our village so he could murder one of us. A *Renegai!*"

Absalm tugged at his earlobe, then dropped his hands to his lap. The calm, remote expression dropped over his face again. "Who died for the greater good."

She had heard that before. "*What* greater good? What are you planning? Tell me!"

Even to herself, she sounded hysterical, and she wasn't surprised when Absalm shook his head. "I'm sorry that we're having this conversation now." He didn't sound sorry, though. He sounded tolerant and paternal. "You weren't meant to discover the truth this early. I wanted to wait until I was sure. . . ."

"That I was like you?" She brushed a clump of hair away from her cheek and hoped it hadn't left blood on her face. "One of them? That was never going to happen."

"No?" He said it very softly, and she was suddenly sure he knew about everything: the celebration, the fighting lessons, and—most of all—Sorin. Blood rushed to her cheeks.

"Come, Ileni. You must have realized by now that the assassins are not precisely the way the Elders painted them." Absalm leaned forward, his gray eyes soft, and went on in that terrible, kindly, inexorable voice. "I think you should take some time. This has been a lot to absorb. When we talk again—"

She didn't wait for him to finish. More than anything in the world, she wanted to be away from this room where she had taught killers, where one of her own Elders had trapped her in the master's mysterious plans. She was through the door before she could think, footsteps pounding in her ears, running down the stairs and through the passageways and toward the only person in these caves she could even think of trusting.

Sorin was fast asleep when Ileni flung open his door, but only for a second. Then he was across the room, pressing her to the wall, holding a blade to her throat. Ileni froze, her breath coming in painful gasps.

His eyes met hers, cold and deadly, and the dagger's edge pressed against her skin. Then his expression shifted into horror. He lowered the dagger and stepped back. "Ileni. That was not smart."

"I know. I'm sorry. . . ." And this time, she didn't even try to stop the tears.

But this time, he didn't watch her sob from across the room.

"He's not dead," Ileni gasped against Sorin's shoulder, his arms tight and strong around her. His lips brushed her hair. Her blood-streaked hair. "Absalm. He's here, and he . . . he . . ." She pulled back slightly at his jerk of surprise. "Irun is, though. Dead, I mean." She burst into louder sobs and buried her face in his tunic again.

To Sorin's credit, he waited until she had calmed down before saying, in a very tight voice, "Why don't you start from the beginning?"

So she did, starting from Bazel's knock on her door. The only thing she left out was the worst thing that had happened that night: the final loss of her magic. She thought about telling him that, too, but she choked on the words.

By the time she was done, they were both sitting on the bed, side by side. Sorin held both her hands in his, and squeezed occasionally. When she was done, he said, "And you have no idea what he wants of you?"

Ileni shook her head. Her face felt tight with dried tears and blood. "But it's part of something he's been planning since . . . since before I was born, I think."

"He said it was time for the Renegai and assassins to combine their talents? How is that supposed to happen?"

"I don't know."

"But the master knows." Sorin let out a relieved breath.

Ileni jerked her hands out of his. "That doesn't make me feel any better."

"If we go to him—"

"He'll tell me the truth? Even though Absalm wouldn't?"

She scrambled off the bed. "No. The best person to give us answers is still Karyn."

Sorin shook his head.

"We know now that she didn't kill anyone. Or, well, she didn't kill Absalm and Cadrel. So she has no reason to kill me. She's here for something else."

"Like what?"

"I don't know. But it has something to do with Absalm's plan. He's the one who contacted her, and it wasn't just because he wanted chocolate. Bazel said he was asking her about magic. . . ." Ileni took a deep breath. "If she's still here, I have to find her. And I can't do that without your help." She reached for his hands again. "Sorin, *please.*"

Sorin leaned closer, his face all lines and shadows by the dimmed light of the glowstones. "Why do you need my help? Can't you use magic?"

Ileni hesitated. She should tell him the truth, finally. She had come to him because she trusted him . . . but that was before he had brought up the master. "I have nothing of hers to use in a finding spell. If she's somewhere in these caves, we'll have to rely on your skills to find her."

"And what skills would those be?"

"I don't know. Can't you track her or something?"

"Starting where? The caverns extend so far that no one has explored them all, not even me. Karyn could be anywhere. We could spend years looking and never find her." Sorin stood. "Couldn't you try to detect her magic use?"

"She knows I'm here. She'll be shielding against me."

"And you're not powerful enough to break her shields?"

She couldn't find her voice. Fortunately, Sorin misread the reason for her silence, and held up both hands. "I'm sorry, Ileni. I didn't mean—"

"Will you help me, or not?"

Sorin let out a breath and said, his face remote, "We're thinking about this the wrong way. If Karyn is still here, she didn't come back to hide somewhere in the distant regions of these caves. She wants something. If we go back to the river, maybe *she*'ll find *us*. Or at the very least, be close enough for us to find her."

Ileni swallowed a *thank you* she suspected he didn't want to hear. "You might be right."

"Well, then." Sorin pulled her to her feet. "Let's go."

The riverbank was dark and silent when Ileni and Sorin made their way down the narrow path along the cliff. Ileni, who had used Sorin's basin to wash the blood off her hands—

and, less successfully, out of her hair—stepped off the ledge with a breath of relief and wrenched her eyes away from the large dark smear on the white rock.

Sorin partly unrolled the thick coil of rope he had retrieved from a storage room on their way and tied a loop at its end, then closed his hand around the four-pronged hook at the other end.

"The rope Bazel used is gone," he said. "Does that mean she came back and pulled it up?"

"Not necessarily. She could have created it with magic, and it would have vanished shortly afterward." A feat that would have drained even Ileni at the height of her power. If she was wrong about Karyn's motivation, it would take a sorceress that powerful less than a second to kill her.

Ileni swallowed hard. She was carrying a knife, strapped to her side beneath her tunic—Sorin had insisted—but she felt completely defenseless. She resisted the urge to step closer to Sorin.

He nodded, leaned back, swung the rope in a few rapid circles, and flung it up over the cliff. The metal hook at its end thudded sharply high above them. "Do you want to go first?"

She looked at him incredulously.

"Right." He had a way of smiling without smiling. It was her favorite of all his expressions. "There's only one rope, so we'll have to go one at a time."

"Couldn't we just go around the path?" Ileni suggested weakly.

"Straight up would be easier for a sorceress, no? If Karyn wanted to hide deeper in the caves, she would have gone straight up the cliffside. If we go that way, too, I won't miss anything." He tugged the rope twice and turned to her. "I'll pull you up after me. It's not that hard."

"Right."

Sorin put one foot up against the cliffside, leaning back. The rope went taut. "You should probably have your own magelight, or it will be pitch-black once I'm gone."

Ileni shook her head. "I should conserve my magic. If I do have to fight her, I'll need every bit of power I have."

"Right." Sorin blew out a breath, and a new magelight flared to life above Ileni's head. Then he turned and was gone, shimmying up the rope with a speed that made her heart catch in her throat.

For a few moments she was alone, the rock flat and white except for that dark bloodstain, the black river whispering past. She turned in a slow circle, staring warily at the shadows, imagining the sound of someone else's breathing. Then the rope went still. Sorin had reached the top.

She fitted herself into the loop with some awkwardness, grasped tightly with both hands, and closed her eyes. That proved to be a mistake when the rope's first upward jerk slammed her head against the rock wall. She opened her eyes hastily and used her feet to push herself away from the cliff as the ground and the river receded below. Sorin's magelight traveled with her, and from this height the water looked like flat black marble, as still as the white rock that cut sharply against it.

When she finally scrambled onto the clifftop and untangled herself from the rope, Sorin gave her what seemed like an approving nod before re-coiling the rope and stuffing it into his pack. He tilted his head at the ground. "Looks like you were right."

A pair of narrow footprints was barely visible in the dirt covering the rock.

"Those weren't here last time," Sorin said.

Ileni stared at him. "Last time, when you were chasing down Bazel? I think you might have missed them."

"No," Sorin said flatly.

She opened her mouth, then decided not to argue. "All

right. Apparently Karyn *is* still here." She drew in a long breath. "Let's find out what she can tell us."

Sorin reached over and touched her cheek. He rubbed a finger against her skin, then flicked off a sliver of dried blood.

Heat rushed to Ileni's face. "Sorry."

"About what?" Sorin grinned at her. "You should be proud. You bested Irun."

A wave of nausea rolled through her. She could still faintly smell blood, as if it was caked into her nostrils. "Don't *compliment* me. It was self-defense. I didn't want to. . . ." Except she had. When she had driven the knife in, she had *wanted* to kill him. She had hated him and wanted him dead.

She turned away, and Sorin said roughly, "I didn't—Ileni, don't. It doesn't matter. If you hadn't killed Irun, I would have done it for you."

And he wouldn't have pretended it was anything but revenge. It wouldn't have bothered him at all.

"It's a good thing you didn't," she said, more harshly than she had intended. "Whatever this thing is between us, I'm certain it wouldn't survive my watching you murder someone."

Sorin went perfectly still, then turned his back on her. "Let's hope you're powerful enough to make Karyn cooperate, then."

Ileni took a deep breath. It wasn't fair, to lead him into this blind. "I can't—I can't fight her. You don't know—"

"Don't worry," he said stiffly. "If Irun could best an imperial sorcerer, so can I."

"Or she could kill you."

He shrugged. "Of course."

Ileni fought to control her breathing. He was being reckless, yes, but also brave; and he was, after all, doing it for her. She gestured at the stretch of rock ahead of them. "After you."

The trail led steadily downward along the unevenly sloping rock. The footprints disappeared after a few minutes, but Sorin kept going, his eyes darting from the ground to the boulders piled around them to the stalactites hanging above. Whatever hints of passage he was following, Ileni couldn't see them, but she walked behind him silently. Once the way was wide enough for them to walk side by side, she reached for his hand, and was relieved when his warm fingers closed around hers.

Suddenly she found herself blinking back tears, and was glad he was concentrating too hard on the ground ahead of them to notice.

After another few minutes, the trail hit a wall, and Sorin let go of her hand so he could squeeze through a narrow crevice and climb onto a ledge. The ledge became a tunnel, so low Ileni was forced to pull herself forward by her forearms, her body scraping along the stones.

The tunnel seemed to go on forever. She had to keep her head down to avoid banging it on the craggy ceiling, so it was impossible to get a sense of how far she had to go or even of how far they had gone. Twice she thought about calling ahead to Sorin, asking him to slow down. Each time, she opened her mouth and then forced it shut, pulling herself onward.

Then the scraping of Sorin's body ahead of her came to an abrupt halt, and she pulled forward so hard she scratched her arm on a sharp rock. A moment later, she was able to get to her knees, and then to her feet. Relief swept through her as she stood upright, before she saw the empty space in front of them.

The ground dropped away abruptly, as if it had been sliced off by magic. Below them was a vast darkness, a space so wide and deep she couldn't see any hint of rock formations either across or below.

"She must have gone another way," Ileni suggested hopefully. But Sorin already had the rope out, and was tying it firmly around her legs and waist.

"You'll have to go first this time." His fingers skimmed over her tunic as he tied the rope, and lingered briefly at her waist. "It will be easier for you if I'm controlling the rope from up here."

Ileni looked down into the chasm, then at Sorin.

"All right," she said.

His quick, surprised grin kept her from balking, until the rope was secured around her and she balanced at the edge of the cliff, her back to the gaping emptiness behind her. Then panic rose in her, so swiftly she couldn't fight it. "Sorin—"

"Lean back. Once you can feel the rope holding you, you won't be afraid."

He actually seemed serious. She started to twist around, and Sorin said sharply, "Don't look down. Look at me."

She looked at him. His eyes were as black as the space behind her, his features sharp, shadowed lines. He looked fierce and dangerous, but he was waiting, patiently, for her. His strong hands were clenched firmly around the rope.

She kept her eyes trained on his and leaned back, even as her instincts screamed at her to stop before she fell.

Sorin was right. As soon as she had passed the point where she should have fallen screaming into the abyss, she felt the rope tighten around her, holding her aloft. She braced her feet against the cliffside, suspended horizontally above the emptiness.

Sorin's eyes sparkled, and suddenly he didn't look dangerous at all. "Push off with your feet."

She bent her knees and pushed her feet away from the cliff. Sorin let the rope out, and she arced out into the darkness before landing back against the side of the cliff, several yards lower. She laughed aloud, and pushed off again even before she heard Sorin's answering laugh.

It felt like flying. Exhilaration surged through her as she pushed herself harder and harder against the cliffside, flew out farther and faster, until she could barely see Sorin's form above her.

And then the cliffside ended.

She realized it a moment before her next swing took her down and under the rock. Her head grazed the lower edge of the cliff, and then she was swinging uncontrollably through the darkness, waiting for the crash that would tear her loose and send her plunging to her death.

"Ileni!" Sorin shouted from above.

Her reply was a strangled gasp. The cliff had veered inward so sharply she could no longer reach it, so she had nothing to brace her feet against, no way to slow her motion. Panic seared through her.

Then, as she swung wildly away from the rocks again, the rope jerked upward, bringing her back up to where the cliffside was within reach. She put her feet out and they thudded against rock. She whimpered, bending her knees, swinging away again without wanting to—but not as far, this time, and not as fast. Another two swings and she was stable again, her feet braced against the rock, the rope trembling but still.

She would never have believed this could feel like safety. But it did. She didn't look down at the cavernous emptiness below her.

"There's no more cliff," she called up. Her voice trembled.

"Then I'll lower the rope slowly until you hit the bottom. Hold on tight."

"Wait—" But the rope was already letting out, and her feet slid across the rock and dangled into emptiness. Her body jerked as she clung tighter to the rope, and it began to twist, swinging her sickeningly from side to side as she was lowered deeper into the cave.

Then, with a jerk, the downward motion stopped. The twisting didn't, and Ileni's stomach turned upside down. Luckily, since she hadn't eaten for hours, there was nothing to spew up.

"Sorin?"

"We're out of rope." His voice was distant but clear. "Just a second."

Something whizzed past her, and she heard a splash from below.

"Good," Sorin said. "That distance should be safe to jump."

Ileni thought wistfully back to the time when she hadn't cared much whether she died. Then, trying not to think about what she was doing, she began extricating herself from the harness.

She needn't have worried about giving herself time to think. In the struggle to untangle herself, she lost hold of the rope. A brief, terrifying plunge downward, a short scream, and then frigid liquid sprayed into her face as she pitched forward on her hands and knees into shockingly icy water.

Icy, but shallow; it only came halfway up her forearms.

She knelt in it, gasping, then got to her feet. Another freezing splash hit her side as Sorin landed beside her.

His magelight illuminated an underground lake so still that it was almost invisible. She could see the white rock formations beneath the water as if there was no water covering them at all. Around the banks were more structures, like tiny castles and fortresses, formed of sparkling fernlike rocks. Tendrils of stone as thin as flower stems were scattered over the ground, also in that unearthly white. Ileni drew in her breath. She felt like an intruder, heavy and awkward in a place where no human beings were ever intended to go.

"Sorin. Maybe we should—"

"Hsst!" he whispered sharply, and she clamped her mouth shut just as a new light flared ahead of them. It illuminated a chasm several feet from the edge of the lake, and beyond it a flat white rockface lined with deep cracks and framed by a vast archway of pearly stone.

Karyn stood beneath the archway, waiting for them.

CHAPTER
18

The sorceress stood with her legs braced apart, her face remote and calm. Her green tunic and black leggings were now dirt stained and torn, but somehow she looked almost majestic. The magelight floated several feet above her head, below a white ceiling pitted with holes and sparkling with tiny liquid droplets.

Sorin surged out of the water onto the white rock shore, moving with such grace that Ileni didn't even hear a splash. Karyn raised one hand, and a line of thick white stalactites snapped away from the ceiling and fell directly in front of him in a series of echoing crashes. Sorin stopped short, and

Ileni scrambled out of the lake to stand next to him. Water squelched in her shoes.

"Well," Karyn said pleasantly. "Here we all are."

Ileni shut her eyes briefly, trying to sense Karyn's power. But the sorceress felt completely mundane, not a spark of magic in her.

Something was wrong.

Sorin stepped around the fallen rock in front of him, and Ileni followed, as if getting one step closer might make a difference. It didn't. The chasm between them and Karyn was wide and deep, a wedge of blackness among all the ethereal white, and she still couldn't sense any magic.

"We're here to talk," Sorin said.

"So am I." Karyn smiled. "But not to you."

She swiveled to face Ileni. Ileni's stomach tightened, and she lifted her chin.

"Confused about me, aren't you?" Karyn dipped her hand under her tunic. "Allow me to enlighten you."

Sorin hissed and crouched on the balls of his feet. Ileni reached for the knife under her tunic. But all Karyn did was hold up a perfectly round stone, so small it fit neatly into the palm of her hand.

The breath went out of Ileni's body in a *whoosh*. The

stone was beautiful—glassy and clear, with dozens of shimmering colors swirling beneath its surface—and it lit up all her senses with the feel of magic, of power. Of everything she had lost.

"What is *that*?" Sorin demanded.

"I don't know," Ileni whispered, and didn't care what he thought of her ignorance. She couldn't take her eyes off the rock. The power within it, too vast to be crammed into something so small, called to her with hypnotic urgency.

Karyn held the rock out, as if to give her a closer look. "We call them lodestones. They store magical energy."

Black magic! Ileni tried to look away, and managed it just long enough to see the eagerness in Sorin's eyes, the predator's focus as he slid one foot forward.

Karyn saw it, too, and laughed. "It can only be used by someone with no power of his own. So don't bother."

Ileni's heart pounded so hard it hurt, and her breath caught every time she drew it in. All that power, trapped and waiting . . . she could imagine drawing that strength into herself. Being full of magic again, able to do anything.

It wouldn't last forever. She would use it up, and it would be gone, and then she would go through that loss all over again. She didn't care. She had never wanted anything so badly in her life.

Karyn lifted her eyebrows. "More interested in talking to me now?"

Ileni's mouth was too dry for speech.

"I think we'll be taking that," Sorin said, and pulled two knives from beneath his tunic.

The knives flashed in whirling silver streaks over the chasm. Magic flashed from Karyn, blindingly powerful, and the knives flew back, straight at Sorin.

Sorin dodged them as if they were in slow motion and took off at a dead run, straight for the chasm between him and Karyn. At the very edge, he launched himself over the black space.

Ileni couldn't help a brief, strangled scream. It was an impossible leap. But Sorin's hands thudded onto the rock on the other side, and he tucked himself into a ball and rolled. When he unfurled himself, sleek and swift, he was on his feet, another dagger in his hand, its point inches from Karyn's throat.

Karyn lowered her hands and sighed. Smoothly, she tucked the lodestone away under her tunic. Ileni felt a ward flare up, and then the stone went silent to her senses. Its sudden absence made the cavern duller. "You bore me, assassin."

"Ileni," Sorin said, very calm, "break through her wards."

Ileni opened her mouth, then closed it. The silence stretched for a long, terrible moment. Sorin glanced at her, a swift look stark with betrayal.

He didn't know she couldn't do it. He thought she was choosing not to.

Sorin. No. But Ileni couldn't speak. She could barely breathe.

Karyn laughed again. She turned on her heel as if Sorin wasn't there, and he lunged and struck. His dagger slid across the side of Karyn's neck as if along marble rather than flesh, leaving her unharmed. As he finished the lunge, he twisted and tangled his legs with Karyn's, throwing both of them hard on the flat rock.

They rolled once, and then Sorin was on top, kneeling over the sorceress, fingers wrapped around her neck. The dagger was gone, but he didn't need it. His fingers dug hard into Karyn's throat. Her eyes fluttered dazedly—she had knocked her head hard on the rock—and she opened her mouth, but all that emerged was a croak. His fingers tightened, and her heels kicked frantically at the rock, her mouth open in a soundless plea. Sorin leaned down, arms taut, a hunting animal lunging in for the kill.

And then he hesitated. He turned his head and looked across the chasm at Ileni. Their eyes met, and his weren't deadly and focused at all. They were . . . afraid.

This thing between us wouldn't survive my watching you murder someone.

Sorin's face hardened. He turned back to Karyn and pressed down.

But that momentary hesitation had been enough. Karyn twisted her head to the side and gasped out a word. A burst of power erupted from her, flinging Sorin through the air, his body twisting as he arced down into the chasm.

Ileni screamed as he fell into the darkness, and reached for her magic. It was like scraping the insides of her soul.

Sorin jerked to a stop and hung suspended between the white rocks and the empty blackness. A sob broke from Ileni's throat. For an insane moment, she believed that somehow, she had done it; she had saved him. Then Karyn surged to her feet and beckoned with one hand, and Sorin turned helplessly in midair to face her.

"Now," Karyn said pleasantly, "perhaps we can reopen our discussion."

"Don't waste your time, Sorceress," Sorin snarled. "I'm no traitor, and I'm not afraid to die. You might as well drop me now."

Don't. Ileni had never felt so helpless. She had betrayed everyone, ruined everything, and now Sorin was going to die. Dropped into a dark canyon, gone forever, his death *wasted*. Because of her.

"How noble." Karyn's neck was mottled red with bruises. "But I'm still not speaking to *you*."

Ileni tore her eyes away from Sorin.

"Ileni," he said. "Don't. She'll kill me anyhow."

"Why would I do that?" Karyn murmured. "Some of us prefer not to kill, if it's unnecessary." She gave Ileni a small smile, including her in that *some of us*. "I wouldn't expect an assassin to understand."

Ileni forced herself to straighten, to meet the sorceress's eyes. Sorin was defying Karyn despite the abyss beneath him. How could she do less? "What do you want to know?"

"Many things. But mostly, I would like to know how to get through the Renegai wards around these caves."

Ileni froze. She could feel Sorin struggling to use magic against Karyn, like a fitful breeze against the strength of her spell.

She hadn't betrayed *everything* after all. She hadn't betrayed her own people yet. But in exchange for Sorin's life, she would.

"You think I can tell you that?" Ileni said finally. "Right now?"

"Can't you?" Karyn rolled her shoulders back. "Then let's start with an easier question. Why have your assassin friends been killing off sorcerers? Do you know the answer to that?"

"I do," Ileni said. "I'll tell you when you let him down."

Karyn lifted an eyebrow. "I could still kill him, if I wanted to. So what does it matter?"

"It would make me feel better," Ileni said, through gritted teeth. "If you want this to be a friendly conversation, let him down."

Karyn considered, then nodded. Sorin floated toward the sorceress, landing roughly near the edge of the chasm, and promptly fell over on his side. He lay perfectly still, not allowing himself the indignity of a struggle.

Ileni couldn't see his face. Her last glimpse of it had been that stricken look he gave her right before he failed to kill Karyn.

"All right," Karyn said. "Let's be friendly."

"Let's not," Sorin growled.

The surge of power caught Ileni by surprise. She had never felt Sorin use his full strength before. He was more skilled than she had realized, and his magic had an edge to it, an untamed tremor pulsing beneath the perfect, clean precision of his spell.

The spell holding Sorin captive shattered, with an impact that made Ileni gasp. Karyn doubled over with a sharp cry. Sorin was on his feet and across the rock before the sorceress could recover. He slid behind her, yanked one arm around her neck in a chokehold, and clamped his other hand over her mouth.

"Nice spell, isn't it?" Sorin's smile was sharp and feral. "Absalm *did* do some teaching, you know, in between his . . . extracurricular activities. And now I think this is going to get a lot less friendly."

Karyn twisted against his grasp, once, futilely. Sorin pressed his forearm against her throat, ignoring the fingers tearing desperately at his arm.

This time, he didn't look at Ileni.

Karyn let out a broken, throttled cry that reminded Ileni of Irun's hands pressing on her throat. She forced herself to stand and watch as Karyn's face turned purple-red and her struggles grew weaker. There was nothing else she could do.

Then Karyn opened her hand and flung the lodestone wildly.

Sorin let go of her and leaped to grab it. He landed in a crouch, holding the glowing stone in one hand. Its swirling lights played across his face.

Then he grunted as Karyn's magic hit and forced him to his knees. He managed to hold onto the stone, even as his face twisted in agony.

Karyn threw her head back and laughed.

"You can't use it," she said. "But I still can, from this distance. You should have killed me when you had the chance."

She lifted a hand and began chanting. Ileni didn't recognize the spell, but the cadence made her stomach twist. It was dark and ugly and vindictive, promising terrible pain. The colors in the stone twisted violently as Karyn drew on its power.

She knew what this was, even though she had never heard it before, except in whispered rumors: a deathspell.

"Sorin!" she shouted. "*I* can use the stone."

He looked up at her, and she saw him understand what that meant. *It can only be used by someone with no power of his own.*

His eyes widened in shock, even through his pain.

He threw her the stone.

Karyn let go of the spell in mid-chant and threw herself at Sorin, slamming into him as he released the stone. The shimmering orb arced across the chasm, and Ileni ran to intercept it. It was going into the abyss, it was going to fall—she threw herself after it, and her fingertips brushed its smooth surface.

Power tingled through her hand, just from that small contact. But the stone slipped away from her and down.

Her cry turned into a scream as she plummeted after it.

Something thudded behind her, and a hand clasped around her ankle. Sorin's grip jerked her to a stop, almost yanking her leg right out of her hip. She dangled against the cliffside, fingers scrabbling against slick rocks. She could no longer see the stone. She had never even heard it hit the ground. It was gone, gone, gone.

Sorin pulled her out bit by bit, her body scraping against the rock, until she was on solid ground. Then his hands closed around her waist and he pulled her up. She had just enough time to see that Karyn had vanished before he pulled her roughly around.

They looked at each other. Ileni's legs felt like jelly and

her heart felt broken, and she was afraid of what she was going to see in his eyes. She let out a sob.

Sorin yanked her to him and held her tight, so tight it hurt. But it still felt better than anything else she was feeling. She closed her eyes and buried her face in his shirt, breathing in dust and sweat and the faint, metallic scent of blood.

"I'm sorry," she whispered. "I'm sorry I didn't tell you—"

His hand touched her cheek, a faint nudge. That was all the encouragement she needed to lift her face so his mouth could land on hers. She clung to him desperately, trying to find what she had found in his kisses before: forgetfulness.

But it didn't work. She couldn't stop thinking about the lodestone, tumbling away into the darkness. About how it had brushed her fingers, sending tingles of power through her, making her feel, for a second, like herself.

The dark power she had abhorred her entire life. The source of the Empire's evil.

It can only be used by someone with no power.

But someone who knew how to use magical power. Someone who had the skill to use spells, but no power to fuel them.

Someone like her.

That's why this deception was necessary. So you could be trained in earnest.

Absalm had gone through all this to create a Renegai who could use a lodestone. But why?

She pulled away, and it was a moment before Sorin let her go. She could feel the force of his gaze even though the shadows hid his eyes.

"We should go after Karyn," she whispered.

Sorin shook his head shortly. "I don't see the point. We know what she wants—a way through the wards. And the master has to know about that, Ileni. This has gone too far."

She didn't have the energy to argue. His voice was curt and remote. Already the memory of their frantic kiss was fading away.

"So what do we do now?" she asked. She immediately wished she had waited longer, until the tremor in her voice was gone.

Sorin stepped back, letting go of her, leaving her cold and alone in the vast cavern.

"Now," he said, "we go back."

CHAPTER 19

Sorin stared up into the darkness where the rope was dangling several yards above them, eyebrows furrowed. He must have expected that once they were done with Karyn, Ileni would be able to fly them back up. Ileni bit her lip, awkwardly silent, trying and failing to come up with a useful suggestion.

Finally Sorin strode over to one of the feathery rock formations at the side of the pool. He examined it for a second and then, with a swift, efficient kick, broke it off at its base. It cracked at once, shattering into a jumble of white rock. He dragged the larger pieces into the pool.

By the time he had constructed a haphazard mountain of stones, the chamber was full of broken rocks, scattered and shapeless, its ethereal quality gone forever. The destruction sent a pang through Ileni: a place of beauty and grace turned into a twisted, senseless mess.

Ileni climbed silently after Sorin to the top of his construction, not making a sound even when rocks fell away under her feet or when Sorin tied her into the harness and then shimmied up the rope so he could pull her up.

Sorin was silent, too, during the climb back down to the river and the laborious journey through the maze of boulders. It was more difficult than the way there had been. He lowered her down the cliffside and helped her over some of the more precarious rocks. But the few times he spoke to her—out of necessity—the neutral tone of his voice made her want to cry. Or hit him. Anything, to make him look at her with a real expression on his face.

"Sorin," she forced herself to say when they dragged themselves through the narrow tunnel and crouched below the low ceiling at its end. He stopped. "What can the master do, even if we tell him?"

"I don't know," he said, in that same removed tone.

"But he'll figure something out. Something we haven't thought of."

"Sorin—"

He vaulted out of the tunnel, then stopped short, only his head visible to her. Ileni rushed after him, once again banging her head on the rocks above her.

Absalm was waiting for them in the cavern, his arms crossed over his chest.

And a caveful of assassins stood behind him.

Ileni stumbled to a stop next to Sorin. Absalm's face was hard and angry, and the assassins were a mass of gray tunics and blank, intent eyes.

"How could you be this foolhardy?" Absalm snarled. "She's an imperial sorceress!"

The Renegai part of her shriveled before an Elder's wrath. "How did you know—"

"*I* have my magic," he said pointedly. "But even if you did—even at the height of your power—she still could have killed you. And then your entire life, *my* entire life, all our plans, would have died with you."

Fury lanced through Ileni, making her spit out her next sentence with vicious pleasure. "Your plans are already ruined. The lodestone is gone."

Absalm stared at her for a long moment, and she glared back.

"The lodestone?" Absalm said. And smiled.

A cold foreboding rushed through Ileni. She opened her mouth, and nothing came out. She felt Sorin's hand slide across the small of her back, supporting her despite his anger and hurt, and gratitude rushed through her. She leaned back into him.

Absalm saw Sorin's hand, too. A muscle in his cheek twitched. "Do you know how many lodestones the imperial sorcerers have? They are powerful objects, yes, but very limited. One person's power. One person's death. What can that accomplish against the might of the Empire?"

From the assassins behind him came a soft, approving murmur. *They know,* Ileni thought, and a chill ran through her. Why would they know what Absalm had planned? Why were they all here?

She wrapped her arms around herself as the cold in her bones deepened.

"No, Ileni," Absalm said. "We are going to need much more than that. Enough power to strike the imperial sorcerers at their base, blast through all their defenses. To cripple them so badly they won't have the strength to retaliate."

He was asking Karyn about the method for transferring power.

"You must have realized," Absalm said, "that if magic can be drawn from death, there is another source of great power in these caves."

Behind him, the faces of the other assassins were young, hard, and inexorable. Her eyes fell on one, who stood out because of his bright red hair: the boy who had played the flute so exultantly during the assassins' celebration.

No.

"They are here willingly. They will sacrifice themselves, and their power will be yours." Absalm's voice was so soft that if not for the utter silence in the caves, she would not have been able to make out the words. "Imagine the power of a hundred willing volunteers. Imagine what you, the most skilled sorceress alive, could do with it."

She did imagine it, despite herself. Power rushing through her, as she had once thought it always would. Magic rising in her, coursing through her blood. Hers to command.

And then it would be gone. But the Empire would be gone with it.

She *could* do it. She could fulfill the dreams of her people, exceed all the hopes they'd had for her, free them from their exile, finally bring an end to the Empire. Change the world.

The cavern was small and dim, deep beneath the earth, crowded with the faces watching her. Waiting for her to say yes. *Wanting* her to say yes.

She didn't turn, but she knew Sorin's expression was the same. Everyone she knew would want her to do it, even those far away from this cavern, up where the sun shone and people hesitated to die. The Elders. Tellis. The deaths of these killers, who they believed were evil, wouldn't give them pause.

And the deaths of the imperial sorcerers wouldn't give anyone pause. Because everyone knew they, too, were evil.

"No," Ileni said.

"They want to do it." Sorin's voice was low and urgent. Pleading. "*I* want to do it. We are all marked for death anyhow. Let our deaths accomplish something." She felt the brush of his fingertips and didn't move as he closed his hand around hers. "Help us put an end to the Empire."

She couldn't look at him. She wished she didn't have to look at any of them. Once she would have leaped at the chance to kill them all, put an end to these caves. Back when they had been made of stories and dark legends. Before she had lived among them and learned how much more complicated the reality was.

"I won't do it," she said. Her insides twisted with shame—*coward, traitor*. "I won't."

She looked at Sorin at last. He stared back, his eyes cold. He looked lean and grim and feral.

A killer.

"You will do as the master commands," he said.

The bottom dropped out of Ileni's stomach. She told herself that he was lying—that he was trying to protect her, that this was to fool the others—but his unwavering, closed-off expression told her otherwise. He had never been that certain about anything concerning her.

His face was the same as the others', as Absalm's, united in their vast purpose. She was the only one who was different, the only piece of the master's brilliant plan that didn't quite fit.

She wasn't going to be given a choice.

"Sorin," she said. It wasn't hard to sound hurt and confused, but his expression didn't change. "Can I . . . can we talk, before I . . . in private?"

Sorin exchanged a glance with Absalm, who nodded.

The smug expression on the Elder's face made Ileni want to hit him as she and Sorin walked past. She had been right, back in the training cavern. Absalm did know about her and Sorin.

What fools they had been, thinking they were keeping a secret from the master. This had been part of his plan all along, just like everything else. Her feelings for Sorin were yet another of his tools, a backup in case she needed extra convincing.

Did Sorin realize it? She couldn't tell, when they finally stopped around a bend in the passageway, out of hearing distance of the others. His face was soft, his mouth gentle. But his eyes remained dark and cold.

"Ileni," he said. His voice made a shiver run through her, and she realized abruptly that the master had been right about this, too. He *could* convince her. "I understand—"

"No, you don't," Ileni said, and threw herself at him, fingers curled into fists.

Her attack was slow and clumsy. Sorin moved under the blow easily, lightning fast and deadly, and sliced a hand at her hamstring.

His hand never connected with her body. The air around Ileni exploded in a flash of green light, throwing Sorin backward. He landed against the rock wall and slid gasping to the ground in a cascade of rocks and dirt.

She was past him then, and running. Only when she reached the next bend in the passageway did she glance back, briefly. Sorin was getting slowly and painfully to his feet, small bits of rock scattering away from him. He didn't try to chase her; he must have figured out that even if he caught her, there was nothing he could do to her.

"How?" Sorin demanded. His eyes were wide and a bit wild. "You said you got rid of the warding spell!"

"I lied." She smiled at him. "I love you, Sorin. But I'm not stupid."

The gentleness was gone from his face, his mouth hard with betrayed fury. But there, for just a moment, in the depth of his dark eyes, was a gleam of admiration.

Ileni turned and kept running.

Ileni ran out of breath when she reached the Roll of Honor. She stopped, panting, leaning against the rock wall. It didn't sound like anyone was following her. Which didn't mean much; Sorin could probably run silently, and certainly could catch her, even with her head start. But if he tried, her ward would protect her.

The column rose through the center of the cavern, covered with small carved names. Ileni hated it. If she'd had the power, she would have melted the outside of the stone, blotting out all those proud names carved into its whiteness.

She gasped in air and kept running, past the Roll of Honor and toward the steep stairs, up to the black room where the master of assassins was waiting.

Waiting for her.

He sat in his chair, hands clasped in his lap, completely calm. As if he had known she was coming; as if this, too, was part of his plan. Ileni hesitated then, but it was far too late to turn back. She bent, hands on her knees, fighting for breath. When her heartbeat no longer hurt, she straightened.

"I won't do it," she said flatly, before he could speak. "Even if they all die, I won't take their power. Everyone tells me you don't deal death for no reason. Go ahead with this, and you will be wasting all their lives."

The master laughed. It was all she could do not to shudder at the sound.

"I'll take that gamble," he said. "If I order them to die, it will be your decision whether to waste their deaths or not."

The silence stretched, long and dreadful. Within it, the narrow empty window seemed filled with the echo of screams. *Death is simply one of his tactics.*

He's bluffing, Ileni told herself. But he wasn't. He knew what she would do. He knew what everyone would do, and he had planned this to perfection. Jastim had died so that, at this moment, she would believe him.

And she did.

She tried her own bluff anyhow. "That would be a good thing, I think. The death of a group of murderers."

"Yes." The master leaned forward. "Each and every one of your students, dead."

She shouldn't care. They were killers. But she *did* care, and he knew it.

"Every one," he said. His mouth lifted in a half-smile, coldly amused. "Including Sorin."

Her insides twisted, and she struck back. "I wouldn't be so sure Sorin will follow that order."

The master didn't move; he didn't drop his eyes. But fear flashed across his face, so fast it was gone instantly. If she hadn't learned to read Sorin so well, she might not have seen it at all.

"Of course he won't," he said, still utterly calm. "Why do you think I was expecting you? I knew Sorin wouldn't try to stop you from coming here."

But he was wrong. Sorin *had* tried to stop her.

It was as if the stone floor dropped away from under her. This *was* part of his plan, yes.

But he had gotten it wrong.

The master didn't know everything about Sorin.

And he didn't know everything about her.

"Sorin did try to stop me," Ileni said. Suddenly she wasn't faking her confidence. "He wasn't counting on my magic."

The master maintained his serene expression. "Absalm told me your magic was gone."

"I'm sure he did," Ileni said, and lifted her left hand, palm out.

The master's hands moved to the arms of his chair. Was that fear again on his waxy face? She couldn't tell. "It won't work, Sorceress. I have wards—"

"They're not strong enough," Ileni said, and curved her upraised hand in the beginning motion of a spell. The master stood.

He probably saw her other hand flick under her tunic and out. She wasn't that fast, despite all those hours of lessons.

But he wasn't on guard against a knife. He was expecting magic.

The knife flashed through the short space between them, and when he tried to leap aside, his aged body was too slow.

Sorin would have been proud of the throw. The blade

sank cleanly into the master's chest—a few inches to the right from where she had aimed, but good enough.

"It's not hard to kill," Ileni said softly, as if discovering it all over again. "Not if you hate someone. It's so very easy."

But it shouldn't be.

She tried to feel victorious, even as she breathed in the now-familiar smell of blood. A part of her wanted to go over to the master's body, to check that it was true, what she had just discovered—that he was merely a man. And now a dead one.

Instead she turned away, toward the door and the next problem.

Because right now—and, probably, for a long time after—this man, or his memory, still had power over hundreds of trained killers. Who, once they discovered what she had done, would have their strongest reason ever for hating anyone.

She would be the easiest kill any of them had ever made.

So she had better hurry.

When she reached the cave entrance, Sorin was sitting atop a short rock pillar. Ileni stared at him through the twisted columns of colored rock, feeling oddly blank inside.

"Shouldn't you be with Absalm?" she asked.

"It seemed a waste of time. I knew even the master wouldn't convince you to take our power." Sorin shook his head. "You're not ready yet."

Ileni looked at his sharply planed face, so familiar and so foreign. She started walking again, circling to the edges of the cavern so she wouldn't have to pass right by him. Her hastily filled pack, misshapen and lumpy, thumped against her back.

"Ileni."

She didn't stop.

"You could stay."

Almost, he managed to keep his voice expressionless. She stopped walking. He sat poised and powerful, both hands clenched at his sides.

"No," she said.

"No one will force you to do anything. I'll protect you." His throat convulsed. "You can trust me."

Until he found out what she had done. She had no illusions about whether he would protect her then.

"Sorin." Her chest was so tight she could barely breathe. "No."

His dark eyes searched her face. "But you love me," he said finally.

She had no reason to deny it. Ileni lifted her shoulders. "I'll recover."

He flinched, and the intentness turned to anger. "You think it will be that easy?"

"I do not," Ileni said, "think it will be easy."

His eyes were like dark fire now, and she willed herself to be afraid—it would make this easier—but she couldn't, despite his rage, despite what she had seen him do, believe he would hurt her. Even when he pushed himself off the rock and strode toward her.

They walked side by side until they reached the narrow opening to the outside world. Ileni looked out at the vast gray-blue sky, the wisps of pale pink clouds floating across it. Then she realized she was only standing still because Sorin had stopped walking.

The first step was the hardest, wrenching herself away from his side. The second took her under the sky, steadily lightening and stretching forever. A stray breeze brushed hair away from her face, something she had once—a few weeks ago—thought she would never feel again. The breeze was gentle and warm. She blinked away the blurring in her eyes.

On the third step, she stopped and turned around.

"You could come with me," she whispered. Not entirely sure she meant it, but not willing to leave it unsaid.

From the darkness of the cave entrance, Sorin shook his head.

In the silence that followed, Ileni thought he was going to say he wasn't letting her go. She didn't want him to . . . oh, yes. Yes, she did.

Their eyes met. Sorin took a deep breath. "Ileni. You're the most important person in these caves." His words emerged in a sudden rush. "What Absalm said . . . you could change *everything*. You could destroy the Empire in a stroke. Bring us the victory both our people have been working toward for centuries. You could think about it. You could change your mind."

And she probably would, eventually. If she stayed.

"I can't," Ileni said. "I can't just let myself believe what everyone else believes. I need to see for myself."

He blinked. "You're not going back to the Renegai?"

"No." After all that had happened, she was almost startled he would ask. Then she realized what he was really asking. "There's nothing for me there. And no one."

Sorin's expression didn't change, but his shoulders relaxed the tiniest bit. He stared at her, and then he smiled in sudden realization, a grin that made the dimness look bright. "You're headed into the Empire."

"I am."

"You think you'll find answers out there?" He shook his head. "I can tell you from experience, you won't."

"Maybe not." She lifted her chin and met his black eyes. "But nobody in these caves even knows there's a question."

He was silent for a moment. Then he said, "When you do find those answers, you'll be back. All you'll have done is wasted your time."

She couldn't deny it. She couldn't say he was right. She turned on her heel, shifted her weight to take the fourth step.

His voice was so quiet she almost didn't hear it. "I'll be here, Ileni. When you do come back."

She didn't turn around. She took the fifth step, and the sixth, and the seventh, and then she stopped counting. The sun was rising in the gray sky, scattering the clouds. She set off down the road, toward the end of the shadow cast by the black mountains behind her.

✵ *Acknowledgments* ✵

Death Sworn is the first book I ever wrote with the knowledge that it would more likely than not be published. This was both reassuring and frightening, and I owe an extra measure of thanks to the people who kept both me and the book on track throughout the process.

First and foremost, to all my readers.

To my editor, Martha Mihalick, for making me cut the things that didn't work and improve the things that did, for always pushing me to be better, and for pictures of jumping sheep.

To Anne Dunn, for careful copyedits and an email that made my week.

To everyone at Greenwillow, especially Virginia Duncan, Lois Adams, Patty Rosati, and Mary Ann Zissimos.

To Sylvie Le Floc'h, for an amazing cover that perfectly captures the feel of the book.

To Bill Contardi, for being in my corner.

To my family, for their excitement and enthusiasm, and for Googling me and then forwarding only the good stuff.

To Leah Clifford, for invaluable caving expertise. I'm sorry for fictionally destroying Lechuguilla Cave.

To all the Codexians, for everything, and especially for helpful answers to panicked mid-revision questions.

To Shanna Giora-Gorfajn, for supplying me with hot cocoa, even if she didn't have to row through an underground river to do it. (You would have anyhow, right?)

To Autumn Rachel Dryden and Janina Wilen, for throwing knives. I mean, not really. Okay, yes, really. But not at *me.* Actually, thanks for that, too.

And last but most definitely not least, to everyone who commented on this manuscript in its various stages (especially the frantic I-didn't-realize-this-was-the-last-revision stage): Tova Suslovich (x2 or 3 or 100!), Christine Amsden, Cindy Pon, Bethany Powell, Brant Williams, Anaea Lay, E. Catherine Tobler, Kat Otis, Deva Fagan, Gwendolyn Clare, Laurel Amberdine, Sol Kim-Bentley, and Sharona Vedol. Your input and advice were invaluable.

◎ ◎ ◎

EXTRAS

ARRIVAL: Sorin's Story

The Inspiration for the Assassin's Caves

An excerpt from *Death Marked,*
the sequel to *Death Sworn*

ARRIVAL
SORIN'S STORY

Sorin heard the girl coming before he saw her, which was no surprise. The angle of the rocky passageway magnified and twisted small sounds, and he had been trained to interpret those noises. He could tell that she was walking slowly, that she was wearing leather shoes, and that she was afraid. She stopped and breathed deeply after the third step, the slight hitch in her voice very familiar to him, especially after his mission.

This time, though, the sound sent a surge of grim purpose through him. It was appropriate that she be afraid.

He didn't even have to articulate to himself how he knew she was a girl. He didn't doubt that for a second.

It didn't matter that she was female, of course. Even so, the sight of her delicate face and wide brown eyes, and the lightness of her body when he slammed it against the wall, surprised him.

He shifted slightly to make up for the weight difference and drew his blade, pressing it lightly against her throat as he met her dark eyes.

In his mind, Irun taunted him: *Too soft for the kill?*

One of the many reasons Irun was a fool. This girl had, somehow, found the hidden entrance to the Assassins' Caves. The important thing was to find out how she had done it.

Killing her could come later. Right now, he needed her afraid, not dead.

She pushed against him ineffectually. He kept his face impassive and his blade a whisper away from her skin. A thrill ran through him, the thrill of putting his training into action, of doing things *right*. He held onto that, to give him resolve when she began to show true terror, and waited.

The girl's hands went down to her sides. She tilted her face up and said coolly, "The knife seems unnecessary, then, doesn't it?"

As she said it, a small round light flared up above her.

Shock, disappointment, and then a surge of satisfaction shot through Sorin in quick succession. He made sure none of that appeared on his face. So she had some magical ability, and enough self-possession to try and mask her fear. A challenge. The morning had suddenly turned exciting.

"I'll decide what's necessary," he said. It was an empty statement, but it gave him time to reassess her. Physically, she wasn't much of a challenge, and magically, all she had done was call up a simple light. Her expression, defiance drawn over fear, was complicated by the angry set of her mouth. Who was she angry at? She must have known she would be attacked, coming here.

He slid the knife a fraction closer to her skin. "How did you find the entrance to our caves?"

She rolled her eyes. "How do you think? The Elders told me."

It was the cool contempt in her voice, as much as her words, that made him step back. He twisted his arm lightly as he let go of her, to keep her off-balance, and eyed her while she struggled to regain it. She didn't use magic to right herself, the way Absalm would have.

Then again, there was quite a lot about her that was different from Absalm.

"I'm a Renegai sorceress," the girl snapped, once she was standing upright. There was still that anger beneath her words—too vast to be intended just for him. *Angry at the whole world*, he thought; and heard Lasin's voice, wry and lilting, saying that about him. "Who did you think I was?"

"I didn't —" He forced himself to focus on her claims, not on her. This was all wrong. She had to be lying. "The Renegai have never sent a woman to serve as our tutor before."

She shrugged. "Is there something in our agreement that forbids it?"

Several facts clicked into place in Sorin's mind. It had been months since he had been assigned to guard the entrances; this morning's order had been a surprise, though of course he hadn't questioned it. Cadrel had died only a few weeks ago, which made this about the right time for a new tutor to arrive. He had thought the Renegai would stall longer, after the suspicious deaths of the two previous tutors . . . but obviously, he had guessed wrong.

The master wouldn't have guessed wrong.

The master had known the new tutor would arrive today,

and he had known she would be a girl. And the master had assigned Sorin to guard duty without telling him either of those things.

This was a test. And Sorin suspected he was failing it.

The girl was watching him. Her face was impressively impassive, but she still gave herself away with little signs he had been trained to recognize: the too-even breaths, the tension in her jaw, the long spaces between her blinks. He even fancied he could smell her fear, beneath the clean breezy scent she had brought into the caves with her. But if she was the next tutor, why would she be afraid of him?

He *had* slammed her against the wall and held a knife to her throat. Outside these caves, people weren't used to that sort of thing.

"Come with me," he said finally. He still wasn't sure if it was the right thing to do, but he was certain that letting the silence stretch any longer was the wrong thing.

If this was a test, what were the consequences of failure?

The girl drew in a deep breath, and he felt a flash of hatred, which he immediately suppressed. It wasn't her fault that she was being used to challenge him.

Which didn't mean he had to go out of his way to make her comfortable. He walked at his usual stride, stretching his legs to their fullest, a walk he had practiced for so long that it now came naturally to him. She, of course, would have to quicken her usual pace to keep up.

Except that she didn't. She maintained a normal slow pace, as if she was taking a pleasure stroll through the dark narrow passageway, not hurrying even when he turned a bend and she could no longer see him.

Magefire, she was going to be irritating.

He refused to slow down, but when he reached the Entrance Hall, he hopped onto a pillar. He was waiting there when the Renegai girl arrived. She rounded the bend in the tunnel and stopped short, her sharp face slack with awe.

The Entrance Hall was familiar to Sorin, but every once in a while he saw it the way he once had, when he had been a wild, terrified, furious boy dragged into this cavern kicking and screaming. He had a flash of that memory now: how majestic and unearthly the pillars had seemed, like an entrance to another world. The shock of its beauty, his first experience with awe.

One of the stalagmites, near the left wall, was a discordant note: a thick stump that ended in a slanted, jagged swirl of colors. Apparently, in all the hundreds of years of angry feral boys being dragged into these caves, Sorin had been the only one who had managed to break something.

He was a different person now. He shouldn't still feel a flush of pride at that thought. He should be ashamed.

"Pretty, isn't it?" he said, so smugly it almost made him want to slap himself. Since it was too late to stop, he went on in the same tone. "Didn't the Elders tell you about this?"

"Of course," the girl said, with an inflection that made it clear she shared the desire to slap him. "I didn't realize I would see it so soon."

So there were two of them working with insufficient information.

"We built the entrance here on purpose," he said. "It impresses the . . . impressionable."

"Such cutting wit," she said. "You had better take me to my rooms so I can recover."

He blinked, then regained his scornful expression as fast as he could. *Should have been faster*. Irun's voice mocked him. *Should not have been necessary*, the Old Man said gravely, disappointed.

"Of course," Sorin said, and he couldn't resist adding, "I'll walk more slowly this time, but let me know if you have trouble keeping up."

He said it partly to see if she would react as he had predicted, and he was pleased when she did: lengthening her stride with an obvious effort. But then she ruined it by doing something he hadn't expected, something that sent a tiny sharp pain pinging through his scalp.

He whirled, quicker than thought, his fingers closing around her throat. That part was instinctive. What required effort was holding back, resting his fingers against her soft skin without tightening them even a little.

He felt her pulse quicken, and her eyes were wide. But instead of flinching she held still and glared at him. "Attacks at knifepoint are one thing. Impudence is another. I won't tolerate that from my students."

It was clearly a cover. He knew what she had done: plucked a piece of his hair. Only a sorceress could possibly have a use for something like that, and what she wanted it for . . .

He couldn't even begin to guess. True fear lanced through him, for the first time—fear of this thin, short girl. She looked up at him with the sort of self-assured arrogance that only came with power. He thought about tightening his grip just enough to make her as afraid as she should be.

"It is not wise," he said finally, letting his hand fall to his side, "to surprise an assassin."

"Sometimes I'm not wise."

He put the fear away and gave her the coldest look in his arsenal, just long enough to see fear leap into *her* eyes. It didn't take long at all. Then, slowly and deliberately, he turned his back on her again.

It was one of the hardest lessons he had learned, back when he first came here: sometimes, you had to turn your back on your enemies.

A few minutes later, with the Renegai sorceress safely in her room, Sorin stood outside the closed door and listened. Instead of the rustle of clothes, he heard a series of distinctive, sharp thuds—rocks tumbling onto the thin rug.

She wasn't unpacking. She was working a spell.

She wouldn't have plucked one of his hairs if the spell wasn't meant for him.

He didn't know enough magic to guess what she was doing, but the Renegai were notoriously pacifistic. He doubted she would harm him immediately. And he had more important dangers to face right now.

As he turned from her room, he felt a return of the sentiment he had been ruthlessly suppressing. Except this time, instead of pure hatred, it was mixed with . . . something else. Excitement?

She was pretty. He wasn't blind. But no, that wasn't it. He had wanted the same things for so long: to be the best assassin in the caves. Serve the master. Fight the Empire. All things he desired as desperately as he had once desired food and warmth; and the way to achieve his desires was a clear, straight path in front of him. That should make him happy—it *did* make him happy—and one thing was clear: whatever this girl's purpose, whatever her secrets, her presence in the caves was going to complicate his life.

If he wasn't a fool, he would be upset by that.

He had to bite down a grin—bite *hard*—as he strode down the dimly lit corridor and went to face the master. To find out whether he had passed this test.

And whether it would be the first of many.

THE INSPIRATION FOR THE ASSASSINS' CAVES

It was great fun writing a book set in a system of caves. I've always been a fan of caves and caverns (in a strictly amateur sense—I've gone on guided caving expeditions, but nothing requiring actual skill), and of murder mysteries in claustrophobic settings where the rest of the world is shut out. Long before *Death Sworn* was a glimmer in my mind, I sought out caves everywhere I went and wrote extensive descriptions of each one. Someday, I knew, I would use those descriptions in a book.

Death Sworn, of course, ended up being that book. These are some of the real-life caves that influenced me:

1. The Cave of the Winds in Manitou Springs, Colorado. This is one of my favorite caves, in part because during my visit there I went for the first time with a guide into the non-altered parts of the caves, with hard hats and flashlights. A lot of that experience went directly from my travel notebook into the first draft of *Death Sworn*—in particular, the experience of squeezing through a tunnel that seemed to get narrower and narrower . . . which, as it turned out, was the guide's idea of a joke. *That* tunnel never widened, and he wanted to see how far we would go before calling it quits.

2. Venado Caves in Costa Rica. Here, our guides thought it would be really funny to lead us into a cavern full of bats without warning us. (I'm going to go out on a limb here and suggest that many cave guides have a perverse sense of humor.) Needless to say, my first reaction (well, maybe

my second reaction) was to pull out a notebook and write a description. In the original manuscript of *Death Sworn*, Sorin did exactly that to Ileni. Sadly, the scene didn't make it into the final version; when Leah Clifford, fellow YA author and caving expert, read an early manuscript, she pointed out a number of reasons why there couldn't be bats in the cave system I had set up. (You can currently find that scene online, at http://katetilton.com/reader-special-deleted-scene-death-sworn-leah-cypess/).

3. Avshalom Cave, in central Israel, has the densest concentration of stalactites and stalagmites I've ever seen. It is definitely one of the most beautiful caves I've been in, and a fabulous source for descriptions of cave formations.

4. Lechuguilla Cave in Carlsbad Caverns National Park, New Mexico. This is a cave I haven't actually visited, but it was featured in a gorgeous *National Geographic* documentary called *Mysteries Underground*. It is the deepest cave in the continental US, with strange and beautiful formations just begging to be placed in a fantasy novel; in fact, the original explorers named many of its formations after items from the *Wizard of Oz*. This is the cave that Ileni and Sorin discover near the end of *Death Sworn*. In the book, the cave doesn't survive the encounter well. In real life, fortunately, it is as pristinely beautiful as ever, and maybe it will be the next cave I visit. . . .

READ ON FOR A SNEAK PEEK INSIDE THE SEQUEL,

DEATH MARKED

The mirror shattered into a hundred pieces, a sudden explosion followed by a cascade of jagged shards. Ileni whirled, throwing her hands up in front of her face, but nothing hit her: no sharp pieces of glass, no sting of cut flesh. After a moment, she lowered her arms and crossed them over her chest.

The broken fragments of glass hovered in the air, glimmering with rainbow colors. Then they faded back into the mirror, smoothing into a shiny, unbroken oval.

"Impressive," Ileni said. She had no idea who she was talking to, but it wasn't difficult to sound unafraid. After six weeks in the Assassins' Caves and three days as a prisoner of imperial sorcerers, false courage was second nature to her. "But since I'm the only one here, it seems a waste of effort."

The colors flattened into a vaguely human-shaped form.

Before she could make out the face, the form spoke. "Absalm said this was the only spell that could get through the Academy's wards."

Ileni froze. She dug her fingers into her upper arms.

The image in the mirror sharpened, revealing a blond young man with a sharply angled face and dark eyes. His grimly set mouth curved up slightly in the hint of a smile. "You were expecting someone else?"

Ileni tilted her head. "I wasn't expecting anyone. Given that I am, as you pointed out, in a rather heavily warded room."

She almost—almost—managed to keep her voice cool. But it shook just a little, and of course Sorin noticed. The slight curve turned into a real smile. "It's good to see you, Ileni."

She pressed her lips together before they could betray her with an answering smile. "How did you know where I was?"

His smile deepened. Ileni's jaw clenched. "You shouldn't be trying to contact me. You might have pushed this spell through the wards, but the imperial sorcerers will know it happened."

His dark eyes narrowed. "Will that put you in danger?"

More danger than I'm in already? "No. I can protect myself."

"I hope you're right." He leaned forward a fraction. "I'm glad you're alive."

Ileni forced a laugh. "Why, thank you. I'm glad I'm alive, too."

"I wasn't sure you would be." He seemed about to say more, and her breath froze in her throat. He must know, now, that she had killed his master. He knew, and yet he had said, *I'm glad you're alive.*

She hadn't realized, until this moment, how afraid she had been of him finding out. Not because he would kill her—she should have been afraid of that, but she hadn't been. She had only been afraid he would hate her.

Sorin shook his head slightly. "Things have been complicated here. I couldn't force Absalm to track you down until now."

"*Force* him?" Ileni stepped closer to the mirror. She was sure he could hear the sound of her heart hammering, but there was nothing she could do about that. She didn't know herself if it was from excitement or fear. "I like the sound of that. You have been busy, haven't you?"

"So have you. How did you manage to infiltrate the Imperial Academy itself?" The admiration in his voice was unfeigned, and Ileni was dismayed at the thrill that ran through her. She had left him behind. She was supposed to be past this. Even if it had only been three days.

Irritation sharpened her voice. "I'm not *infiltrating* anything. I'm not on your side, Sorin. Don't forget that."

His expression didn't change. "How did you get in, then? What did you tell them?"

Nothing. I'm a prisoner. The truth twitched at the edge of her tongue. If she said it, he would save her. He would find a way.

Instead she said, "It's not important."

"Isn't it?" His mouth tightened. "Do they know—"

"That I have no magic of my own anymore?" She got it out without a tremor. She was proud of that. "Yes. It's not exactly something I could hide. Not here."

A silence fell between them, and stretched too long. Ileni was acutely aware that she was finding it hard to breathe. Sorin's black eyes searched her face, looking for—what? She didn't know, and she also didn't know whether he was finding it.

He seemed different, somehow. Just a week ago, he had been

teaching her to fight and making her laugh and kissing her in hidden corridors. But the face in the mirror was inscrutable and dangerous. If even Absalm was following his commands, he must have swiftly secured his position as the new master of the assassins. He had always been a killer, but now he was a leader of killers.

"So," she said finally, when she couldn't bear it anymore. "You just wanted to check on me?"

He let out a breath. "Yes. And to see if you needed help."

She almost laughed at that—or maybe it was a sob. She couldn't ask him for help. They really *weren't* on the same side. "I don't. Thank you for the dagger, though."

"You're welcome," he said, with a light bow.

Ileni had found the dagger in her backpack the first time she opened it on the mountain path. She had no idea how Sorin had put it there without her noticing, but she had immediately stuck it into her boot. It was still there, alien and heavy, yet comforting at the same time.

Their eyes met. His gleamed, like sunlight hitting black stone, and an answering spark lit in Ileni. She almost reached for him, as if she could touch him, as if he was right there in the room with her.

"Are you absolutely certain you don't want help?" Sorin said. "If you need me, I will come. Once the imperial sorcerers find out you lived here in our caves, your life won't be worth much."

She hesitated, wondering if he had seen through the casualness. He *could* help her. He had hundreds of assassins who were his to command. He had a sorcerer, who apparently obeyed him at least some of the time. All she had to do was say yes, and he would bring her back.